I0598585

The Omega's Alphas

TAMED BY
THE ALPHAS

JAYCE CARTER

Tamed by the Alphas
ISBN # 978-1-83943-894-3
©Copyright Jayce Carter 2020
Cover Art by Erin Dameron-Hill ©Copyright May 2020
Interior text design by Claire Siemaszkiewicz
Totally Bound Publishing

TAMED BY
THE ALPHAS

Dedication

To my husband, who introduces me to people as
'My wife, the literary pornographer.'

Chapter One

I'm handcuffed, and I'm not even going to get an orgasm out of it.

Kara twisted her hands as she sat on the hard chair in the conference room she'd been stuck in since the night before. What she'd expected to be a quick in-and-out job had bitten her in the ass, as all quick jobs tended to do.

She brought her foot up, pulling the bobby pin from the cuff of her boot. A vibration of her watch let her know she'd gotten a text, and only one person would have sent it. Her ride, who no doubt had gotten an alert when a certain blue-haired omega had been arrested.

The pin let her pop the cuffs open, and she could have moaned as the metal dropped from her sore wrists.

'Steal some files. It's easy money!' When would she learn that easy money was never easy? The moment she'd read a few of the files she'd been hired to steal, Kara had known she couldn't turn them over to the asshole who had hired her. Most of it was so far above

his paygrade it would be like handing space station schematics to an especially slow five-year-old, and honestly? She didn't like him enough to give him anything useful.

She worked hard to not learn much about her clients, because when dealing with criminals, she'd rather not know. Money was money, and she did what she had to. She had no one else looking out for her.

The door to the room opened, and she turned to find a face she'd missed. *Well, almost no one looking out for me.*

Liam wore a suit so fancy he might almost pass for harmless. *Almost.* When he cracked a familiar smile, though, Kara saw him for who he'd always been to her. "How many times have I had to save you?"

Kara stood, dangling the cuffs on a single finger. "From a police station? Never."

He chuckled, catching her chin between his fingers and lifting her face toward him. Anyone who saw it might think he was about to kiss her, but she knew better. That wasn't them.

They'd had sex before, but it had never been serious to either of them. If anything, it had been a favor to her. So, she wasn't shocked when he used the grip to twist her face and check for injuries.

"You sure? I recall having to help you out of handcuffs before."

"Those were recreational handcuffs, thank you very much. I learned how to pick them after that."

He released her chin, stepping backward once he'd satisfied himself that she wasn't hurt. "You are impossible." Liam removed something from inside his coat, shaking it out. "Lucky for you, I'm always prepared."

Kara laughed as he pulled the item around her — a jacket. It was her size. *Hey, I think it might actually* be *mine.* A quick look in the mirror hanging on the back of the door showed the plan. Dressed in the fitted gray blazer, she looked like anyone else. A second item had her rolling her eyes, but Liam ignored any complaints as he brushed his fingers through her hair to push the bright blue strands back and hide them beneath the black wig.

"I hate this thing," she groused.

"Well, I think the blue hair is a dead giveaway, kid, and this is all I have."

"Why do you even have a woman's wig? Are you and your twin into some weird roleplaying shit when you double-team girls?"

Liam yanked softly on the front of the wig to seat it at her hairline, hiding her trademark neon tresses. "Even if I was, we both know you'd out-kink me. Now, head up and use all those skills I taught you. The detective who brought you in here is up a floor, so we should be able to slip out, no problem."

Kara tucked the cuffs into her blazer pocket, and when Liam lifted an eyebrow, she shrugged. Handcuffs were expensive. *Waste not, want not, right?*

He stepped out first, his attitude instantly transforming into that of a man who had shit to do and not nearly enough time in which to do it. Kara didn't pull that off, and in women, it tended to make people pay attention. Instead, she grabbed a notepad and pen off a file cabinet just outside the room she'd been kept in, holding them and scribbling as she made a point of struggling to keep up with Liam. They made the perfect image of a high-powered lawyer and a secretary trying her best not to get yelled at.

It irked her to play the part but, *fuck it, better than landing in jail.* Not just being held in a conference room because men felt bad for omegas and assumed she'd been roped into her little indiscretion, but real-life metal bars. It was much harder to break out of jail.

Not that Liam, his twin and their cousin wouldn't break her out of there, too. In fact, a part of her thought it sounded like a hell of a lot of fun. Plus, she could see the frown of Liam's cousin when they managed the breakout, when he lectured her calmly on making better choices while knowing damned well she'd never do it.

No one gave them a second look as they walked through the police station. That was the benefit of being outed as an omega, she guessed. No one had expected much of her. It meant that instead of planting her ass in an interrogation room or a holding cell, they'd put her in a meeting room with nothing but a pair of cuffs on and no one watching her.

It's almost insulting.

At least it made for an easy getaway.

The elevator doors closed, and Kara breathed in relief.

Liam hit the button for the third floor. "I trust you can manage to find your way out from here?" He flashed her a wide smile, one full of all the mischief they'd gotten into over the years. "As long as you don't run into any good-looking alphas on the way, at least."

Kara tugged at the wig, trying to ignore how it made her scalp itch. "Well, at least I won't have to worry about that problem while you're still around."

Liam laughed as the doors opened. He left her, and that gained him extra points. Just one night of having people treat her like a useless, fragile omega had her grateful that Liam didn't think twice about letting her get herself out the rest of the way.

The elevator closed again, leaving Kara on her own. The shiny doors let her catch a glimpse of herself in the ugly wig, which was too similar to her natural color for her liking.

It had been at least a year since Liam, his twin or his cousin had needed to step in and rescue her. Not that she ever asked. The eldest of them, Torrin, always kept tabs on her. It meant that as soon as she'd gotten herself arrested on this job gone south, she'd known someone would show up even without her asking.

The button for the second floor lit up, and Kara didn't bother to hold in a groan. The odds of anyone recognizing her were slim, but she still didn't need any sort of slowdown. The longer it took to get out, the better the odds someone would notice her missing and send up alarms.

The elevator rumbled to a stop, and Kara dropped her gaze to her list, pretending to be highly engrossed in the scribbles there.

Three men entered the small space, but it wasn't their size — large as they were — that hit her first. Nope, it was the unmistakable, mouthwatering scent of alpha.

When was the last time she'd indulged in an alpha? Months, at least. Alphas tended to get territorial and possessive, neither of which she needed in her life. Sleeping with betas was safer. Every once in a while, though, she'd give in. She'd let herself drown in the scandalous touches, the lust, the scent of an alpha that nothing else could replicate. Hell, that bone-deep need to dominate they had could make the most restrained of omegas beg for a taste. Not to forget, of course, the way they stretched her when the knots at the base of their cocks swelled.

So when the three alphas crowded into the small elevator, so close that the waves of heat their bodies threw off warmed her in places that had grown far too cold, she didn't bother to disguise how she drew the scent into her lungs.

A soft laugh from one pulled her gaze up, and she realized she'd zeroed in on the way his built chest showed through the white of a button-up shirt beneath a black suit jacket. "You know, you're writing gibberish."

Kara found she had, in fact, been writing random letters, too busy ogling to make sense with her fake note-taking. "So I am."

The alpha twisted fully to face her as the elevator moved. "Distracted?"

"By what?" She tried for flippant.

His dark eyebrow cocked up toward his long chestnut hair. It reached just past his shoulders, the messy waves of someone who had wanted to be in a band at seventeen and hadn't ever let go of that spark of craziness. His lips looked soft, and lines beside them hinted that he smiled often. "Why don't you meet me tonight? Harbor Hotel, nine o'clock, in the bar on the bottom floor. We could have drinks, or we could skip that entirely."

How she wanted to… He was amazing, with the sort of body she could spent hours exploring. Each dip between his muscles, only hinted at by his conservative clothing, made her tongue thick and eager to trace them. She could picture herself flicking each button of his shirt open and tasting every new inch revealed.

And beside him? The other two alphas, while silent, mirrored the want in his hazel eyes.

To his left stood a man who seemed the same age — late thirties or so. He had his light brown hair buzzed at the sides and longer on the top, pushed back and gelled into place. The lines between his eyebrows said he frowned. A lot.

Lastly, the odd one of the group, the youngest alpha, stood to the right. He couldn't be more than twenty-one and must have gotten carded without fail whenever buying alcohol. Black-rimmed glasses perched on his nose, the sort that made him look brilliant and caused his deep brown eyes to appear even larger. His short and messy hair was so dark it would've appeared black if not for the bright elevator lights. He was thinner than the other two, but she'd never call him small. Due to the hormones in alphas, they were rarely ever small, and they tended toward fit, even when they didn't work at it. The strap across the young alpha's chest that connected to a laptop case told her what she'd already expected—tech guy. Not that she cared. Even tech guys had working cocks, and given his age, she'd bet he didn't tire easily. *Stamina for the win.*

The casual alpha with the long hair released a playful growl, setting his hand above her, caging her in with his body without touching her. "You smell delicious," he whispered. "I really wish we could blow off this meeting and take you back to our suite right now." He made no secret of the way he inhaled—slowly, as if savoring every last molecule of her scent.

"Meet us later?" This from the green-eyed alpha, the words less of a question and more of a demand. He struck her as the type who would prefer orders to requests. *I bet he gives great orders.*

The shake of the elevator woke Kara up. She'd met them in the police station she was currently escaping from. They had a meeting there, meaning that while they weren't police—she could spot a cop a mile off—they had some connection to the law. The last thing she needed was to meet them anywhere, to risk them opening their big mouths and pointing the finger at her and getting her caught.

There is no shortage of dick, Kara. Keep it in your pants and move along.

When the doors slid open to the lobby, Kara twisted down, beneath the alpha's arm, toward freedom. "Sorry, boys, but I've got plans."

The first alpha turned as she moved, as though he couldn't stand the idea of not having her in his sight. "We'll make it worth your while."

We'll. Oh, that sounded promising. She could almost see the way they'd work together, how exhausted she'd be afterward, how sated. She'd never given that particular deviancy a try.

But no matter how their offer might tempt her, Kara wasn't stupid. She was reckless a lot of the time, impulsive and short-sighted, but no matter how much she wanted to give in, meeting those alphas would be horribly, irrevocably stupid.

So Kara gave them her best smile and tossed a playful, teasing wink. "I'm sure you'd *try*, but I've got more bite than most of your playthings. Good luck, though."

She left them as she turned and headed for the front doors, their gaze predatory and wanting and making her feel like the prey she'd just claimed she wasn't.

Too bad she'd never see them again.

* * * *

Reese rolled his head, trying to ease the mounting tension in his neck.

Sleeping in hotels sucked, because no matter how much money he dropped on them, they were never *his* bed. They always smelled wrong, felt wrong and he never managed a full night's sleep.

The fancy place Cullen had picked for their work in that city a few hours from where he and his fellow alphas called home was no different. Even with the expensive, high-thread-count sheets and luxurious bedding, he'd spent most of the late hours in the bar.

Not drinking, at least not the entire time. Instead, he'd nursed a single beer while he'd buried himself in his headphones and thumbed through the pages of a stupid magazine he'd found in the room.

"Are you ready?" Cullen asked.

Reese shoved his hands into his pockets. "I was ready an hour ago. I don't know what you expect me to do with all this waiting around."

Cullen pressed his lips together into the displeased line he so often wore. "We aren't dealing with people we can trust here. These are the kind who will stab you in the back without a problem."

"And sitting around in a car for two hours is going to change that how?"

"It's going to let me be sure we aren't walking into a trap."

"Why would this be a trap? *We* contacted the thief, not the other way around."

Cullen always worried, having experienced the ugliness of the world far too early after two tours overseas. It had left him suspicious and uptight, but perfect for security.

Reese was good with people. Not many others could read them like he could, could sniff out a lie or a secret with his skills. Which meant he should really just shut up and listen to Cullen. They both had their lanes, and he'd do well to stay in his.

His exhaustion and general bad mood made him unlikely to actually do so, though. They'd been friends for too many years for Reese to just roll over. Instead, he lifted his lip in a half-hearted snarl.

"Complain all you want. I'm not going to get my ass handed to me by some underhanded thief just because you don't like to wait," Cullen said.

They'd already had *that* fight, too. No matter how much they disliked it, they needed this so-called infamous thief. They knew little about him beyond that he'd come highly recommended. His skills didn't come cheap, and while it had taken more than a few favors to set up the meeting, Reese had no doubt this man could do what they needed.

As long as he agreed, and Reese planned to make it impossible for the asshole to refuse.

"Okay, let's go."

"I don't like this. We should have picked a better spot." Cullen's gaze darted across the street, to the bodies going in and out of the busy bar.

"This is where he meets people. I'd guess he's more worried about what we might do to him. Can't be easy to trust clients in his line of work. Lot of people probably want him dead. Standing here isn't going to get this done any faster or any safer. Come on, let's get it over with."

Cullen followed Reese when he pushed away from the building they'd been watching from. A busy, public place like this wasn't Reese's idea of a good plan, either. Too much noise made it hard to study people, to get a feel for them.

Just get in, hire the asshole and get the fuck out.

The music hit Reese with the force of a body slam, followed by the thick mixture of scents when he entered. Lust, sweat, body odor, liquor—all of it assaulted him. It wasn't a good thing, not like the playful scent of an aroused woman, like the one he'd seen in the elevator at the station a few days prior.

Damn, he would have happily drowned in that woman's scent, in the spice of it, in the images it brought forth.

Forget her. She didn't show that night, and the last thing I need is to go into this distracted and hard.

Sometimes being an alpha sucked. He didn't have the nose of an omega — they could identify designations in addition to other basic body changes like lust — but he did better than a beta, who couldn't smell shit.

And right then, in the crowded bar, he envied the betas.

"Damon would have been miserable." Cullen stood beside Reese, speaking loud enough for the words to carry over the noise.

"He's young. I bet he'd fit right in."

Reese almost grinned at how wrong that was. Damon, the newest and youngest member of their happy little trio, had stayed back at the hotel room doing what he did best — burying his nose in his laptop. He'd have hated the loud music and sweaty bodies, but fuck if hormones didn't get riled up at that age. If he'd stayed for more than an hour, those alpha urges would likely wake up and want a piece of something.

And judging from the bodies writhing around on the dance floor, he'd have had no problem finding a willing partner.

They made their way past the dance floor and the bar. Near the back of the large central room, a set of stairs led up to the private rooms, and a hulking guard stood in the way.

The guard's gaze drifted from Reese to Cullen, slow and suspicious and with enough attitude that Reese doubted they'd get past.

Except, just when Reese readied himself to talk his way past, the guard stepped back. "Take a left at the top of the stairs, then head to the end of the hallway. Don't cause me any problems."

Reese let out a soft laugh. "Problems? Me? Never."

Cullen made the same grumble he always did when he didn't appreciate or approve of Reese's comments. Cullen's gaze moved to take in the doorways as they traversed the hallway, probably taking in the details.

That was what he was good at, though. Always had a plan, always knew the exits, the dangers.

Reese preferred a 'let's hope this shit works out' method.

It often didn't, but he'd reached thirty-five alive, which had to mean something, right?

The last doorway led to a room with a large open window overlooking the dance floor. Light and music poured in, but muffled compared to downstairs.

A figure stood with its back to the alphas, tiny and thin, dressed in a black sweater with the hood pulled over its head. *This has got to be a joke.* There was no way *this* was the dreaded thief people had told him about, the one who could get in anywhere, who stole from anyone no matter how unwise. This guy had to be small enough that a good breeze could knock him down.

The figure turned toward them, and all three froze.

The thief was the woman from the elevator.

Chapter Two

Kara wanted to laugh at her shitty luck. The alphas from the elevator — or at least two of them — were her clients? These were the men who had called in so many favors just to get into a room with her?

If I'd known I was going to run into them again, I'd have just fucked them to start with.

Live and learn, right?

Kara moved quickly, her size a benefit when it came to speed. She was never the largest in a room, but she was usually the fastest. She had her pistol pulled from the holster at the small of her back and pointed at the alphas before she'd fully decided what to do about them. She was sure they'd run into each other in the elevator by accident, and this meeting had been set days before that.

Still, the idea of it being a coincidence didn't sit right. *How unlucky can a person be? Even me?*

The alpha with the short hair and impossibly scrumptious physique reacted with a speed that nearly matched her own, bringing his own weapon out. She wasn't shocked to find he hadn't gone for small and easily concealable. No, he'd picked a much bulkier and more intimidating 9mm.

The desire to remind him that bigger wasn't always better struck her, but she smothered the urge somehow. That was a miracle, as keeping her mouth shut wasn't a skill she'd ever bothered to hone.

"You were in the elevator," the one with the long hair said. The surprise in his voice helped sell that this *was* just a big clusterfuck of coincidences.

"What? Me? Never been in an elevator in my life."

The alpha with the gun grunted, a sound that didn't scream trust. "So why'd you pull a gun?"

"Because I don't like you?"

"Like I'd forget how you smell." The alpha with the long hair curled his lip into a smile which made Kara's stomach flutter.

Fucking *flutter*, as though she were some idiot omega who was smitten by a big strong alpha. The reaction annoyed her worse than the asshole's gun. *I might shoot him on principle.*

"This was clearly a mistake," Kara said without lowering her weapon. "Let's just chalk it up to shitty planning and go our own ways."

The alpha with the gun narrowed his emerald eyes. "You know, after we saw you, before we left the building, they closed down the whole station."

"Well, with the world the way it is, that sort of thing happens. Hope you boys weren't too scared."

The man kept going as though her snarky words meant nothing. "They were looking for a woman. Apparently, she slipped out when no one was looking." *Woman?* So the police must not have released that they'd lost an omega, because the alphas would have said it otherwise.

"She must have had shitty guards."

"No guards, from what I heard."

"Well then, who could really blame her for blowing that place? Sounds like a smart girl. Don't know what it has to do with me."

The man with the gun lifted his eyebrow. "I doubt you were on any of their visitor logs, were you? They haven't put much work into finding that woman, because what does one lone woman matter to them? However, I'd bet that would change if they connected their missing suspect with an infamous thief. That might get them a lot more interested in the case."

Kara's arm ached. It wasn't the weight of the pistol—though to be fair, she rarely held it out straight for so long. Normally, if she pulled her gun, she shot someone. Instead, it was the tension that ran through her shoulders and back as she argued with herself.

I could shoot them.

Even as she considered the option, she knew it wasn't really a choice. Despite Kara's less than savory life, she'd never killed anyone without good reason. She just didn't have it in her, and she wouldn't start with a couple of alphas who didn't seem any more eager to kill her than she was to kill them.

The guns were all posturing.

"So what do you want from me?"

"The same thing we wanted when we walked in. We need you to steal something for us."

Well, that I can do.

Cullen couldn't relax. He might not have a gun pointed at him anymore, but he knew the feisty little female still had possession of it, and she didn't mind waving it around.

However, unless he planned to disarm her personally, he supposed there wasn't much he could do about it. The idea of disarming her had merit. He wanted to smell her again, that playful, spicy scent that signaled her arousal. Still, if he got close enough to pat her down — and she was the sort to need a full frisking to be sure she was clean — finding weapons would be the last thing they'd end up doing.

Which was a complication they didn't need. When she was some faceless woman in an elevator, sure. He and Reese always shared females, and she seemed well worth the effort. Now, though? They needed her help, which had withered the opportunity. Plus, the woman had escaped a police station and was a well-known and feared thief. Not exactly the sort of no-complications sex he preferred to indulge in.

For the best. Reese is looking at her like he could eat her up already. We can't afford distractions, and she's nothing but one big distraction wrapped in black and lies.

Reese took a folded piece of paper from his pocket and slid it across the table. "We need one of these."

The woman opened the paper, her pink tongue stroking gently against her bottom lip as her eyes — too clever for his comfort — darted back and forth. "This is from the lab on the west side of town. Hythen Pharmaceuticals?"

Smart girl.

"That's right. It's what a security clearance badge looks like. The address of the person to get it from is on the bottom of the paper. From what I've seen, he's got no alarm system, just a deadbolt and maybe a dog."

"If that's it, why do you need me? I get hired for bigger game than this. Seems like a two-bit kid from the streets could grab this." She leveled a look that said she didn't trust them any more than they trusted her. "Hell, even you might be able to manage a job this easy."

Her barb stirred Cullen, rousing his interest further. Why was it that each little insult she threw had his cock perking up? Cullen preferred demure women, those who listened, who fawned, not the sort who pulled guns on him and challenged him, so what was up with his dick?

Reese answered, which was good, because Cullen's attention remained on the woman's soft pink lips and not the conversation. "This needs to be done right, quietly. The last thing I want is to risk getting caught. This is delicate, and if they realize the card is gone, the lab will be on higher alert."

She leaned back, pulling her hood off. The light from the window caught on her hair, and Cullen's back straightened. It was blue. Not a deep, dark blue but a neon that shone even in the dimness. "No more brown?" The question came out before he'd had a chance to silence it.

Her eyes met his, and he noted they mirrored her hair. Bright blue and sparkling from the lights. "Brown is boring."

And she was anything but boring, wasn't she?

"What's your name?"

The woman released a long-suffering sigh. "Kara."

The name was odd, short and harsh on his tongue. It seemed to fit her well.

"I'm Reese, and this is Cullen." Reese nodded back at him.

"And your young groupie?"

Cullen couldn't stop the soft huff of laughter at the way she spoke about the other alpha, who was still taller and much larger than she was. "That's Damon. He doesn't like this sort of thing."

"Fun?"

"No. Bars and noise."

She did that eye-rolling thing again that made Cullen's hand itch to swat her ass. How did she manage to rouse that in him? When was the last time he'd felt so strongly for any female? Maybe it was the challenge of it, the alpha in him scenting prey that might actually be worthy of the chase.

"Can you do the job?"

She folded the paper and tucked it down the front of her shirt, into the cup of her bra. *How can I be jealous of a damned piece of paper?* "Yeah, I can do it. What're you paying?"

"Other than our silence?"

"Silence keeps me out of jail, but it doesn't put sex toys in the nightstand."

Her vulgar joke sparked to life the sizzling embers of lust inside him. He wanted to take each of those damned toys and break them into pieces, to replace them with his own body, to show her she didn't need them. Before he'd even realized it, his throat vibrated with a deep growl.

Reese jumped in. "One grand, and we won't tell anyone about you. That's more than fair for all of an hour of work."

"A grand for lifting one little key?" She crossed her legs, the action drawing Cullen's focus to where her thighs now pressed together tightly. "Money that big means you're desperate. Who are you?"

"Does it matter? I didn't figure you'd be that picky." Criminals rarely were.

"Take the wrong job enough times, and you realize some questions are worth asking. If someone is willing to pay too much, I want to know why."

Cullen leaned back on the couch, trying to look comfortable despite the lust swimming through him. "We're private investigators. The key is for a case involving a missing person, so time is of the essence."

"Lot of money for a missing person case. Trust me, there aren't a lot of people worth it."

"It's a missing omega."

And that said it all, didn't it? Omegas were rare, and the alphas around them would do anything to obtain or keep one. In this case, it had been her friend who had called them when the omega had fallen off the grid.

Kara didn't respond right away, the silence thick and full of things that flashed in her gaze but didn't leave her mouth.

Was she annoyed by omegas? Many beta females were, just like beta males often resented alphas.

Which Cullen had never fully understood. There were some advantages, he supposed, but overall the world seemed simpler for betas. They got to live their lives, never worrying about heats, about bonding, about the incessant and insidious truths that alphas and omegas dealt with on a daily basis.

People always wanted what they didn't have, though, and it seemed one's designation was no exception to that universal truth.

Kara tapped her foot on the ground, the action causing her legs to shift, drawing his attention there. "Did she run? Because if an omega ran, I'm doing exactly jack shit to help the alpha she ran from."

Reese leaned forward, resting his elbows on his knees. "We wouldn't take the job if that was the case. I looked into it deep, but there's no evidence of abuse. Hell, the alpha looking for her was her best friend, not a mate. Her family is worried as well, and they made it clear they had no reason to believe she was running from them or him."

Again, silence ate up the space. No one said the ugly truth—missing omegas were rarely found. Omegas fell off the grid for two reasons. They were running, which she didn't seem to be, or they'd been abducted or murdered. Either way, they didn't often have a happy ending.

The knowledge of that showed on Kara's features, her gaze darting away for a split second before returning. "Okay. I'll scout the place tonight, and if it looks good, I'll grab it. If not, I'll give it a few days of surveillance."

Cullen rubbed his hand over the back of his tense neck, trying to massage away the stiffness. What was it about Kara?

Why did he still want to fuck her as badly as he did? Maybe he and Reese just needed to burn off some steam with a warm and willing body.

Reese pulled an envelope from his jacket. "Half the money is in here, the rest when we get the keycard."

"Who are you taking it to, to alter?" At Cullen's look, she smiled, stuffing the envelope into a bag that hung from her hip. "This badge has a picture and name on it. It's useless to you unless you have a new one made with your own information. I'm not an idiot."

"Terry Grimes," Cullen shoved through gritted teeth. He didn't like giving away secrets, but then again, both Kara and Terry were criminals. Hell, they probably knew each other. *One big happy illegal family.*

Kara let out a huff but didn't comment on the choice. Instead, she hopped to her feet, the move quick and graceful, like a cat leaping onto a table. It made him reconsider the way her black leggings clung to her toned thighs and showed off every inch of her form.

"I'll get back to you when it's done."

Cullen pulled a business card from his back pocket, their cell numbers printed on the white cardstock, and handed it over. "Call us when you're ready."

Kara's deft fingers brushed his when she took it, and he swore sparks flew at the innocent touch. His cock hardened and her scent increased, as if that was all it took for both their bodies to get on board with the plan.

And just when he thought she'd pull back, that she'd retreat from all the waves of desperate lust and aggression he knew he was throwing off, Kara's grin only widened. "I don't shit where I eat," she whispered. "And I don't fuck clients."

With that, she was off, twisting past him and out of the room before he'd picked his jaw off the floor.

Reese chuckled, a deep rumble as though he was amused by the entire exchange. "She's a handful."

Cullen nodded, gaze pinned to the doorway she'd walked through, as though he could still see the way the leggings had clung to her perfect, heart-shaped ass. "Yeah, she is."

Reese slapped Cullen's shoulder, shaking loose his intense focus. "Come on, let's get back to Damon and fill him in."

Cullen rolled his shoulders to get rid of the need to chase the female, to shove her against a wall and taste her, to bask in all that attitude and snark.

She was a criminal and even if he wanted to fuck her—and boy did he ever—he might end up missing a kidney by the end.

It might just be worth it.

Chapter Three

Kara flicked the keycard, holding it up to the light as if that would tell her a damned thing.

Getting it had been her easiest job in months. She'd picked the deadbolt on the back door—no alarm system at all—crept through the dark house while the owner of the coveted little piece of plastic snored away in his bed, and stolen the card from the briefcase.

It wouldn't be missed anytime soon, since his calendar showed he wouldn't be back for at least a month. The keycard was a visitor badge for one of the many companies who supplied test subjects for experiments. The companies screened potential subjects and connected them with the lab.

Hythen Pharmaceuticals worked on a number of things, most far above her level of schooling—which was fuck all—and surrounding alpha and omega biology. They worked on drugs specially formulated to the hormones of alphas and omegas, and also on things like birth control options or heat suppressant medications.

Why the alphas needed it, she didn't know and really didn't care.

Justin walked into the small back room behind a hole-in-the-wall cafe that served horrible coffee and worse food. The beta was quiet and always nervous around her. He'd asked her out once, after she'd slept with him on an especially bad day of hers, but she'd turned him down.

He was too sweet, and it would mean too much to him. He wasn't the type to hit it and quit it like her. Despite the whole criminal thing, she'd actually call him a good person.

"Kara," he said, a timid smile crossing his thin lips. He pushed his glasses up his nose, though they remained askew as they usually were. "I didn't expect you."

Kara held up the keycard she'd swiped. "I need your help."

He took the card, flipping it over and studying it carefully before walking toward a table full of a few computer monitors and random bits of technology she didn't come close to understanding.

Kara could manage security systems and basic computer usage, but anything this complicated? *Nope.*

He slid the card through a reader, then glanced at the laptop connected to it. "How soon do you need this? It's surprisingly complex."

"I need that one or an exact copy immediately. After that, I'll take four ones already encoded but with the name and picture blank whenever you can get them to me."

He turned a disapproving look on her. Not a glare, because Justin wouldn't ever glare at her. "Please tell me you aren't double-crossing a client again."

"Not exactly. They're going to get what they paid me for. I'm just making some copies because you never know what that will come in handy." Kara offered a smile that she'd bet wouldn't reassure him, but he'd always melted easily for her. "Besides, the client is going to Grimes."

"Grimes?" Justin snorted, his cheeks turning red afterward, as though he hadn't meant to do something like that in front of her. "He'll never make a decent copy of this."

"I know, which is why I came to you. Hell, maybe I'll sell them one of your good copies for an even better profit after Grimes fails."

Justin shook his head, his gaze dropping back to his screen. "Give me an hour and you can have the original back. They'll never know I did a thing."

Kara waited in the small café out front, a cup of their horrible coffee in front of her.

"How do you drink that?" The new, disapproving voice of Torrin had her smiling.

She lifted her gaze to his familiar face. "Pour enough cream and sugar into anything and it becomes tolerable. Besides, it's three in the morning—what else are you going to do but drink coffee?"

Torrin undid the buttons of his suit jacket before sitting across from Kara. He always looked regal, no matter the situation or place. One lift of his finger had the waitress hurrying over, another cup of coffee in her hand.

He grimaced when the black liquid touched his lips, then put the cup down and pushed it toward the middle of the table.

"Did you really need to check up on me? I called Liam and thanked him, told him I was fine." With that, she glanced out of the large glass windows to spot both

Liam and Erik standing beside the dark town car. Liam's lips twisted into a smile when he met her gaze, though Erik only nodded.

Torrin folded his hands and set them on the table. "Yes, they told me you were fine, but I wanted to see for myself. I've never had to rescue you from a police station before."

"It was nothing, just a job gone wrong. They happen."

"Well, now I need to know the story."

Kara sighed and leaned back in the seat, kicking her feet up onto the bench beside Torrin. Refusing to tell him would only make the protective alpha need to know all the more, and it would go easier if she just told him and made him leave. "Mario Navarro hired me."

Torrin showed no reaction, which was pretty much on par for him. She knew him well, or as well as she suspected anyone knew him, given how tight-lipped he tended to be. "To steal the files held by Tracy Pera."

Kara should have been shocked he knew, but nothing much surprised her when it came to Torrin. He knew *everything*. "Mario thought it was just a few things on him, maybe one or two other people, but Richard Pera had files on everyone."

"Mario never got them, so what happened?"

"I burned them. I couldn't risk letting Mario, or anyone else, get hold of what was there, and I didn't have time to get them all out."

A tic in Torrin's jaw was his only outward reaction. "You burned such useful information?"

Kara took another drink, allowing the sickly-sweet coffee to slide down her throat and keep her awake despite the late hour. "I might have taken a few pictures of important things we'd find interesting." She offered a grin full of mischief. "Which is why it took me so long before I could destroy them."

Torrin only stared, his startling bright green eyes trained on her. "What did you do with the photos?"

"I sent them to our private email. I think you'll like it. Got some blackmail on a few politicians, figured out who was behind the hit on your pill shipment about three years ago, and a handful of other things."

Torrin nodded, his gaze finding the coffee as though tempted to try it again. "Tracy came to find me a few days ago. She wanted to make a deal. Her silence about the contents of those files in exchange for my protection of her, her mates and her child."

Kara huffed softly. "Well, I never figured that omega would have it in her. Good for her."

"I've found omegas to be far more resilient than we give them credit for." Torrin didn't say it as though he were happy about the fact. "I agreed, and even had our man who worked for Navarro save her mate and offspring."

"And Mario?"

"Dead."

Kara frowned at that, given that Torrin rarely killed people without good reason, and Mario was a useful patsy. "Why?"

Torrin's shoulders lifted, the subtle movement he did when an answer might reveal too much. She suspected anyone else would have gotten only that, but for Kara, he offered a hair more. "Mario struck the child."

Ah, that explained it. While she didn't know much of Torrin's past, or much about the past of his cousins, she knew it wasn't pretty. While he easily stomached all sorts of violence, he never had dealt well with the idea of children being hurt.

"Are you going to honor her deal, even though you know there aren't any files?"

"Yes. The hard work is already done. She's already played me, and I sent out word that they are not to be touched. If I revoked it now, it would be more work and make me look weak. I suppose I have to give her credit on this one. Not many outwit me or manage to lie to me."

Kara swirled the coffee in her mug, chuckling at the annoyance in Torrin's voice. He didn't like being beaten, especially at his own game. Though, if Kara were being honest, she'd suspect he knew all along that Tracy didn't have the files. Torrin had a soft spot, and while he rarely showed it and few would ever believe it, he did good every now and then. With him, though, who knew?

After a long moment of silence, Torrin released a soft sigh, one of the rare shows of anything other than the unflappable and ruthless businessman he displayed to the world. "You could have been hurt, Kara." The words came from Torrin in a low voice, the way he always spoke when he set aside that face, when she saw what was underneath the monster other people feared.

"It wasn't a big deal." She played it off. "Besides, I wasn't about to let that sort of stuff get into the wrong hands, not when it could have come down on you, since your name was on quite a few of those pages."

She tried to let that say what they never would outright—Torrin was important to her. He and his cousins had taken her in when she'd had nothing, protected her, given her a family of a sort, a purpose, a life.

"You should know better. I would have much rather taken that risk instead of you. Liam and Erik would agree." He leaned back, though still alert, on edge.

Torrin always did that. Despite all their years of friendship, she wasn't sure she'd ever seen him relaxed. "I think sometimes about the night we met."

She winced at the reminder, at the story he so rarely brought up.

After the night she didn't think about, and sure as hell didn't talk about, after the subsequent hospital stay, she'd had no pain pills. Broke and living on the streets, she hadn't been able to afford anything, and once what the hospital had pumped her full of had run out, Kara had been so desperate, she'd broken into an expensive townhouse in the center of the city. She'd expected some waspy woman hooked on opioids to have something in her medicine cabinet worth a damn.

Instead, she'd found Torrin.

Her silence allowed him to continue. "I wonder sometimes if I did the right thing."

"You helped me."

"Maybe, or maybe I ruined you. I could have easily afforded a boarding school for you, could have set you up for a good life. I wonder if bringing you deeper into my world didn't cause more harm than good."

Kara fidgeted in the seat, the heart-to-heart uncomfortable and unsettling between two people who had as much emotional depth as shallow puddles. "If you'd done that, I would have snuck out. I was never going to be strait-laced. I would have tried to do exactly what I'm doing now, except I wouldn't have had the training, so I'd probably be dead or in jail."

Torrin met her gaze with a hard stare, his eyes bright in the empty cafe. "Are you ever going to tell your brother you're alive?"

"Who?" she asked in a not-at-all-convincing squeak.

Torrin's gaze never shifted as he said the name Kara tried her hardest not to think about, not to remember. "Kane."

* * * *

Damon traced his gaze over the other people at the park, mostly children and the stressed-out and over-tired mothers who chased them.

The three alphas stuck out, but Kara hadn't budged on the meeting place. Then again, she knew they worked as private investigators, so she probably figured they weren't likely to do anything that might endanger the sort of people who were at a park at ten in the morning.

A smart choice, if he had to admit it.

He'd spent more than a few hours on his computer the night before, searching for any concrete information about her. Rumors had credited a few jobs to her, but nothing definite. Her name floated around like some bogeyman no one wanted to tangle with. She seemed to be a ghost, something talked about in the shadows but without solid form.

It made Damon nervous.

He liked plans. He liked knowing what was going to happen and having a contingency for any potential problems.

He did not like meeting some female criminal who had pulled a gun on Cullen and Reese and escaped a police station.

Not the sort of woman we should be trusting.

Reese kicked Damon's foot, scolding him softly. "Stop worrying so much."

How many times had someone told him that? Countless.

Damon was a born worrier. He'd lived his life always knowing everything that could go wrong and working hard to keep it from doing so.

People liked to poke fun at him about it, but then again, he'd never been caught with his metaphorical pants down. No one had ever needed to bail him out of anywhere, to save him.

Nope, Damon was on top of shit. *Always.*

"I'm not worrying. I'm just aware of how terrible this plan is."

"It's just some female thief. No need to get this worked up. It's not like we're waiting for an assassin here."

Just some female?

"Some female thief is just as capable of putting a bullet in each of us as anyone else," Damon pointed out.

Cullen grunted softly from the other side, leaning against a tree in the shade. "Just as capable and probably more likely. Nature made women smaller because they were already more vicious. It had to give us men a shot at survival."

Damon pressed his lips together instead of responding. The two alphas had become his friends, but that didn't change that they were very different. Both liked to mention how young Damon was, as though he were some kid in need of their help.

Which amused him as much as it annoyed him, since the two of them could barely use the GPS on their phones to find an address. They weren't in a position to mock him for a lack of knowledge.

Still, having them around filled a void for him. He'd never had the stability before, and they offered a counter to his slightly neurotic nature.

From around the corner came a small figure, dressed in a bright red shirt that clashed with the absurd neon blue of her hair. *Kara.* Cullen had mentioned that the brown she'd had in the elevator had been fake, but Damon hadn't believed it would be *this* obnoxious.

Not that the blue dampened the instant shot of attraction as he took in her narrow waist and her toned thighs clothed in black jeans. Her chest wasn't large, and the front of her shirt read *nice truck, sorry about your dick.*

She held an ice-cream cone, one of the cheap ones bought from a fast-food chain. When she darted her tongue out to stroke up the side, Damon nearly dropped his water bottle to the sidewalk.

"You know, you three look like creepy predators here."

"Maybe next time, don't schedule a meeting at a park."

"Well, the good thing is, even if you get picked up by the police, I've heard they don't have great security." She grinned, her lips damp from the ice cream and glistening in the sunlight. It made her hair impossibly brighter.

Reese laughed, the man always so easily swayed by a pretty face.

Cullen chimed in, as though trying to silence his clearly smitten friend, "Do you have the card?"

Kara reached down the front of her shirt, pulled the card free and held it between two fingers as though keeping it in her bra were in any way normal.

Cullen plucked it away and handed it to Damon.

"So, this is the whiz-kid?"

Damon ignored Kara as he studied the card, looking for signs of damage or trickery. He wouldn't put it past the woman to try to pull one over on them.

"This is Damon," Cullen said. "Any problems getting the key?"

"None. Easy job. In and out. They'll never know I was there. He'll assume he lost the key the next time he needs it, but when I took a glance at the planner in his briefcase, he isn't scheduled back there for a month."

Damon nodded and tucked the keycard into his laptop case. "It looks good." He removed the envelope of cash, already prepared for her, and held it out.

Kara grabbed it, folded the envelope over and stuck it into her back jeans pocket. "I can expect a five-star review from you, right?" That damned tongue of hers darted out again, like a thing with a life of its own, and gathered up more of the white ice cream.

A similar groan left the three alphas at once, the sort that always happened along with the hardening of someone's dick.

And Kara, the minx, curled her lips into a sharper smirk and did it *again*.

Reese gave in first, always quicker to break when it came to women. He crossed the short distance, the two large steps it took to stand just before her, close enough that she had to look up—way up, given he had over a foot on her—to meet his gaze. "Come back to our room."

"I don't fuck clients."

"Job is over. We aren't clients anymore."

Damon shifted on the bench, openly staring at the play between the two. He wasn't a virgin by any means, having spent his time exploring like any guy his age, driven by the higher libido of an alpha, yet he wasn't sure he'd ever felt a pull like this.

He had no idea if he was even part of *us*. Cullen and Reese routinely fucked women together. The alphas seemed joined at the hip, like some strange married couple who just didn't have sex with one another. Damon hadn't joined in, hadn't tried or been invited to.

Still, in those brief moments between Reese and Kara, Damon knew he'd either join in or bare his teeth for a shot of his own.

Which was absolutely insane. It was just a woman, one he didn't even know. Why would he react like this?

She lifted her ice-cream cone and twisted that teasing tongue along the swirled top, making a show of slowly swallowing it down. And didn't that fire up Damon's filthy thoughts about what else that wicked tongue could do?

Reese responded the way they all probably wanted to. He leaned down and captured a tiny speck of ice cream that rested on her lip.

Damon would have taken the kiss. He wouldn't have been able to stop himself, not so close, not with how much temptation sat there, or the teasing, mocking promise in Kara's eyes.

Reese didn't give in, though. After he licked clean the spot of dessert, he pulled back.

Kara's pupils spread until they ate up the blue.

Her scent… It was probably something that shouldn't have happened at a damned park, but the soft breeze drew it to him.

He'd never smelled anything more amazing, more succulent. Full of spice and heat and something so distinctly female. A beta had never drawn him in so deeply, but she couldn't be an omega.

Omegas weren't common and, being in high demand, tended to keep a low profile, especially ones of her age. By the time an omega reached twenty-five, they were mated or running. Either way, they didn't parade around like she did.

Which made his reaction all the stranger. Not that his cock would listen to reason.

Kara leaned in, as though she would kiss Reese, like she'd cross that threshold, but just before they touched, she lifted the ice cream between them. She pressed the cone into Reese's hand and moved backward, a playful bounce in her step that made her look like the best kind of prey. "Enjoy that." She nodded at the dessert clutched in Reese's palm. "It's the closest you're gonna get."

She backed away, tracing her gaze over each of the alphas in a very slow perusal. She caught her full bottom lip between her white teeth, openly enjoying the sight of each alpha.

And Damon was included, despite not being nearly as aggressive or obvious as Cullen and Reese. As the youngest, as the planner, the nerdy one, Damon was used to women not noticing him.

In Kara's hungry gaze, though? She noticed him.

And no matter how much he told himself all the good and valid the reasons it was stupid to consider anything, for him to even want to see her again, he did.

Chapter Four

Kara shuddered, her hormones raging inside her. Her skin burned, her forehead was coated in a slick of sweat and her cunt was damp.

I fucking hate this.

Was it those damn alphas? She'd spent plenty of time around alphas before, so what was it this time? Had it just been too long?

Temptation tore at her to call Liam. It had been years since she'd been that desperate, since she'd called him up to help her through the mindless lust, but she knew he'd come.

She snarled down at her hand when she realized she'd already dialed the number.

"Hey, kid." Liam's voice came out with that purr it always had, since he radiated sensuality even when he didn't mean to.

She leaned against the wall, the night air not enough to cool her heated skin. "Hey, Liam."

A rustle on the other end of the line and a muffled exchange let her know he was stepping away from the others, Torrin and Erik never far from him. A moment later, he responded, voice low. "You don't sound well. Do you need me?"

The question made her pussy clench and her chest ache. God, *yes*, she needed him in the worst way, but she couldn't bring herself to answer.

"Talk to me."

She swallowed past the lump in her throat, the one made of all the frustration. "I hate this."

"I know. Let me help you."

His voice took her back to the other times he'd helped her, the times when they hadn't kissed, when he'd spread her thighs and fucked her because she'd needed it, not because either had wanted it.

The idea of doing that again hurt more than the cramping of her stomach. It wasn't a heat, not exactly, yet these episodes plagued her, often only weeks apart. She'd try to hold them off, to sate them with scraps of flings, but they always rose up again.

Blame it on my fucked-up body. The scars on her lower stomach burned, ugly and raised and proof of the injury that had broken her.

Kara closed her eyes and let her head strike the wall of the building softly, trying to rattle loose her brains.

It's just instinct. Suck it up, cupcake.

"Where are you? I'll come get you."

"I can't do this with you again."

The softest sound echoed through the line. *A purr?* Only Liam would purr for her, as if the sweet sound would somehow make things better. "So we won't fuck. You can come home, still. You always can."

Home, meaning the house Liam shared with Torrin and Erik, the house she'd had a room in for years, no matter that she hadn't slept there in so long.

Instead, Kara pulled in a shaky breath. She had no idea if it was her own will or the thought of another awkward round with Liam that had her reining in her hormones. "It's okay. I'm okay."

His sigh was loud and clear, but he didn't push. When had pushing ever worked between them? Kara was the far more stubborn of the two. "You will call me tomorrow," he demanded, using the tone that usually brooked no arguments and the one that never worked on her.

"Is that an order?"

"Yes."

She smiled. "Then you know I'm not going to now."

His chuckle said he heard the renewed control in her voice. A goodbye ended the conversation, and not a moment too soon. Kara had no desire to further showcase her weakness. No matter how good she was at what she did *now*, she'd screwed up before, and if anyone knew that past, it was Liam.

Mistakes like getting caught by the police, or fucking up a job — those were mistakes that didn't sting. They happened.

This mistake was her body, and it struck a chord so much deeper than any other.

It made her feel broken, and there was no worse feeling.

But since that wasn't likely to change, Kara relegated it to the little spot in her brain where it squatted, the place where it would reach out to swipe at her from time to time.

The lights of the cafe were bright and harsh, spilling onto the sidewalk.

She needed to pick up the cards, Justin having sent her a message that morning about having them ready.

She focused on the task, on what needed to be done. She'd pick up the cards and store them away for future use.

While she'd considered getting a pretty penny by selling them to the alphas, the thought of seeing them again made her want to groan in need. Why she reacted so strongly to them, she didn't know, but the last thing she wanted was to throw her body even more out of balance.

Those alphas undid her, and while she loved herself some wild, no-holds-barred sex, she didn't need what *they* did to her.

Kara walked past the waitress and into the kitchen, then used the code Justin had given her for the door tucked away near the back.

The moment she walked past it, she froze.

Something's wrong. It was a sense she'd developed from living in places where she needed to watch her back. She couldn't pinpoint what it was at first, an overall feeling of discomfort closing in around her. She hadn't brought her pistol, never did when heading around town because getting picked up with an unregistered weapon was a quick way to get attention she didn't need. Instead, Kara reached into the pack at her thigh and pulled out her heavy pocketknife, using her thumb to slide the blade out.

Her steps were silent and light as she ventured deeper into the room, as the details that had set her off started to come together. The lights were off, and Justin *never* left the lights off. Even the constant glow of the computer screens was black.

Her eyes adjusted to the darkness, the only light slipping in from small barred windows that hovered near the ceiling. Pieces of his beloved tech were strewn about the floor, a chair turned over, the desk with all its drawers opened.

Amateurs. A professional wouldn't have made such a mess. Each thing they touched, each item they moved increased the likelihood of leaving behind something to get caught. Kara's best jobs happened when no one even knew she'd been there.

She passed the largest desk in the back corner where Justin kept his main computer, and she didn't have to look closely to identify the body on the floor.

Justin.

Even if she hadn't wanted anything serious with him, he was far too sweet a man to meet that end. Blood pooled beneath him, and a long open wound on his throat told her what had happened. Worse? A few of his fingers sat at angles they weren't supposed to.

Her stomach rolled, and it almost made her proud that she could still feel sick when witnessing such violence.

Justin was always on her case about double-crossing people, about taking dangerous jobs, but it seemed he'd pissed off the wrong client. A person could only swim through their world so long before attracting the attention of sharks, and it seemed Justin had done just that.

Kara leaned down and brushed her fingers over the man's arm. He had no mate or children, but he had a mother whom he cared for. She'd talk to Torrin and make sure the woman got the care she needed. They all owed Justin at least that much.

Even criminals stuck together.

When she pulled in a breath, knowing she could do nothing else, she rose. There were benefits to knowing those one worked with, and right then? It showed itself in Kara knowing exactly where Justin kept his sensitive data.

He'd never have told another person, guarding that location more than his own life. Dying was one thing, but pissing off a few of their clients by outing their secrets? That wasn't something she wanted to even consider.

On a bookshelf on the far wall, Kara moved the sci-fi books he'd loved, revealing the wall behind. She pressed in the bottom corner, the panel popping free to show a keypad.

She put in the four-digit code—Justin's mother's birthdate—and the safe clicked open.

From inside, Kara pulled the contents. A few folders, three plastic cases with hard drives in them and a handful of USBs with number sequences on top she didn't understand.

She found the four keycards, complete with blank fronts as she'd asked for, and the papers wrapped around them with information on how they worked. After folding them, she placed the items she needed in her bag, then sent a message to Erik about the rest. Torrin would love to get a look at anything left over there, and he could ensure the place was properly cleaned. She would have contacted Liam normally, but after their phone conversation, she couldn't bring herself to do so. Erik would make sure everything was handled. They didn't need the cops getting involved and finding potentially incriminating information.

On the top of a filing cabinet sat paperwork, part of the endless collection of horribly organized things Justin kept. What caught her attention was her name on the top file, or at least one of the many variations she used.

Kara Hamilton. The paper was wrinkled as if it had been handled often, with an old number of hers she'd gotten rid of long ago scribbled beneath it. She could almost see how Justin would hold it, crumbling it in his anxiety as he talked himself out of calling her. The idea that she'd never see him again hit her hard, but grief wasn't something she had a place for in her life.

She left the cafe when Erik said he'd get there in ten minutes. She might have waited to see him personally, but the idea of seeing any alpha made her shudder. While she didn't think about Erik like that, she didn't need the temptation. She also wasn't thrilled with the thought of watching someone dispose of Justin's body.

There was a reason she'd always preferred work that didn't deal with dead bodies—finding them, creating them or disposing of them.

She walked back to her apartment, trying to use the chill and random people to erase the entire night, to tell her she didn't care about…anything.

This was why she'd never moved from the city—she needed the noise. Being alone with no sound to distract her beyond her own scattered thoughts terrified her. No, she'd take the loudness, the busyness, the fact that even at three in the morning, folks walked the streets.

The suburbs weren't the place for her.

The front door to the lobby of her building had no doorman, because she didn't want someone noting her comings and goings. She took the stairs two at a time, ready to swallow down enough vodka to fall into such a deep sleep she didn't have to think anymore. Not about Justin. Not about the alphas. Not about any of it.

Inside her apartment, she threw closed the locks and tossed her bag on the table.

She grasped the hem of her top, ready to pull it free and strip down, when her gaze landed on the window, the one that sat open despite her always closing and locking it before leaving.

An arm closed around her throat before she could react.

The body behind Kara was large and solid, the strong arm tight around her neck. She smelled beta and male, with hot breath full of garlic turning her stomach.

"Stay calm and you won't get hurt."

The thought that he'd broken into *her* apartment irked her. Sure, she stole things, but she stole them from other people. Someone stealing things from her seriously pissed her off.

The man loosened his grip slightly when Kara didn't resist. *Always underestimating me.*

With the new grasp, Kara had room to maneuver.

She'd never been a patient person, and that was no different. She lifted her boot and stomped on the man's foot with her heel as hard as she could.

A grunt left him on a whoosh of exhaled breath, and his arm loosened more.

Just enough. Kara dropped her weight, unsettling the man's balance further, and drove her elbow backward. She struck him in his side, too low to hope for broken ribs, but hell, she could only do what she could do.

She darted forward, but before she made it a step, something yanked her backward.

He'd gotten his fingers into the back of her shirt. The fabric tore.

Damn it, I like this shirt!

She slammed into his front, and when she twisted to land a jab, something struck her cheek. The hit was solid but weak enough that she knew he'd pulled it.

Despite the ringing in her ears, she wanted to laugh at the idea that he had bitch-slapped her.

"Stop fighting me," he snarled as they toppled to the floor, bodies twisting as they fought for purchase.

Kara didn't give in to shit, and she wouldn't give in to him. Her knee hit him in the balls, and she took a good chunk from his forearm when she bit down.

Even so, Kara wasn't a close-quarters expert. She was small, which meant she lacked the strength and stamina for a prolonged hand-to-hand fight.

She couldn't overcome the sort of bulk the man carried if the fight lasted long.

Which meant she needed to finish this fast or it wasn't going to end in a way she liked.

The man hissed out more commands, telling her to settle down, to relax.

"Fuck off," she snapped, twisting to slam her elbow into his jaw.

He caught the move, pinning her arm down, effectively ending the battle. She could hardly draw breath, let alone move, his large body above her, trapping her.

"Who hired you?"

The words stilled the fight. This wasn't just a random break-in?

It made her feel mildly better.

"Your mom."

"I don't want to hurt you. My name is Thompson, and I am only trying to find out who hired you to steal the keycard." He leaned in close.

She saw her chance.

Kara whispered, and he frowned, coming even closer.

She threw her head back, striking him as hard as possible in the nose. A crunch sounded, the thing so damned rewarding, even as blood poured from Thompson.

He released her arm and sat up, grasping for his face. She twisted, then pulled her knees toward her chest and drove her heels against his chest.

Thompson tumbled backward, and she rolled to her feet, a throbbing in her shoulder she could cry about later.

She was quick as she darted, grabbing her pack from the table.

A crash echoed behind her, as though he had risen and knocked into something.

Fuck him, she wasn't about to turn around and look.

The locks gave under her quick hands, and she yanked the door open.

A shot rang out, a bullet striking the wall beside her.

Well, there goes my security deposit. Suddenly the noise didn't seem like enough.

She darted out, but the gun went off once more and a searing pain in her arm said it had grazed her.

She left Thompson in her wake, her speed finally helping her as she took the stairs to the lobby, then darted into the darkness before he could follow.

This was all the fault of three alphas, and she would damn well make them pay for it.

Chapter Five

Cullen tossed the keycard onto the table as soon as they walked into their hotel room. "Fucking worthless," he muttered.

Damon walked past him, picking up the keycard from the table as though it mattered anymore. "Be careful with it."

"Why? Grimes can't do a thing with it."

"He isn't the only person who can work on this. We'll find someone else."

Cullen lifted his lip, not annoyed with the young alpha, but he was as good a spot as any other to place his frustrations.

Reese closed and locked the door to their suite, then shrugged off his jacket. "Would you two stop fighting?"

They'd been at each other's throats for days. Ever since Kara had walked away, if he had to be honest. It was as though, when she'd left, this uncomfortable tension had started to grow.

Cullen couldn't settle. He couldn't sit still, couldn't sleep. His body remained alert and tense, as if waiting for something he couldn't identify.

And judging from the snarls passing between the other alphas through the day, he wasn't the only one.

How could that female still be affecting them?

Part of him wanted to find her. They'd found her once, so they could find her again. No matter how she might have objected, he'd smelled her, knew she wanted them, too.

Just a little more, and she'd give up whatever stupid reasons she'd had for turning them down.

Fuck, he wanted to see her naked. The picture of her stripped to nothing, that wild blue hair and those even wilder blue eyes beckoning him. He'd take her until she was too tired to toss any snark his way.

Would she be sweet? Once worn down and sated and blissed out after he'd made her come a couple of times, would she purr for him like a contented pet?

Probably not, but fuck if I don't want to give it a try anyway.

Cullen carded his fingers through his hair, ready to snap back at Reese just to release some of the pressure building inside him. He drew in a breath and went still.

Reese mirrored the action, as if they were connected and he'd caught wind of the same thing. Damon was the last, but the moment he'd done it, the same predatory look came into his eyes.

Kara.

Her scent was faint, but it was there. Had she broken in?

A deep growl vibrated from his chest at the challenge it posed to him, at the desire to hold her down and fuck her for the insult.

Reese was first, always better with his nose than Cullen had been. They entered the room the scent was strongest in, where it seeped from the closed door.

Damon's room in the suite.

Once they walked in, something else struck him.

Blood?

It leashed some of the lust, but damn if a rage he was unaccustomed to didn't take its place.

On the bay window sat Kara, the light from the desk lamp illuminating her.

He stopped in his tracks, something unfamiliar swamping him as he stared at her.

"What the fuck did you guys drag me into?" She twisted to look at them, and the sight of her swollen, darkened cheek squeezed his chest.

The more he looked, the more he saw.

Her lip was split and fat, and her shirt was torn, the strap hanging loose and showing off the lines of her bra.

Reese moved forward first. He caught her chin and turned her face.

Kara reacted like an angry kitten, hissing and swatting the touch away.

"What happened?" Reese asked.

"You assholes lied to me. Whatever this is about, it's bigger than one missing omega. People don't send brutes to my apartment over one little missing omega."

Reese exchanged a loaded look with Cullen. *This is our fault?*

He didn't care for guilt, but guilt over this? Even worse.

Damon spoke up, his steps slower than Reese or Cullen's had been. "Someone attacked you in your apartment?"

"Nice job keeping up. His name's Thompson. I don't recognize the name, so he probably works privately. He wanted to know who hired me to steal the keycard."

"That doesn't make sense. The keycard couldn't even be read. No one would have known about it unless you were caught stealing it," Damon interjected.

She cast a withering glare at the youngest alpha. "Trust me, pup, no one caught me."

The two faced off, and Damon dropped his gaze first.

Interesting.

"It wasn't when I stole it. It had to be when I had these made. To make a copy, my tech guy had to break into their system to code them right so when the company scanned them, it all showed aboveboard. They must have caught him, because I found him dead." She reached behind her and lifted something, holding them out to Damon.

He took the items and flipped through the keycards. "How did you get these? *Why* did you get them?"

"I knew Grimes wouldn't be able to do the job. Believe it or not, I'm pretty fucking good at this sort of thing, and I know everyone who needs to be known."

"But why have these made?"

"I figured I could sell them to you after Grimes failed."

Vicious. Cullen hated to admit that he really liked it. He shouldn't, especially since he normally hated cutthroat people, but hell... Kara looked good when she was scheming.

And now that they knew she wasn't seriously hurt, his libido decided to start ramping back up.

Damon took the cards from the room, as though the rest of them had become unimportant when he'd gotten a new piece of the puzzle.

Which was impressive, because Cullen couldn't think about anything beyond the female seated there.

Reese sniffed, then frowned. "What have you drunk?"

"Raided the minibar. Enjoy the hundred-dollar bill, because you owed me at least that much."

Reese stood. "I'm going to guess you haven't eaten, and you'll want ibuprofen for when that all starts to hit you after the liquor wears off. I'll get some food."

Once he left, Cullen took a seat on the bay window beside her.

He nodded at the gauze on her arm. "Cut?"

"Bullet graze." She shrugged then winced. Her cavalier attitude about the wound set his teeth on edge. *Exactly how much trouble is she usually in?*

"Is the man who attacked you dead?"

"Nope. Broke his nose, though." She curled her lips into a vicious smile that gave him a hard-on so fast it made him dizzy.

"Why is it I can't seem to stop thinking about you?" The words came out before he could censor them.

"Because you're an alpha, and they're pretty much led around by their dicks." She leaned backward, stretching her feet out until they rested beside him.

"Other females don't distract me like this." The words came out like an accusation, but he couldn't help his annoyance. "Other females don't smell like you do, don't do this to me." He wanted to understand exactly why she did this to him. Reese might be happy to be smitten with her, but Cullen needed to know why.

She sighed as she lifted her tiny bottle of pilfered mini-bar liquor and gulped it down. The way she wiped her mouth with the back of her hand, with a slight grimace as it probably irritated her split lip, was anything but classy, yet it fit her.

She didn't give a fuck what anyone thought, and that was the exact sort of woman he normally disliked.

Finally, she met his gaze again. "I don't know what you're expecting, but let's be clear. This isn't a long-term thing."

"I'm not looking for forever."

"We're going to discuss your case, figure out what the hell you dragged me into, and then I'm gone."

The words made an objection simmer inside him.

Because he knew she was right—this wasn't going anywhere—he leveled a look filled with all the heat that had clawed around inside him since he'd first caught sight of the wild woman days before. "Sure, Kara, that sounds fine. During that, though, make no mistake. We *will* fuck you."

Her eyebrow lifted, and he expected her to argue. She'd argued with everything else, and if there was anything a sane woman would argue against, it was a declaration that they'd be fucked by three alphas, against the assumption that they'd *let* three alphas do it.

Instead, she smiled, the action pulling her split lip despite even though it had to hurt like hell. "That's the first smart thing you've said so far."

Good thing I don't fall in love, because this woman is fucking dangerous.

* * * *

Kara stared at the ceiling, the fold-out couch in the living room of the suite surprisingly comfortable.

Each alpha had offered her their bed, despite the tension when it had happened. If she'd have picked one, she could have guaranteed a fight.

Which wouldn't have been all bad. *Those three all sweaty and rolling around? Sign me up for that show.*

The only reason she hadn't agreed was that she wanted to remove herself from as much of their scent as possible. Lying in one of their beds, with their masculine, lust-creating smell, was the last thing her overworked body needed.

Instead, she'd planted herself on the spacious couch, which shifted into a bed, and tried to ignore the demands her body made.

Silence pulled at her. At home, she'd have played music or just stayed up until morning, when the traffic and noise of the city could lull her to sleep. The suite was so nice—however, she couldn't hear a peep from anywhere else.

Instead, her brain ran rampant. It drifted to Justin's still body, to the man who had dared break into her apartment, to the alphas asleep in their rooms.

She shifted on the mattress, the action dragging her already stiff and aching nipples against the sheet.

She slid her fingers down her stomach, pausing on the raised scars there, the evidence of the reason her body didn't work right.

For a split second, she remembered the piece-of-shit beta who had made those cuts, his sadistic grin as she'd screamed and cried. That was what stuck with her some of the time—maybe because it was easier to remember that than the pain—but the beta had enjoyed it so much.

Worse than any of that, though? Lying there, barely awake—hell, barely *alive*—and seeing Kane walk in.

The memory of him hurt, of the knife plunging into his chest, was the last straw. She'd just lain there and watched it happen, watched as her only family had nearly been ripped from her while she'd been able to do nothing. The laughter of the men as they'd waited for Kane, telling her how they'd carve him up too...

She couldn't do anything to shake loose the nervous energy inside her created by stress and hormones and the maddening scent of the alphas.

Instead, she rose from the bed and crept into the room on the left, the door open like an invitation.

She could have picked any of them, all of them, but she made her choice with ease.

Cullen.

The hard-ass, the one she liked the least but who could give her what she needed.

Reese was funny, sweeter, easier to fall for. Damon? The pup would have bent for her, and while she enjoyed putting an alpha in his place beneath her, it wouldn't wipe clean the ugly images in her head.

For what she needed, Cullen was the right choice.

The light from the rising sun poured in through the window. The room was almost identical to Damon's, except Cullen had no computer set up and didn't use the desk.

The scent of him and gun cleaner struck her, both alluring.

He rested on the bed, body still, blankets pulled up to his waist, his broad, solid chest on display.

God, that man is beautiful.

Maybe beautiful wasn't the right word, and she'd bet he'd bitch if he'd heard the thought, but what else could she say? Tribal tattoos crawled up his right arm from wrist to shoulder, then spread over that pectoral, black against his tanned skin. When she'd met the alphas, she'd never have expected that he'd be the one to have tattoos beneath his suit. His hair was messy, the longer part on top no longer perfectly falling backward with the help of gel. Instead, the light brown hair had a wave from the shower he'd taken before sleep.

Kara shimmied out of her already drenched panties, her body beyond ready. She could have crawled on top of him and mounted him without any foreplay.

She'd been ready for hours as she'd lain in the living room, trying to do anything else.

But why resist? Why keep trying to avoid it?

This wasn't the pathetic thing she did with Liam, with Justin, with friends who didn't really want her or, worse, wanted things she couldn't give them. This was just like any hook-up, and they'd both walk away from it happier for the few moments of stolen pleasure.

What the fuck is wrong with that? She told herself the same lies she told herself every time.

She moved forward, crawling onto the bed and over him in a quick motion that let her steal her first kiss before he woke.

When he did, he came to ready to fight. Fight, fuck or flight, that was what bodies did when stressed, and his first reaction was violence.

Cullen flipped them, his hand around her thin throat, his green eyes fierce.

What the fuck was wrong with her? If he'd woken with a sweet kiss, she'd have snarled, but like this? That fire and violence and the threat of his hand at her throat had her all but purring as she wrapped her legs around his waist, the blanket tossed aside in his attack.

Awareness came to his eyes, his forehead creasing and his eyebrows pulling in. "Kara?"

He removed his hand as though her skin burned, but she took advantage, as she always did, and leaned up to take his lips in another kiss.

A deep growl left him, and she swallowed it. Even if it had taken him a minute to catch up, the grinding of his cock as he rolled his hips forward said he'd figured shit out.

More, her mind cried at how his hard dick fit against her cunt, nestled there and grinding against her clit in a delicious spark of pleasure.

It seemed he hadn't worn anything to bed.

Did he always sleep naked or was he just hopeful? Maybe if she'd been someone else, his assumption that she'd show might have bothered her. She wasn't someone else, though, and Kara only basked in the coursing pleasure as he thrust against her drenched pussy.

"You're so damned hot," he growled as he moved his lips from hers and attacked her throat. His facial hair scratched her, but even that only lit her up, only energized each nerve ending of her body. "Fuck, how can your cunt smell this good?"

Because it was broken. Because a fire raged inside her that never fully went out.

Kara reached between them, dragging her nails down his chest and abs until she could stroke his cock. She didn't wrap her fist around it, not willing to lose any of the contact between it and her needy clit. Instead, she danced her fingers along the top of his shaft, teasing the head and collecting the wetness there. She didn't bother to hide the way she took the pre-cum smeared on her fingers between her lips and licked them clean.

A more vicious sound left Cullen, as though the action had woken something deeper inside him, something primal. He reached for her shirt, but Kara swatted his hand away.

She never removed it during sex.

He stilled above her, though his chest rose and fell in heavy breaths. "What's wrong?"

Words stuck in her throat, words she almost wanted to say but wouldn't dare. *Deflect.* "Are you going to fuck me already?"

His emerald eyes hardened at the challenge. "Why don't you want me to take off your shirt?"

"If you can't manage this, there are two other alphas in this suite who can."

That snapped his control, stole away his questions. It seemed he didn't care for her threats, but the way his cock, impossibly harder, pressed to her sex said maybe he did.

Kara's eyes slipped closed at the feeling, as she prepared for that wonderfully full stretching when a hard dick would plunge deep, taking up every inch of space inside her and driving everything else away.

His warm breath still held the tang of mint from his toothpaste as it fell over her face. The moment she waited took forever, as though the seconds turned to hours, before he slammed into her with a thrust so strong it stole her breath.

The tightness of Kara's body nearly made it so Cullen didn't hear her lusty cry. He struggled to pay attention to anything beyond the clutching wetness of her pussy and the way her scent drove all rational thought from him.

She'd not let him remove her shirt, but maybe she was shy. In the end, the call of her body had been more important than one little obstacle. Let her keep the damned shirt on if it meant burying himself this deep inside her sweet cunt.

Her face twisted into almost pained lines of ecstasy, like his dick was the only thing she needed right then.

She came to me. That stroke to his ego helped — when she could have gone to either other alpha, she'd crawled into his bed. He didn't mind sharing with Reese, and hell, he had every intention of fucking her right along with his best friend, but it didn't erase the possessive pleasure at her choosing him.

Damon? Well, they hadn't taken a woman together before, but he had a feeling it would happen. The kid was becoming more family than coworker.

None of that mattered right then, though. That was for another night, another time.

Cullen waited as her pussy squeezed down around his cock, trying to give her time, not wanting to risk hurting her. He wasn't a gentle alpha nor a small man, and Kara was a tiny beta.

Tiny and the hellion Reese called her, it seemed, because what couldn't have been more than a handful of heartbeats later, Kara rolled her hips toward him and gouged her nails into him to urge him to move.

Verbal demands accompanied the physical ones. "Fuck me already," she ordered in a voice that held the same authority as any alpha he'd dealt with.

"Gladly, thief," he responded, using the name like a reminder, pulling back until only the tip of his thick cock remained.. He paused, the sensation as her greedy pussy seemed to pulse around him to keep him inside too wonderful to ignore. He grasped the short blue strands of her tresses to tip her head backward before he plunged into her again.

He took her hard and fast, his grip on her hair keeping her still as he fucked her with everything he had.

His knot ached, the sensation strange and familiar. He was driven by a need inside him that made him feel out of control, as though he had to sate her, had to spill deep inside her and nothing in the world could pull him free.

Kara responded with the same frenzied motions. Her eyes never opened, and she never looked at him, but the flush on her pale skin, lit up by the rising sun, made her look like some filthy fantasy. Her small breasts, covered in a thin top, bounced as each brutal thrust moved her, as she took everything he had to give, trapped beneath his larger body as she was.

Cullen didn't bother with more kisses, instead using his teeth on her throat, tasting her sweat from her heated skin. She was divine. Wild and untamed and as lost to lust as he was.

Her hips moved on their own, her hands clutching in the same way, as though each part of her fought for him. He'd have scratches down his back when they were done from where she'd raked her nails over him, and he'd fucking love it.

Her body went haywire when she came, her cunt tightening around him so much he sank deep and remained still, enjoying the way it seemed to want to pull him deeper.

He lost his battle to stave off his release as her back arched and he caught a nipple with his teeth through the fabric of her top.

It wasn't the orgasm that shocked him, though. It was way that aching in his knot became all too clear, how the base of his cock swelled and locked him inside her, behind her pubic bone, deeper than ever. Each squeeze of her cunt, accompanied by another gasping whine from her, milked his knot as he emptied hot seed into her body.

It took him until his brain started working again, until a shift of his hips tugged his solid knot against her entrance, that he realized the truth.

Kara was an omega.

Chapter Six

Reese had openly glared Cullen's way when Kara had grabbed a cup of coffee and headed off to the shower first thing in the morning.

The moment the water turned on, Reese zeroed in on Cullen, who was pouring his own cup. "You fucked her?"

It wasn't jealousy exactly, but rather annoyance that he'd been left out.

Cullen didn't hurry as he finished his coffee. Finally, he lifted his green eyes. "She's an omega."

The words reached into Reese and gripped him. *An omega?* He guessed it explained a few things, like their instant attraction to her.

While alphas couldn't scent designations like omegas could, he suspected they might still know on some instinctual level. The unbearable lust, the possessiveness...it all hinted that the alphas had been aware of her status as an omega.

And it only made his need for her grow, building inside him.

"You're sure?"

Cullen took a slow sip of his black coffee before setting it down. "I might not always be observant, but I noticed when I knotted her."

The thought of Cullen stretching her in that way, of him claiming the female so fully, had Reese groaning.

"Don't get any ideas."

Reese lifted his lip. "You already had her. Are you really in any place to tell me not to?"

"That's not what I'm saying. You want to fuck her? Go for it, but I know you, Reese. Don't let it go to your head."

"I'm not stupid." Even as he snapped, that niggling inside him said Cullen wasn't out of place for saying it.

Reese knew what they'd always wanted. They lived a dangerous life, and they needed a sweet, quiet mate who would stay home where it was safe. It was best to stick to one-night stands until they found the right female, and that wasn't Kara.

They'd seen what could happen to mates who ended up too close to the work they did. The lucky ones got quick deaths and the not-so-lucky ones didn't. The only way a mate of theirs would make it was if she flew under the radar, and if she listened. Since Kara wasn't likely to do either, she didn't fit what they needed.

Which meant that, sure, Reese would give in to the urges that had swamped him since he'd first seen her. He'd tease and tempt her until he was buried so deep inside her sweet little body that he might just manage to quench the fire she'd started in him, but that was as far as it could go.

The door opened to the bathroom, and she came out, her hair appearing darker due to the water. She wore the same pants from the night before but had on one of Damon's button-up white shirts, since he was the smallest of the three. It was tucked into the waist of her pants, showing off her toned figure, and the billowy fabric of the shirt teased the figure beneath.

He could fuck her and let her go...*right?*

The subtle ache between Kara's thighs thrilled her. Cullen had more than lived up to her expectations, and when she'd crawled from his bed and back to her own, she'd fallen asleep without a problem.

He'd managed to force her body back to center, to let her regain control.

She hadn't spoken to Cullen all morning, managing to grab her coffee and jump into the shower before having to. The night before, when his eyes had widened just like his knot, when he'd realized what she was, he'd tried to talk to her. Kara had shut that shit down, because being stuck on an alpha's cock was so *not* the time to have a heart-to-heart.

Hell, she was pretty sure there was really no good time to have one.

By the time she left the safety of the bathroom, she'd rebuilt her armor.

He was nothing but a convenient knot, and she was the snarky omega who didn't give a shit what he thought. In fact, she figured all three of them were nothing but thorns in her ass, causing her problems, which meant that using them to slake her lust seemed fitting.

Besides, they had other things to deal with. Most importantly, Kara needed a hell of a lot more details about whatever case they were working on. Clearly, these alphas were idiots. She couldn't trust that they'd handle the issue themselves, meaning she needed to know exactly what they'd gotten themselves—and her—into.

That had left them back at Grimes' place. He was inept for handling the actual coding of the cards, but even that moron could add the names and pictures to the ID badges Justin had created. Part of her didn't want him to touch the cards, like they were Justin's final masterpieces, but she shut down that strange, sentimental instinct.

While he worked, they sat in his shitty little waiting room out front. His shopfront doubled as a locksmith, which always made Kara roll her eyes.

"The omega's name is Grace Singer," Damon said, his computer away for once. His glasses were ever-so-slightly askew, and it added to his almost puppy-dog cuteness. "She's been missing for two weeks."

"Two weeks? She'd probably just out having a good time."

Damon shook his head. "I doubt it. Her friend, Bran, hired us because he spoke to her the night before she took off. She was nervous and told him she appreciated everything he'd done before she'd gone home."

"Well, that sounds like she left on purpose, since she gave him the famously vague goodbye."

Reese picked up the story. "We know she left on her own. The alpha searched her place, and she took a journal she never went anywhere without."

"If she left on her own, why the hell are you trying to find her?"

He sighed and rubbed his fingers against the bridge of his nose. "Because in addition to running, she stole

Bran's pistol. He hired us because he wants to make sure she's safe, because obviously she needs help."

Kara leaned back in the shop's hard plastic chair, crossing her legs to show just how little she cared. "So you are going to come along all white-knight and rescue the poor damsel?"

Cullen spoke up, and she hated that his words sparked back to life every fire he'd started the night before, as though his voice alone could bring forth those memories and make them real again. "She was working as an intern at a pharmaceutical company in her home town, the same company whose main location is here. We were able to get a bank statement showing she pulled cash out here in town, and Bran said in the last week or two she'd become obsessed with researching information about the lab, but she refused to tell him why. The best lead is that lab."

"And that's why you need the keycards?"

"If I can get inside, I can access their computer system, see what we can find out about if she went to the main lab and when," Damon said.

"So your brilliant plan is to go into the place you think she might have been, despite having no idea why she was there, and hope maybe you'll figure something out?"

It was Reese who frowned the hardest in response, telling her who exactly had come up with that crack-shot plan. "Do you have a better idea? Because clearly there's a problem with that lab or no one would have come looking for those keycards."

She pressed her lips into a tight line when she could come up with nothing better. They could sit on the lab, watch it for a few days, but she had no idea what they were looking for. Plus, since people had come to her place looking for *her*, it seemed she was short on time. Getting inside afforded them the best chance of catching that one useful piece of information that would bring everything else together.

She didn't care about the omega — at least, she kept telling herself that — but she cared a lot about her own skin, and right then her skin was on the line, and it pissed her off not to even know why.

She'd done far cooler things in her life to end up in the crosshairs of some bigwig. Why couldn't she be in trouble over the time she'd stolen a car from a mob boss? Or when she'd drawn a mustache on the portrait of the largest tech guru in the country while it hung over the mantel of his highly secure private home? So that one hadn't paid anything, but she'd felt slightly better after having spent hours on the phone with tech support over her newest cellphone not working. Honestly, the whole thing was almost insulting.

If this is what kills me, I'm going to go poltergeist on these assholes forever.

Grimes walked back into the main shop area, his gaze not nearly careful enough for Kara's comfort. Then again, that was why she didn't use him. He was a hack. "Here you go."

Damon took the cards, lifting them to check the craftsmanship.

He didn't need to. Grimes could handle adding a few pictures and laminating a pre-done card. That shit was child's play. Justin had done the hard work, the coding, creating duplicate cards that would function to get them into the building without setting off red flags. Grimes only needed to add the names and pictures to the physical cards.

"Looks good." Damon tucked the cards into his laptop case, then looked over at Kara. "So, are you in?"

Despite everything inside Kara screaming that this was a bad idea, that she should spend as little time around these alphas as possible, she shrugged. "Fuck it, why not?"

Chapter Seven

Reese tried to ignore the omega, but it was hard once he knew she *was* an omega. It explained more than a few things, like why all three of them couldn't forget about her.

By the time Grimes had finished the cards, it had been too late to hit the lab. Instead, they'd picked up food and returned to the hotel room.

Kara hadn't been nice, choosing to throw an insult of one kind or another every chance she got, as though it put her on steady ground.

Then again, maybe it did.

She didn't act like any omega he'd dealt with before, and he'd had his share of them. They were sweet, even the feisty ones.

Kara was *not* sweet. She didn't seem to be affected by them the way he'd grown used to. No leaning his way instinctually, no seeking approval, no reaction to praise.

It all confused him, yet that uncertainty didn't dull his want. If anything, it made him need her more, made him want to break past her exterior and find whatever was beneath.

Not that she seemed interested in that.

The moment she'd finished eating, she'd headed out. When Cullen had forbidden it as too dangerous, she'd tossed him the middle finger and not slowed her steps at all.

Unless they planned to tie her to a bed—which wasn't out of the question when it came to options—it seemed they'd have to deal with her wild streak.

That left him and Cullen in a corner booth in the small restaurant of the hotel as Kara sat at the bar and worked her way through her second martini.

And flirted.

That was the worst, that she beamed that smile at anyone who showed an ounce of interest in her.

"She's going to be the death of us," Cullen said.

Reese nodded. It seemed a damn likely option, though if he got to go after being buried deep inside her sweet cunt, he had a feeling he might consider it a fair trade.

Which was stupid, because it wasn't as though he hadn't slept with omegas before. He knew he could find it elsewhere. "What is it about her?"

"She's different." Cullen took another drink of his water, both of them choosing to remain sober despite Kara's quickly deteriorating state. "She's also a menace."

"What does it say about us that we like it?"

"We'll get a good taste of her and be done. She's just an infatuation, and we'll get over that novelty fast. That's how it's been before, and it's always worked.

Just have to get her out of our system, and we'll remember why we don't claim omegas like that."

Because it was too risky. Kara had proven time and time again they couldn't trust her. She lied, she went behind their backs, she was forever looking for a way to one-up them. What sort of life would that be? What sort of future could he have with a woman who was never honest?

Reese thought back to Gabby, the only woman he'd ever thought he'd have as a mate. A familiar aching started in his chest at how wrong he'd been, at how she'd stolen so much from him and left him bitter.

He shoved away the hurt, as he always did.

The male beside Kara on the barstool set a hand on her leg, a hand that was quickly creeping up toward the juncture of her thighs, toward that spot Reese wanted to lavish with attention, that he wanted to lick until he could taste nothing else.

Alpha possessiveness was legendary, and the twin growls that left Cullen and Reese said Kara had just pushed it too far.

They were up and out of the booth before the asshole at the bar could move his hand another inch.

He'd be lucky if he didn't pull it back with just a stump.

Kara didn't find the beta next to her all that interesting. He'd prattled on about himself, and he'd thought she wouldn't notice the wedding ring he'd recently removed, but tan lines always gave it away.

Still, the attention usually helped. Her day around the alphas had once again sent her body responding, and normally a quick roll with a beta could quench some of that.

And, if she were being honest, the nearly-foaming-at-the mouth alphas in the corner booth watching her made it all the more fun.

They'd arrived just after she had and taken a seat in the back, as though she wouldn't notice them.

Which was absurd, because she'd been able to focus on little else. Maybe the beta was boring, but it wasn't as though she'd spent much of her focus on him, either.

Instead, she'd *felt* each small rumble from the alphas, the way their gazes traced her and the wave of fury so hot it scalded her when the beta had touched her leg.

It was enough for her to end up drenched, and it had nothing to do with the fumbling fool beside her. It was some weird foreplay between her and the alphas.

The alphas stalked through the small space, and she wasn't shocked when Cullen grabbed the beta's hand and yanked it away.

His control did surprise her, though. Sure, he was snarling. And, yeah, his teeth were bared like a pissed German Shepherd, but he didn't break the beta's arm or even throw a punch.

Pity. I'll have to try harder next time.

"Don't touch her," Cullen growled in a rumble so low and feral it sent delectable shivers up her spine.

If that wasn't a *she's mine* declaration, she didn't know what was.

And while she had no illusions about anything long term, fuck if his tone didn't rev her engine even more.

The beta's eyes went wide, that 'oh shit, this was a bad idea' freezing thing people did when fight or flight were both bad options. "I didn't realize," he stuttered.

She should feel bad. She'd put him in that spot, but a little fear never hurt anyone, and he'd been boring and self-centered enough that guilt didn't get within a mile of Kara.

Cullen peeled his hand from the beta's wrist but didn't pull his threatening gaze away until the beta had run from the bar.

"Oh, no, that wasn't an overreaction at all," Kara said, turning in her barstool to face the two alphas who surrounded her. It reminded her of how large they were, so that even on the tall barstool, they towered above her.

She should not like that as much as she did.

Reese spoke, which didn't shock her, because Cullen's jaw twitched from the way he was grinding his molars together. Cullen wouldn't be saying anything until he unclenched. "You know exactly how alphas are, so don't pretend this little show wasn't for our benefit."

"Show? What show? He was a charming, handsome man, and I could use some company." She cut a dismissive look Cullen's way. "Seems last night didn't do the trick."

Which was such a lie, she was amazed she could get the words out without busting into laughter. Cullen had done everything right the night before, but her body rarely stayed happy for long. Besides, it was these alphas' fault it was currently having a hissy fit, since they seemed to make her control take a swan dive out of the window.

Cullen caught her chin, his grip strong but careful, as though walking his line of control. "I don't recall any complaints. In fact, I recall you coming around my knot so hard, you cried out."

"Maybe we remember it differently. Men are always thinking they're better than they are." The back and forth lit Kara up better than any romantic gesture or candlelit dinner.

He could have lifted her onto that bar to fuck her right there, and she'd have been so on board with that plan.

Reese pulled in a deep, noisy breath through his nose before leaning in as though not wanting the conversation to carry. "Look here, hellion. Either you take your ass to the suite, sleep in one of our rooms and stay put, or you're about a minute from getting fucked. You can't expect to smell the way you do and not get a reaction."

Kara inhaled, mirroring his response, drawing the scent of the aroused alphas deep into her lungs, able to identify it over the other smells in the room. The bar, the liquor, the unwashed bodies — those things couldn't stand against that perfectly masculine scent of the turned-on males.

"I'm not going back to the suite," she said, challenge in her voice.

Reese leaned in so his lips brushed her ear, the touch sinful in its fleeting stroke. "No? Because the second option was pretty clear."

Kara grasped him behind his neck, letting her nails dig into his skin, using that bite of pain to soothe her wild nature, and twisted to kiss him.

The kiss was hard, fast and exactly like the sex they were headed for. It lacked sweetness or subtlety, wasn't about teasing or foreplay. Instead, it was a game of who would come out on top, and Kara always won that game.

She broke it seconds later, closing her teeth on his bottom lip in a bite just this side of breaking skin. "The suite is too far away, but there's a bathroom right over there."

He had her up and against him so fast Kara's breath caught.

For a woman who made a lot of bad choices, she'd bet taking them both at the same time ranked up there amongst her worst.

Cullen closed and locked the door to the single stall bathroom, the place surprisingly clean.

The blinding white of the tile didn't show a speck of dirt and made Kara stand out, like a perfect background to showcase her black-clad ass and absurd blue hair.

She hung on to Reese as though he were life, their lips mashing together in something too violent to be considered a kiss. Reese and Cullen had taken females together before, and while it was never rose-petals-on-the-bed sweet, it was altogether more with Kara.

Everything she did called him to dominate her. He wanted to force her to her knees, wrap his fingers in her hair and feed her every inch of his hard cock. He *needed* to see her eyes water as she swallowed down his thick shaft, and better yet, the way he knew her nails would be in his side, in the muscles of his ass so she could take him deeper.

She wouldn't be outdone, not this omega, and it made him want to try all the more.

Reese let her feet drop to the ground, but only so he could reach for her shirt.

As she had the last time, she shoved his hands away, trying to distract Reese by reaching for the button of his pants.

Lines between Reese's eyebrows said he'd caught the movement.

Still, Reese was the same selfish alpha Cullen was and didn't push the issue. He'd say it was respect, but it wasn't. Push her and Kara would walk—possibly with a limb or two of the alpha who had pissed her off.

She used her nimble fingers to tug at the fastening of Reese's pants, but he recovered quickly, undoing the top buttons of the white shirt she still wore then pulling the shoulder enough to bare one of her perfect, perky little breasts.

Reese leaned down to attack it with his lips, feasting as he cupped it with a hand.

Kara dropped her head back, her face drawn into lines of ecstasy that Cullen already found familiar. It wasn't just pleasure, instead reaching deeper, as though feeding something primal and hungry inside her with the touches.

Cullen shook himself from his inaction. He didn't mind watching—hell, there had been plenty of times he'd been happy to jerk himself off as he watched his friend fuck a female, where his voyeur side lived through the detached pleasure.

That wasn't what he wanted right then, though. He took a spot behind Kara and flicked open the button of her jeans. They were snug on her narrow hips and molded perfectly to her firm ass. He peeled them down, leaving her underwear in place.

A black thong cut across the pale tone of her skin, the garment simple, not adorned or fancy in any way. It seemed fitting—stunning and yet straightforward. *Just like her.*

Cullen used his foot to work off her shoe so one leg could come free of the jeans, but left the clothing pooled around her other foot. He traced the thong with a single finger beneath the fabric, teasing her and himself before tugging it down and letting it follow the path the jeans had.

Reese pulled back, releasing her breast with a noisy pop before he traced his gaze down her body. He let out a low whistle. "You are damned pretty." He grasped her hips and turned her, chuckling when she nearly tripped and had to rely on the alphas to keep her standing. "But Cullen's already gotten to fuck you, and I plan on having my turn, now."

Cullen stole a kiss before Kara could complain, and he was sure she would. He moved his large hand to her breast, palming it so he could brush across the hard, damp peak of her nipple.

She moaned against his lips, grasping with her hands for him. Fuck, he liked that, loved that she didn't hide how much she wanted him.

She might snarl some, might make jokes, but she didn't hide a bit of the passion coursing through her fit little body.

Reese clutched her leg and lifted it, setting that knee on the sink. The position left her cunt exposed and her balanced precariously on a single leg.

Not that he'd let her fall.

Her cry had his dick growing impossibly harder when Reese ran his fingers through her slick folds.

She squirmed, as though trying to get closer to both of them at the same time.

Fine by me. We'll be really fucking close pretty soon.

"Ready?" Reese asked with a purr in his voice.

Cullen broke the kiss so he could watch. Kara's back was arched, and Reese had his cock in his fist, teasing her entrance with the blunt head.

Cullen denied Kara any more kisses, wanting to see his friend sink deep into her heat and her wetness.

"Get on with it," Kara all but snarled.

Reese tapped his cock against her like a soft reprimand. "That doesn't sound like being good. Not sure you deserve anything when you can't be good."

Kara's nails sank into Cullen's arms, but he savored that sharp pain.

"If you aren't up to the task, maybe that beta —"

Whether it was to shut her up or because Reese couldn't tolerate the mention of the other man in that moment, Reese plunged into her waiting cunt, grasping her hips to steady her.

The most beautiful moan left Kara's lips, the sort of sound that belonged in a dark room, thick as smoke and twice as lovely.

"Fuck," Reese hissed out. "She's drenched."

Cullen dipped down to capture a quick kiss, her position forcing her forward. Still, he wanted to taste those little mewling cries she made, especially since they were so at odds with how she cut into him with her nails, with how she demanded to be satisfied. The dichotomy thrilled him, that he couldn't quite figure her out, and he liked it.

"Harder," she ordered.

Reese brought his hand down to swat the side of her ass hard enough that the sound echoed off the tiles of the room. "You aren't in control here."

She moaned, her body writhing as though the reminder turned her on as much as it pissed her off.

As quickly as she reacted, she recovered. "Leave it to me to get saddled with an alpha who has no idea what to do with his cock."

Cullen chuckled, using one hand to undo the button and zipper of his jeans, then pull free his dick. He was already rock hard, had been for a while, but he gave himself a nice stroke just to enjoy the sight of Kara's flushed cheeks, her eyes closed again.

That meant that while she bitched, she had no idea she was face to face with his shaft.

Reese must have caught wind, because he slapped her ass again — and fuck if the way it jiggled despite how firm it was didn't just make for the best picture — and chuckled darkly. "You'll take what we give you."

She opened her mouth, but before she could snark at them, Cullen fed his thick cock past her lips.

Kara tasted nothing but heady, masculine alpha. Salty, strong and something her omega rejoiced in.

She didn't need to see what was happening to know when someone had shoved their dick into her mouth. That was the sort of thing she noticed.

Maybe she should have bitten him, or at least scraped him with her teeth as a warning against him taking liberties, but she responded on instinct.

She wrapped her lips around him and sucked, trying to swallow his taste. He twitched in her mouth when she massaged the bottom of his cock with her tongue, when she opened wider to swirl around the head. She traced the ridges where he was thicker, that delicious collection of skin near the bottom. *I could spend hours happily worshiping this cock.*

However, with the way Reese pounded into her, with the steady slap of his hand on her ass every few strokes, she didn't have hours.

She'd teetered on the edge of orgasm since he'd threatened to fuck her — no, even before then, when the weight of their possessive gazes had teased her senses as she'd flirted with that beta.

Kara did nothing half-assed, at least not when it came to sex, so she trusted herself to the grasp of the alphas. She wouldn't trust them for anything else, but they wouldn't let her fall. They were far too over-protective for that. However, when she didn't have to focus on balance, she used the precarious position to take Cullen deeper.

Funny that when he filled her mouth, he seemed even larger. Her lips were pulled tight around his thick shaft, and he teased at the back of her throat. *Not enough.* She let him slide farther back, keeping her throat straight, giving him entrance as deep as he wanted to go.

Cullen didn't thrust, though the hard slams of Reese's body into hers still managed to knock her forward a hair. All of it was perfect.

She couldn't think. The sway of her breasts when Reese's hard dick plunged deep inside her, the burn of her ass from how he had landed the playful spanks, that completely taken-over sensation of Cullen's shaft pressing deep into her throat then back again were the only things she could focus on.

Sex had always helped her ignore the rest of the world, but had it ever done it so fully? Had she ever given herself over to the pure insanity of it?

Or, perhaps more accurately, had she ever felt so powerless to keep any control when she'd done it before?

The growl of the alpha behind her ran along her spine like the sharp points of a pinwheel, but it also let her know he was growing close to losing his battle with prolonging the moment.

Cullen grasped her chin, helping to straighten her out more, then crept his fingers down to her throat. His groan was rough when she knew he felt his cock sinking impossibly deeper.

His touch was almost sweet, coaxing fingers stroking along the straight column of her throat, before he shuddered and pulled back until only the head of his cock remained inside her mouth. The first jet of hot cum to land on her tongue threw her into her powerful release. Her pussy clenched around Reese's dick, though it didn't stop him. In fact, he fucked her harder despite the clutching of her cunt, digging his fingers into her hips.

The taste and warmth of Cullen's cum pooling on her tongue distracted her, at least until Reese's knot began to swell. That pressure, the way the base of his dick grew and stretched her, was impossible to ignore.

Cullen's thick cock muffled any sound she made, the cum still sitting on her tongue as Reese's knot locked inside her when he sank as deep as possible.

Cullen pulled from her mouth, then traced his thumb over her full lips. "Swallow me down, thief."

Kara's throat bobbed as she did so, as she followed the command he rumbled out so deeply yet sweetly. The taste of his hot cum seeped into her, soothing as he stroked her lips.

Meanwhile, Reese massaged her hips with his firm grasp, unable to pull out due to his knot.

Despite Reese's heavy breathing, he held her steady. She didn't so much as waver in his grasp, and Cullen, after tucking himself back into his pants, crouched to help keep her balanced.

Cullen offered sweet kisses, the action odd with how she could still taste his cum, with how Reese's cock would twitch inside her and cause her body to shudder with another wave of pleasure in response.

"How are you?" he asked against her lips.

The question should have been easy. She hadn't felt this good in a very long time. The two of them had satisfied her in ways she hadn't realized she'd even been missing.

That seemed too personal, though, too sappy for a woman like her.

She closed her teeth on his bottom lip in a gentle bite before answering. "It'll do."

His chuckle was deep and surprised. *Did he think one little round in a bathroom would turn me speechless?*

Reese moved his hands to her ass, massaging over the flesh until she drew a gasp at the burning skin. Worse? It reignited the want inside her, though it only shifted like a beast still sated. "You're lucky I think your attitude is cute."

"Oh yeah?"

Cullen answered, dragging his thumb across her bottom lip as though daring her to nip him again. "Yeah, because if we didn't, we'd just fuck it out of you." He pressed that thumb into her warm mouth, her tongue latching on to it out of instinct. "Though, hell, maybe we'll do that anyway."

Chapter Eight

Damon shouldn't have let the others watch over Kara. He'd done it because he had work to do anyway, and because he had no idea if there was a point to him wanting Kara.

She hadn't shown any direct interest in him. She'd flirted, but it seemed she flirted with anything that moved.

Damon was young, inexperienced, eager yet unsure. He was nothing like the steady alphas whose scents she carried.

He didn't blame them, but that didn't stop the resentment as he sat on the balcony of the suite. Resentful for being the youngest, for not having their experience, for lacking that domineering edge they had.

He shouldn't want her, but he couldn't stop himself.

Memories of the betas he'd slept with came over him, the fun of conquest and exploration. They'd looked at him like he should be some he wasn't, as though they expected something from him that he didn't have.

He'd never been 'that alpha.' Sure, he could be possessive and difficult and hard-headed, but he'd always felt like a part of him was missing. That feeling had only been driven home when he hadn't lived up to what the betas had expected from him, when they'd thought he'd be the stereotypical domineering alpha, tearing at clothing and biting and holding them down. They hadn't hidden their disappointment when he hadn't done that.

It was one reason he'd never considered looking for an omega. What one would ever want him? Despite the drive to do so, the few times he'd been around one, he'd ignored any instinctual desires that might have crept into him.

So why is this one different? Even if I managed to catch her attention, what would I do with her?

He shook his head, trying to ignore the question. Why dwell on things that weren't going to happen?

He should focus on the case, on the work. He'd already started to create a nice little rut for himself. He worked hard, learning from Cullen and Reese, pulling his weight. He rented a room from them, making it easy to work together and allowing him to save.

Eventually, he'd open his own business, working on contract for police and private investigators, doing what he did for Cullen and Reese for a wider range of clients.

He liked a plan, and he excelled at making them. Order kept him calm, made him feel in control, and all he had to do was keep his head down and follow the order for his life plans to keep going exactly the way he'd set them up.

Eventually, years down the line, he'd find a nice beta to settle down with. A pretty house in the suburbs, two or three kids — it was all the same thing he'd envisioned as a kid, a life he could control and direct.

He brought his fingers to the bridge of his nose, moving his glasses out of the way. As much as he enjoyed a good plan, they also weighed on him.

Expectations. His, his family's, even the other alphas'. People expected things, but they also expected him to know what those things were and exactly how to get them.

It meant the same people who put the pressure on him also felt the need to poke fun at his highly regimented life. Still, as uncomfortable as it could be, he had no idea how to just let go.

The creak of the sliding glass door for the balcony alerted him a second before a breeze of air from inside carried the delectable scent of the omega.

He didn't turn, unsure what to say. Instead, he kept his gaze on the dark skyline.

The wide outdoor couch shifted when she took a seat. He allowed himself to take in her details in the periphery of his vision. A large black sweater — Cullen's, he thought — covered her body to nearly her knees, and her pale legs showed from there. The question of whether she wore anything beneath popped into his head, but he cursed it away.

Focus. "Did you need something?"

"Air."

Except, with her so close, he suddenly felt like *he* had no air, like she'd stolen it all and replaced it with her intoxicating scent. She smelled like fire and female and the other alphas. It all melted together until he couldn't pick up on anything else.

He closed his eyes, trying to center himself, to remind himself that making any sort of move would be foolish. She carried Reese's and Cullen's scents. What would she want with him?

He could give her nothing the others couldn't give her, had given her, and would probably do better. Seeing the disappointment on her face if he were to try wasn't his idea of a great time.

Not to mention that the last thing he needed was strain between him and the alphas. He didn't want to end up tossed out. That was not in his plans.

"How old are you?" Kara's voice held a wealth of amusement he didn't care for.

"Twenty-one."

"God, you really are just a pup, aren't you?"

He turned a side-long glare her way, unwilling to fully engage but also unwilling to not show some spark. "You're not that much older than I am."

"I've got four years on you, but years don't tell the whole story." She turned fully toward him. "See, you, I bet you had the normal life. For normal people, twenty-one is a kid, just figuring shit out, just getting their feet wet in the world. For people like me? I've been an adult since age thirteen, so my twenty-five is miles away from your twenty-one, *pup*."

He wasn't sure what he thought about her nickname.

Normally, he hated when Reese or Cullen called him 'kid'. He loathed the reminders of his age, of his inexperience. It felt like weakness, and his alpha side deplored weakness of any kind.

Yet, a strange tingle started inside him when she called him pup. It sat between them like a teasing lure, and he really wanted to follow it no matter where it led.

"And what made your life so hard?"

Kara's shoulders lifted in a subtle shrug, hidden slightly by the bagginess of her sweater. "I was on my own early. You figure out how to get along the best you can."

"And that's why you went into your...line of work?"

Her eyebrow hiked up as she curled her perfect full lips into a smile. "Nice way to put it, but yeah. At thirteen, you don't have a lot of options. Can't work a legal job on the books. Had a couple good friends willing to take me in and teach me the trade."

"Thirteen?" Damon shook his head at the thought of her so young. "At thirteen you should have been protected, not taught to steal."

"Do you know what happens to most girls who are on their own at that age? Especially omegas? Without skills, the only thing we have worth a damn to most people is what's between our thighs. I could have ended up a lot worse off. Hell, I make good money, I live on my own terms and I don't owe anyone shit."

He nearly missed the rest of her statement when she mentioned what was between her thighs. His initial reaction was an embarrassingly fast erection, followed by a growl at the thought of anyone taking advantage of her in the way she'd hinted.

Damn, Damon might be young, but he normally had a better grip on his reactions. What was it about her that made him lose it?

And why did she have to know it? Because the curl of her lips said she was aware of exactly how much she affected him.

He shook his head, each deep breath he usually used for control serving only to draw her more inside him, like an infection. "I guess I wasn't there. What do I know about it?"

She tilted her head, the moonlight making her hair impossibly brighter, lit up like a blue beacon in the darkness. Shadows played across her features, making it harder to read her exact expression, and she never made it all that easy.

Finally, she turned her head toward the city, taking the scrutiny off him. "I don't like the quiet," she admitted.

The change of conversation threw him, but he tried to keep up. "What quiet?"

She nodded toward the hotel suite. "It's quiet in there. Out here, I can hear the cars, the city, everything. This many floors up, it's not as good as home-sweet-home, but it's better than nothing."

"Not a fan of quiet? Funny thing for a thief to say."

"I like when I'm quiet, but actually, noise is a thief's friend. Covers shit, makes it disappear."

"What are you trying to make disappear?" The question slipped free from him before he could think better of it, and the instant hard lines of her face said it hadn't landed well.

She isn't the sort to want to share secrets with someone she doesn't know.

"Never mind," Damon muttered, stretching back in his seat and putting his legs up on the table. "Forget I asked."

They drifted in the tension for at least a minute, as though she were deciding if she should bolt or stay. He let her make the choice, gave her the space to do so.

After a minute, she twisted to look into the room again, and the droop of her shoulders screamed her choice.

Noise out here was better than silence in there.

She shifted, stretching out and resting her head in his lap. She did it without asking, without checking, but it wasn't as if he'd turn her down.

No doubt she could tell the effect it had on him, but it didn't seem to bother her, not even as her cheek rested against his hard-on.

She fidgeted, like snuggling—which couldn't be right, because if there was one truth in the world, it had to be that Kara was not a woman to snuggle—before finally huffing out a breath and closing her eyes.

Damon risked a single touch to her hair, the strands impossibly soft between his fingers, before he settled in as well. Seemed he wasn't going any damned place so long as she was comfortable.

And Damon had to admit…he liked the feeling.

* * * *

"Relax," Reese all but purred into Kara's ear, his breath warm and more calming than she'd ever admit to.

"I don't like labs," she said. "Labs, hospitals—"

"Morgues?" Reese's joke was joined by a grin.

"Nope, I like morgues. No one asking stupid questions there."

The conversation helped distract her from the chill that never went away in places like this.

It wasn't just the chill, though. It was that biting breeze of cold that carried the stink of disinfectant chemicals. It was the white walls and perfect tiles—all surfaces made to wipe clean so no traces of the horrors that happened there would stick.

It took her back to the hospital, to her lying in the bed, barely able to move, the beeping of machines surrounding her. The nurses had been kind, but they'd worn pity like a second skin, all wanting to do whatever they could for the poor broken omega who was too young to have suffered as she had.

Or that was what they'd thought. Still, each one who came in, telling her it would be fine, a sheen in their eyes from tears they'd tried to hide had only driven home the point more fully to Kara.

She didn't need anyone, and she sure as hell never wanted anyone who had to watch out for her again. She didn't want anyone paying the price for her actions, for her life.

Nope. She needed to be free.

And standing in the damned lab made her feel like that same young, damaged omega who had been inside that hospital.

The keycards had worked perfectly, Kara's clipped to the lapel of the suit they'd picked up from a store far too conservative for her tastes. The alphas surrounded her, each having dressed in similar styles.

They played the part of businessmen who had access to omegas who might agree to participate in studies for the right price.

And Kara? She was the bait, the piece of meat to dangle as proof they could get what they claimed.

Given how protected omegas were, how rare, finding willing subjects was a difficult job. Labs hired out for the task, letting others do the footwork. Less reputable ones would give in to abduction if needed, or pay off doctors for samples stolen from unaware omegas.

Being just the subject rankled, but Kara had always been good at playing her part when she needed to, so she walked along between the alphas like a good little omega.

She supposed there could be worse places to be. She'd spent the night sleeping on the balcony, curled around Damon like he was a damned body pillow. For his part, he'd been the perfect gentleman — which both annoyed and charmed her — and remained still for her to sleep on. Between his scent and the hum of the street, Kara had managed a little shut eye.

It meant she didn't object to the alphas' presence as she normally did. Hell, she almost enjoyed it. That sexual tension that coursed between them all made her skin sizzle, made every nerve in her feel alive.

Which, she had to admit, was nice.

She'd used temporary brown dye to dull her hair. She couldn't wait to wash it out, to see it streaming down the drain like the boring, useless shade it was. Still, she needed to look meek. Innocent. Forgettable. Just another brainless omega in need of big strapping alphas to care for her.

If I don't stop, I might just throw up.

They all turned in to an exam room, following the beta receptionist whose heels clicked against the tile. As least Kara's snarky thoughts distracted her from her discomfort. Being a bitch had its uses.

"And where did you hear about us?" The receptionist didn't lift her gaze, peering instead at the tablet in her hands, her fingers tapping away at the screen.

"We used to work with another lab, but they had no idea how to handle omegas. A few complained, and we started losing volunteers," Reese said.

The receptionist finally lifted her gaze. "I've heard that sort of thing before. Rest assured, we take very good care of the omegas who choose to work with us."

Kara barely hid her eye roll at being talked about as though she were some pet. *Yes, we take good care of the omegas! We feed them and walk them every day.*

A sharp pain in her side had her looking over to find Cullen ignoring her, but his finger still close, telling her he'd jabbed her in the side so she'd behave.

Joke was on him. She *never* behaved.

"If you'll take a seat, the doctor will come in and explain everything."

The moment the door closed, she let out the loudest groan, one full of all her annoyance.

"Really?" Cullen shook his head. "It wasn't that bad."

"That's because you weren't the one expected to shut up and be good."

"Two things you clearly aren't very good at." He pointed at the exam table, which was padded and much nicer than she'd have expected. "Why don't you sit up there?"

All sorts of *oh hell no* must have crossed Kara's face before she'd even fully heard the request. Maybe it had taken longer to realize it because her heart suddenly pounded so loud and hard she struggled to hear anything outside her eardrums.

Cullen furrowed his eyebrows, then reached for her.

The action woke her the fuck up. A room wasn't about to turn her into the fragile omega everyone already expected her to be. She brushed off his hand, then pushed past him. She wanted to hop onto the table, to do it with enough grace and attitude that everyone would forget her moment of panic.

Instead, she froze. It was only for a breath or two, but damn if it didn't feel like longer, if it didn't feel like the world ground to a halt around her as she faced off against the table.

As it always did, the world pepped right back into action, and Kara forced her unwilling body to move. She didn't hop, but slid one hip up, her hands braced on the sides, and plopped onto the padded top with less grace and more reluctance than strictly needed.

Instead of looking at any of them, she kept her gaze down. *Get your shit together, girl. You lived through worse than this before. You can sure as hell get through one little exam.*

A large tan hand set on her thigh and squeezed. *Reese.* She'd recognize any part of at least the two older alphas, she'd bet. He said nothing, didn't force her to answer or talk about it, just offered the touch like a quiet acknowledgment.

Damon spoke up from beside the computer at the edge of the room. "I'm going to need the doctor to sign in."

Cullen turned his gaze on Damon with a frown. "What? If people just put in their passwords, why do we need you?"

"I could break into it if we had the time, but we don't. It's faster if we get him to log in, then it'll only take me a minute to look up the information."

"And then what? We distract him?" Reese crossed his arms, looking about as amused as Cullen.

Which meant the two really had no idea how information gathering worked. How many times had she served as a distraction for Erik? Or there was that time she'd tripped Liam down the last few steps on a flight of stairs so everyone was looking at him and not her as she'd swiped a security pass for the upper levels of the building they'd been in.

Basically? The distraction bit was a time-tested way of getting what a person needed.

"One distraction coming up," Kara said, rubbing her hands together, shaking off the last of her almost-breakdown from before.

If there was one thing she could do with some level of skill other than stealing shit, it was being a nuisance.

Reese had no idea what to think of Kara. She kept him guessing, and while he liked that aspect, he also couldn't quite get his feet beneath him when dealing with her.

Her moods shifted so fast. When she'd walked into the lab, the stress in her had grown until he'd feared she'd vibrate out of her very skin. She hadn't even seemed to notice just how bad it had gotten.

Why? What caused that sort of reaction in her?

Many omegas disliked hospitals, especially those omegas who didn't advertise their designation. Many were afraid of being found out, and many were in hiding.

Whatever had happened to Kara went deeper.

It took him back to her refusal to remove her shirt. She'd fucked them without a second thought, which meant she wasn't fearful, so what was it? Was completely naked too much? Too close? Did she have some strange tattoo on her?

An alpha's name?

He cut short the growl that threatened to escape before it had a full chance to vocalize.

After she'd stared down the exam table like it might burn her, when for a split second she'd been a different omega, she'd squared her shoulders and set herself up there anyway.

The sort of determination that took wasn't lost on him. People thought being brave was about not being afraid, but it wasn't that. Bravery was about being scared as shit and doing it anyway.

And while he'd be a liar if he didn't admit he wanted to know, that he wanted to crawl inside her head and figure out what ghosts in her past had made her react that way, he knew it wouldn't happen. She wasn't going to say anything, and she didn't owe those truths to him.

Worse, he couldn't read her. Reese could read anyone, like walking lie detector. With her, he felt blind. She never reacted the way he expected, and he could never trust anything she said.

Reese knew exactly where that would lead them.

The door opened before any of them had the chance to continue the conversation, and an older doctor walked in. His white hair was pushed back, and he seemed kinder than Reese would have thought. He'd expected doctors who worked in a place like this to be cold and aloof.

Instead, the man could have played Santa if it were that time a year and he stopped shaving for a while.

He gave a kind smile to Kara before acknowledging the alphas. "I'm Dr. Jessy Kallop, and I understand you're here for a possible research subject procurement contract, correct?"

Cullen nodded, then shook the doctor's hand. Fine by Reese—he preferred to sit back and pay attention, to try to catch any little tell he could. People got uncomfortable when a person studied them. No one liked that sort of scrutiny. It was nearly impossible to do it while talking to someone without them starting to clam up.

Reese would much rather chime in when necessary, but otherwise keep his mouth shut and learn as much as possible.

Dr. Kallop sat on the small rolling stool before the computer. His fingers moved over the keyboard in the rapid sequence that said he used it often and hardly had to think about it. "Ah, yes. Kelly Garden, right?"

The fake name irked Reese, despite the fact that it shouldn't. They'd all supplied fake names on the cards and forms, since none of them knew exactly what involvement with Grace's disappearance the lab might have. Still, he suddenly missed her real name.

Kara nodded, her legs hanging off the exam table. "Yep. That's me."

The doctor squinted and leaned closer to his screen, as though his glasses didn't quite cut it anymore. "Your birthdate?"

"August twenty-nine, 1996." She rattled off the date without hesitation, telling him she either was exceptional at memorizing things in a short period of time or had used that birthday as a fake one previously.

Dr. Kallop sat back, then twisted to face Kara and the alphas. "I'm going to be honest with you and say we need more volunteers. It's getting harder and harder to find omegas willing to come in, especially with so many people pushing for mandatory registration."

The thought of a mandatory registry for all omegas had been volleyed about time and time again, but it never passed. They'd managed a delinquent omega registry, used for omegas who got into enough trouble that the government felt secure in turning them into little more than property.

The idea was used with the bullshit theory that if omegas were properly documented and registered from birth—something capable of being done with specific genetic testing—then they could be best protected. Still, all the discussion had floated between faux fear for omegas' safety and a general undercurrent of anger against omegas, which were often seen as both fragile and temptresses.

Reese doubted the law would ever pass, since none of the others had, but hell, who knew? He'd long ago learned that people were capable of a very special brand of cruel stupidity missing from the rest of the animal kingdom.

The doctor kept talking. "I can assure you, we take excellent care of the omegas who choose to work with us, and our pay is second to none. I thought we would run a few baseline tests, let you get the feeling for how we do things here. I am one hundred percent sure that by the end of the exam, you'll feel confident in continuing to do business with us."

Kara's hand, resting on her leg, twitched. The movement was so slight, he doubted the doctor noticed, but for some reason it seemed that Reese was entirely tuned in to the omega. Each little breath she took, each movement of hers, drew his focus without him having to think about it. When he studied her, though, he saw it.

Fear. It was written in the way her fingers gripped the exam table, in the tightness of her jaw. Still, he had to give her credit. If he didn't know what to look for, he'd never have caught it at all.

A not-insignificant part of him wanted to call the whole thing off. He wanted to snarl at the doctor, toss Kara over his shoulder and carry her the hell out of there. Since that wouldn't be welcome and would ruin their entire plan, he closed his eyes for a heartbeat, then forced his gaze from hers. "That sounds good," he told the doctor.

Damon stepped back, pretending to be moving out of the doctor's way, but subtly inserting himself beside the computer.

The doctor took the other alpha's place, coming forward until he stood just in front of Kara. From beside the exam table, he pulled out a pair of blue gloves, snapping them onto his hands as Kara watched with enough unease, that he worried she might break something on the poor man.

"Relax, dear," the doctor coaxed.

"I'm relaxed."

Dr. Kallop's smile was both knowing and kind. "You aren't the first omega I've dealt with who isn't a fan of doctors."

"Is that why they have betas doing the exams?" Kara's words were rough, a slight bite to them.

"One reason, yes. Also, many omegas come with an alpha"—he turned a quick glance between Reese, Cullen and Damon—"or three. A beta is less likely to rile up an alpha's possessive nature, which means exams and testing go easier."

"Why don't you just get this over with?"

The doctor leaned a hip against the table, his back to Damon. It gave the youngest alpha the chance to slide the last bit and start working on the keyboard, the whir of the air conditioner enough to cover the soft tap of keys.

"You don't trust me, but you'll see, I'm not that bad. I won't do anything without telling you what it is first. If at any time you want to stop, just tell me."

Kara said nothing back, her eyes not softening a bit.

The doctor sighed, the resigned sound implying he wasn't shocked by her disbelief. "You don't seem to want to do this. Why are you, then?" His gaze cut over toward Reese, who had moved closer to the door to help ensure the doctor didn't glance behind him, where Damon worked. "You aren't being forced, right? Because I can have security meet you in here. You don't have to leave with — "

"It's not like that." Kara spoke so quickly, the defense enough to startle Reese. "I mean, they aren't like that. I just really need the money to get me on my feet."

Kallop nodded, folding his arms across his chest. "I've heard that plenty of times. We pay in cash, we keep only the name you give us on record and we don't look too closely into whatever information we're given."

"That seems awfully nice," Kara said, the set of her eyebrows saying she wasn't about to be taken in by the doctors.

"Well, to be fair, from a business standpoint, it's simply smart. Omegas who fear being turned in are less likely to volunteer. Further than that, however, a good number of those who come in do it because there isn't a lot of other work for them. Finding paying work, especially if an omega doesn't have fake papers yet, isn't easy. Labs like this offer something, at least. It may not be much, but it might be the difference between sleeping beneath a roof or not."

The doctor's tone was what got to Reese. He seemed to mean it, to care. Odd, given that betas rarely gave much of a damn about alphas or omegas.

Then again, how many doctors were bleeding hearts? It seemed to go with the profession.

Kara nodded, her face softening just a hair, just enough to say that the man had managed to endear himself to her at least a little.

"So, what sort of exam are we talking?"

The doctor pulled a syringe from the drawer beside the table, and before it closed, a similar unhappy sound left all three alphas.

It seemed they already had a claim on Kara, at least enough for them to not like to idea of anyone harming her, even if just for drawing blood.

The doctor didn't seem fazed. "I can ask you three to stand outside if needed. I don't usually suggest alphas who are intimate with the omegas they bring in remain during exams. You tend to cause problems."

The reminder that Kara carried Reese's and Cullen's scents caused a storm of feelings inside Reese. He disliked the doctor's tone, or any negativity toward Kara that might be there, but damn if he didn't love that she carried his scent.

Cullen cut Reese a hard look. "We'll be fine. Please, continue."

Kara held her arm out, and the doctor drew a vial of blood with ease. After that, he pressed the vial into a machine to the left of the exam table, keeping his back to Damon.

The machine whirred to life, and Kallop started on the rest of the exam. He took blood pressure, heart rate, checked Kara's eyes and ears.

The entire thing reminded him a bit too much of a vet check-up for a dog, with the doctor writing down the results but not communicating much.

After finishing with the baseline information, he took clipboard and pen in hand and faced Kara. "Now for the questions. We have to know if there are any reasons you'd be unable to participate in any specific study. Are you on any medications? Suppressants?"

"Nope."

"Very good." The scratch of his pen against the paper said he was writing down her answers. "And have you had any recent injuries or surgeries?"

She pointed at her face, at the bruising there from her run in with the man who had waited inside her apartment. "Just this. A mugger stopped me on the way home, and I wasn't quick enough handing over my purse." The lie rolled off her tongue so easily and with such certainty that Reese again reminded himself not to trust her.

He almost believed her, and he knew the truth.

"That happens, unfortunately. Your stats all look good. Blood pressure and O2 levels are good. Your lungs sound clear."

She nodded toward the machine that still clicked and whirred. "What's that for?"

"Basic hormone checks. A few betas have come in claiming to be omegas for the money. We like to do a quick test to check first."

Damon worked quickly, his fingers moving so fast, Reese was again impressed. Getting his phone to work was too much for Reese some days, and yet Damon could make a computer sing with a few mindless keystrokes. The set of the younger alpha's eyebrows said whatever he was finding wasn't useful.

Kara must have caught the same thing, because her lips tipped down the slightest bit. "I had a friend who came in," she said.

Cullen gave her a glare over the doctor's shoulder, as if to try to silence her.

Like anything silences her.

"Oh really? I handle exams for most of the omegas who come in. What's her name?"

"Grace. She's the one who recommended you, actually. I mean, I'd already considered doing this and talking to their group" — she nodded toward Reese — "but Grace said she liked it here."

The doctor tapped his pen against his lips before a smile broke out. "Oh, yes, Grace. I remember her. She's the young blonde, isn't she?"

Kara nodded, feigning a delighted smile. "Yes, that's her!"

"What happened to her? She was quite sweet when she came in for a preliminary, but I never heard from her again."

Kara's smile fell. "I don't know, honestly. She's sort of fallen off the face of the Earth."

The frown on the doctor's face seemed honest enough, though not surprised. "I was afraid of that."

"You were? Why?" Reese pipped the question in.

"We get a lot of omegas on the run. Sadly, them disappearing isn't all that uncommon. I don't like it, but it's part of life. She seemed anxious while she was here, asking a lot of questions."

"Don't most volunteers ask questions?"

"No. They tend to want to get their money and get out as quickly as possible. It's why I remember her, because it was so unusual to have someone who wanted to understand what we did so well. Though, she said she worked at another one of our labs, a smaller one, as an intern. I thought her interest was due to that, but she was still nervous, looking over her shoulder a lot." His eyes, aged and kind, met Kara. "Was she in trouble?"

"She didn't say anything to me."

He reached out and set a weathered hand on Kara's knee. "Don't blame yourself. You can't help someone who doesn't tell you the truth." He went to pull back, but Damon made a quick pointing motion from behind him.

Not quite done then, huh?

Reese went to ask a question, to keep the attention away from Damon as he finished, but Kara beat him there.

Didn't it seem they were always playing catch-up when it came to that omega?

She dropped her head in her hands and began to sob. Loudly. "I just should have done more!"

The antics were so quick, Reese fought the desire to comfort her himself. Even knowing it was a scheme, even realizing she wasn't the sort to break into tears, his brain instantly snapped over to *we need to fix this shit now* mode.

Instead, the doctor, who looked more than a little surprised, rushed into action. He came forward and gathered Kara in a hug. Luckily for him, the hug was entirely innocent, with him stroking his hand over her hair—he'd probably end up with some of the temporary dye on it—and offering comfort in a very grandfatherly way.

Which was the only reason Reese resisted the initial desire to remove the good doctor's hand for touching Kara that way.

Reese's jealousy abated even more when Kara lifted her face and, rather than the blotchy, red-rimmed eyes he'd expected, he found a glare from the blue-eyed imp as she mouthed *hurry the fuck up* to Damon.

Reese fought his newest desire, which was to laugh at the entire thing.

Kara's wails were over the top, her hands grasping the doctor's coat. "I just miss her so much," she sobbed.

"I know," he reassured her, patting one of his large hands on her back. "She might still show up. What if I put in your information in her file? So if she comes back, I can make sure to let her know you're looking for her?"

Damon struck a few more keys before sliding away from the computer and giving a thumbs-up.

"Yeah," Kara said on a sniffle, pulling back. "I would appreciate that."

The doctor moved away, and despite the fact that Kara looked rather put together for a woman who had just had such a sudden and ridiculous breakdown, the doctor didn't appear to take notice. He sat at his computer, typing in a slow pecking motion that again showed how talented Damon was.

Kallop frowned. "I don't see her file. It should be here." He leaned forward, clicking a few more buttons, before shaking his head. "This happens sometimes. I'll contact IT and add it when they fix the problem."

A beep from the machine with the vial of blood broke the conversation, and the doctor went to it, taking the small printed sheet it had dispensed.

He held it up, pushing his glasses up his nose. "You function remarkably well," he said, almost mindlessly.

Tension shot through Kara, but her voice was steady when she answered. "What?"

The doctor slid the piece of paper beneath the clasp of the clipboard. "I've dealt with a few omegas in your condition, and without treatment, it tends to be rather difficult to manage. If I didn't have the results here, I'd never have suspected."

Kara said nothing, her jaw tight.

Reese asked the question the alphas hadn't realized they needed. "What condition?"

The doctor lifted his gaze to Reese, eyes confused, as though he wasn't sure why they didn't already know. Then again, they had posed as a procurement company, which meant they would have already done all the needed testing on any omega who worked with them.

What was it that they didn't know about Kara? Would it help them understand her better?

The doctor tapped his finger against the results. "She's sterile."

Chapter Nine

The alphas could all fuck themselves for what little Kara cared. Or each other. Or a rusty keyhole.

Really, she didn't much care as long as they stayed away from her.

She'd used her humor and snark to mask her reaction when the doctor had blurted out the truth, the one she hadn't had to actually hear in years, the one she'd only admitted once in her life, to Liam before he'd fucked her.

She was sterile.

After the attack as a teenager, after the doctors had patched her back up as best they could, the damage couldn't be undone.

They'd had to take her uterus, though one functioning ovary was hanging in there.

Sort of.

The bitch would send signals to her body, wanting to breed, but given her lack of a womb, she never went into full heat. It meant she also never fully went out of heat. She lived her life in that halfway-there state, sated for short bits of time but never free of that clawing need.

She had yet to look the alphas in the face.

What do I care what they think? I'm not their mate, so they can fuck off if they have an opinion.

Repeating that to herself didn't quite fix it, though.

She'd sat in the back seat of the car as the alphas spoke about the lab.

Damon hadn't found any record of Grace. The doctor having talked about her so freely meant he likely wasn't involved, especially because he'd seemed surprised to not find her file.

Someone at the lab was covering up Grace's visit, but who? And why? Given that there hadn't been any movement, any sign of Grace, the lab had to have grabbed her. If they'd sent people after Kara, she doubted the other omega could have kept off their radar.

Even as they'd talked, she'd stared out of the car window, not rising to offer more than a word or two, and only when forced.

No one addressed the huge fucking elephant sitting in the room, though.

Which, yet again, she told herself didn't matter.

She didn't want kids. She wasn't the maternal type, and after her own upbringing? *Fuck that noise.* She wasn't worth shit as a mate, either. If anything, this made it easier, right?

The alphas wouldn't get any stupid ideas if they knew she was useless as an omega.

Broken.

The word carved gouges in her skull as it always did.

Reese and Cullen headed out after getting back to the hotel. Supplies, they'd said, but neither had tried to speak to her. She wasn't an idiot. They were going to go gossip like fucking teenage girls.

It left Damon typing away on his laptop, which he'd set up on the desk in the living room. Normally, he worked in his own room, but she got the sense he didn't want to leave her be.

Afraid I'll bolt?

She wasn't a coward. She didn't run. *Well, I do run, but not out of fear.*

Frustration built inside her, twisting and writhing until it ate her up and she couldn't breathe. She'd be the first to tell people life wasn't fair, yet all of a sudden, the idea of it drove her mad.

Not only was she defective, as so many people had said in her life, but now the alphas all knew it. She wasn't quirky and feisty and wild.

She was just broken. Damaged goods.

And while the idea of Cullen or Reese touching her turned her stomach right then, because they would take and she felt raw and empty with nothing left to give, the movement of Damon's long, agile fingers on the keyboard tempted her. They sped over the keys, the constant clicking making her think about how those fingers could be put to better use.

He slowed, a quiet inhalation reminding her that she couldn't exactly sneak up on an alpha, not when she struggled as she did with her body's reaction.

No matter the problems in her life, sex had always been a quick and easy fix. Angry? Stressed? Sad? None of them were anything a good round with a stranger couldn't resolve, or at the very least, distract her from. And right then? She needed that distraction. She needed to use Damon's body until she forgot how broken her own was, until she felt right, just for a moment.

The clicking of the keyboard continued, though it slowed as if he wasn't fully focused on his work anymore.

Kara rose from her spot on the couch, tossing down the magazine she'd been reading. She wore only the large shirt she'd picked up from the store to sleep in, *boys suck* written across the front. Her cunt was already drenched.

Even when she reached the desk, Damon didn't lift his gaze. He smelled of aroused male, something that stroked along her desires like the sweetest of caresses. Still, he didn't acknowledge her.

Did he not want her?

The thought might have doused the flames inside her if she'd been any other female, if they weren't at least partly based on biology she couldn't control.

"I can call Reese and Cullen," Damon said, voice tight.

Kara leaned her hip against the desk, staring down at the young alpha, his firm lips pressed into a tight line. He wanted her, but what if that was just biology?

She'd done this before with a male who didn't want her. She refused to do it again, especially after what had happened, after having her other secrets and flaws on display.

"I didn't ask you to call them."

He released a long sigh, then breathed in through his mouth as though that might lessen his reaction. "Don't play games with me, Kara."

Her name on his lips was far too sweet. *He* was far too sweet, really.

And it only made her want him more. She wanted his inexperience and his uncertainty. In fact, it was the reason she wanted him so badly right then, because those things made this safer for her.

"Have you ever been with an omega?"

He shook his head, a single quick jerk to the side that said he didn't care for admitting such a thing.

Kara caught his chin and lifted his gaze to hers, an uncomfortable feeling because she didn't tend to care for eye contact. It revealed too much. "Do you not want this? Because I'll leave if that's what you want."

His eyes, so light brown they looked like warm honey, seemed the perfect mixture of hard and soft. They were expressive, begging for something he didn't know how to ask for, and yet solid with want and magnified by his glasses. "I'm not Cullen. I'm not Reese," he said, a waver in his voice.

And that was exactly why she wanted him right then. She slid her thumb against his bottom lip, softening her grasp even as her body nearly screamed at her with need.

She wanted to card her fingers through the short brown strands of his hair and force his head between her thighs, to feel his tongue against her, to let it take away that constant ache she never could quite quench. "I know who you are, and I'm still here. So, pup, do you want me to stay?"

His gulp went straight to her cunt, but damn if his nod didn't nearly make her come.

Damon said nothing when Kara shut the lid to his laptop and tossed it onto the couch. He would have complained if anyone else had dared to treat his most prized possession with such carelessness, but the scent that rolled off Kara meant he'd forgive her anything.

Especially when she slid her ass onto the desk in front of him, spreading her legs so her bare feet rested on the outside edges of his chair. Still, he kept his gaze up, as though playing some game he didn't quite know the rules of.

Though, really, he didn't. He had no idea what to do beyond what instinct told him. That instinct screamed to touch Kara, to taste her, to fuck her until the delicious scent of her arousal reached a peak then died off, until his scent mixed with hers as the other alphas' already had.

He ignored that instinct, though, and fought what he really wanted. The only thing he allowed himself was to lift his hands and wrap them around her calves, the hard muscles there proof she was no wallflower.

No, this omega had thorns and no problem using them to draw blood when she wanted.

She moved her fingers from his lip and slid them through his hair, grasping the short strands tight. Her voice came out like silk, deceptively soft but strong enough to bind a man. "You're not a virgin, I'm sure." She tugged his hair until he came forward, until he rose to his feet. A *tsk* of her tongue made him groan. "On your knees, pup. Show me what other skills you have."

Damon's knees hit the floor without thought or plan, as though she had a shortcut directly to his body, one that bypassed his brain. His cock ached, hard as stone against his slacks and desperate for her. He'd slept with women, but none of them had done *this*. None of them could have sent him to his knees with a few words, could have made him salivate for another order, another demand.

He didn't think about his plans right then. He couldn't care less about plans, not when he could smell Kara's pussy, when only the thin fabric of her shirt dipped between her thighs to cover her from him.

She gave another soft yank to his hair, rewarded by a growl so feral it nearly frightened him. A shudder ran through her, dancing along her bare thighs, telling him it sure didn't frighten her. "Come on, you can figure this out."

Damon needed no more coaxing, no more orders. He used his grip on her calves to spread her legs wider, to open her for him, before he fell upon her drenched cunt. The position of her legs forced her shirt higher, revealed everything to him. Her slit was tight, perfect and pink. He took her plump labia between his lips, sliding his tongue along the folds, tracing each part of her cunt like a painting.

Her scent was so much stronger up close, maddening him, driving him crazy with need. His hands twitched against her legs with the strength of his longing to reach between his thighs and grasp his cock. He wanted to stroke himself until he spilled, lavishing attention on her until she couldn't move, until she couldn't make demands of him because he'd sated her so fully.

Her pussy spread for him as he stiffened his tongue and forced it as deep as he could, as though he could literally devour her.

Her fingers tightened in his hair, pulling him closer, and the loud moans that fell from her lips were a symphony he'd never forget. Her breath would hitch before a deep moan rattled from her, from one extreme to the other, low, then high, loud then tapering off to a whisper.

Damon drew each sound from her like an instrument, though the grip in his hair reminded him who was in charge.

And he wasn't sure he'd ever been happier in any position than there, beneath her. All those unsatisfying encounters in his past had been missing *this*. He sunk into the moment, into the rightness as he moved his tongue to her clit.

The first stroke had her back arching, letting him look up her body. Hard nipples showed through the thin fabric of her top, the sway of her breasts telling him she'd worn no bra. He wanted to pay homage to the tight little peaks, but he refused to relinquish his prize, not yet. Her head was thrown back, one hand behind her for balance.

She was spread out like some fertility goddess, taking what she needed, and Damon was more than happy to give her everything.

He lashed her clit, driving her hard. She rolled her hips up toward him, a rhythm as if she actually rode his tongue.

Perhaps next time he'd lie down, have her seated above him, and just drown in her.

He could think of no better way to go.

Kara cried out, and her cunt pulsed around nothing, twitching as she came, as he drew out the waves by latching his lips around her hard little clit and sucking.

She pulled at his hair but he didn't release her. He *couldn't*. That instinct inside him snarled to keep going, especially when her scent said she still needed him.

Her complaint died in her throat when he scraped his teeth against her hardened bundle of nerves. Instead, whatever she was going to say turned into a gasp, then a groan. Her legs fell wide again, and Damon took that as his signal to move his hands higher. He grasped the inside of her thighs to keep her spread for him, then used his thumbs to pull the hood of her clit out of the way, so nothing hid her from his gaze.

She was flushed, the pink having darkened to a rosy color, and completely soaked, some from her wetness, some from his saliva, and it all sat on her like a claim.

Which was funny, since he still kneeled for her, since she still directed him with a grip in his hair, but it felt like possession.

So Damon feasted yet again. He didn't try for technique, using the sounds she made and the rolling of her hips as his teacher, his guide. The second orgasm was brutal, tearing a cry from her throat so loud, he nearly stopped, her back bowing and her hand clamping down in his hair.

Once more, his mind screamed. Once more and they'd both be sated.

Only, he doubted he'd ever really be sated, not for more than a short while. Her taste sat on his lips and tongue and brain like a tattoo.

The third time he drove her to release was different. Her hips hardly moved, sweat covering her body, plastering her shirt to her. Her noises had turned breathless and labored, and each time he stroked her clit, she whined.

When she came that third time, it was a collapse, as though something inside her had broken — or maybe fixed? Hell if he knew.

He rose to his feet after one last lick up her entire pussy, finishing with a hard flick to her sore nub.

Kara slipped her hand behind his neck as he towered over her, a funny contrast since, despite his size and strength, there was no question who was in charge.

Her eyes remained closed, and he missed that bright blue. He wanted to see her sated and happy and tired from the pleasure he'd given her.

Instead, she hooked a heel around his hip. "You're not done yet, pup."

Pup. It went straight to his cock, and even if he might have turned her down—and he doubted he'd have had the strength to do it—that made it impossible.

Damon fumbled with the clasp of his slacks, undoing them in an uncoordinated rush, then pulled down his boxers far enough to palm his heavy erection.

He set his hand on the desk for balance, crouching slightly to line himself up, dragging the head of his dick against her tight, wet slit just to feel it.

She yanked with her foot, a reminder, a demand impossible to deny.

Damon slid in, taking his sweet time, enjoying the tight grasp of her inner walls on each inch of his cock.

She sighed, swore and moaned as he delved into her, as though each stroke of his cock against her sensitive pussy walls was too much and yet not nearly enough.

When his body pressed against hers, when he'd fed her every hard inch, he paused. The position left his lips just before hers, and he took the chance for a light kiss.

She jerked backward. Perhaps she didn't care for the taste of herself? He hadn't exactly been careful, and he was sure her wetness clung to his lips.

When he might have asked, she drove the questions from him with a lift of her hips and a tightening of her pussy.

Damon groaned and gave in—to instinct, to her, to the demands of both their bodies. He pulled back then thrust in, the slowness of that first advance forgotten.

Instead, he took with that wild side of himself, the one that peeked through his eyes, that hid inside him. He gave himself over to the need of that beast, fucking her with hard, deep thrusts. And for Kara's part, she took each thrust, her legs tight around his waist so he never went far.

Damon's lip pulled back to bare his teeth as the snug wetness of her cunt overcame him. He'd been so close already just from feasting on her that he had no hopes of lasting long. The ache at the base of his cock intensified, and he slammed home as it started to swell.

The sensation of taking her like that, of his knot growing to lock inside her, that impossible grip of her cunt as it stretched around him, overwhelmed him. Even more, though? The spark of pain when Kara bit down on his shoulder seared through it all, even as his cock jerked and rope after rope of cum filled her.

His snarl came out deep, a strange sense of belonging from the omega's blunt little teeth buried in his skin. Even the trickle of blood didn't bother him. Buried as deep inside her as he was, trapped now by her body and his, he doubted anything much could bother him.

Kara released him, pressing a kiss to the mark, then a lick to clear away the smudged blood. Her eyes had opened, though they didn't lift to him. Instead, her eyebrows furrowed, and she stared at the bite mark as though it confused her.

Damon leaned down, nuzzling against the top of her head, the best he could think of since she hadn't kissed him back.

She shook off the touch with the same reaction as when he'd tried to kiss her. Her words held a finely-honed edge when she said, "Don't get any ideas, pup. This was just fun."

Even as she snapped the denial, she burrowed closer, her skin tightening to goosebumps, her sweat having cooled once they'd slowed.

Damon didn't bother trying to sort it out right then. Instead, he wrapped an arm behind her, pulling her against him tightly so he could lift her, even locked inside her as he was.

He took her to the couch and grabbed the throw blanket over the back. A few adjustments and he'd pulled it around her, trapping her between the heat of his chest and the soft fabric of the blanket.

She offered him a soft growl as she adjusted the best she could until she rested her cheek on his chest and tossed her arms around him, draping herself over him.

While sleep didn't take him, Damon relaxed into the odd sense of belonging, the feeling of a sated, happy omega in his lap, her cunt still snug around his knot.

An amoral, sterile omega thief wasn't in his plans, and neither was sharing her with two other alphas.

She huffed, a warm breath heating his chest as she snuggled closer.

It wasn't part of his plans, but suddenly he wondered if it might not still be worth it.

Chapter Ten

Between the sex and a good night's sleep, Kara felt more like herself the next morning. She wouldn't say everything was fixed by any means, but the wounds reopened the day before had managed to heal a bit.

Or maybe the bout with Damon had slapped a bandage on them. *Same difference, right?*

She stole the cup from Cullen's grasp and sipped the hot liquid inside. She'd have expected him to have ordered a black coffee from the small cafe they'd picked up breakfast at, since he struck her as a rather regimented person.

Instead, the sweetness of chocolate hit her tongue, and she almost moaned at the decadent taste.

"You should have ordered one of your own, thief," he said before taking back the cup.

"Then I couldn't steal *yours*. Don't you know things are always better when they belong to someone else?"

Damon broke into the conversation before they could keep arguing. "Are you going to tell us where we're going yet?"

Kara nodded at the motel across the street, a burnt-out *M* on the sign. "There."

"And why are we going to some rundown motel?" Reese blew the tendrils of steam from his cup — tea, which was yet another surprise — as he regarded the shady building.

"Because I was thinking last night. Grace went to the lab, right? I doubt she walked in as soon as she got to town. She'd have needed a place to stay, and what better place than one where she could do surveillance?"

Cullen nodded at the other buildings. "There are eight hotels in the area that overlook the lab. Why would she pick that one?"

"Because it's the only one in the area where someone could pay with cash and not be noticed." Kara gave him a grin, one that was meant to mock him for thinking she couldn't figure this out.

Whether anyone wanted to admit it or not, she was capable. She'd survived a world that hadn't ever been kind, and she'd done it by being smarter and faster than anything else. More vicious, too.

The alphas followed her across the street, toward the dingy little motel she knew all too well. The beta who ran it was the sort Kara would never turn her back on, who would betray his own mother for the right price.

Kara ensured she was his best price and always kept him on a short leash.

The motel never stank of sweat, body odor, or anything but bleach. It was like they hosed the whole place down in a bath of chemicals after each day.

Though, given how many by-the-hour rooms they rented, she couldn't blame them for that.

Kara had used those by-the-hour rooms herself when the need hit her, when her body cramped as though her insides were ripping themselves apart. She never took men back to her apartment, both because of the safety risks and because the idea of those one-night stands in her personal space made her want to retch. Usually she could find a dark corner, or occasionally go to their place if they were local, but some of the time?

A room at a no-questions-asked motel was the best option.

Brendon, the beta who ran the place, had a smile that went past suggestive and into creepy and lecherous as Kara walked in. "Well, if it ain't my favorite little omega." His gaze moved past he, to the three alphas as they followed her in. He huffed a small laugh. "So, just one ain't doing it for you anymore, huh?"

Cullen's reaction lacked subtlety as he let out a low and dangerous growl. It was the sort of sound that warned people off, that sane people backed away from.

Kara kicked Cullen's shin to shut him up. She didn't need anyone causing problems, not in places she had to deal with after the three of them moved on.

She rested her elbows on the counter that sat between her and Brendon, who didn't appear the least bit concerned about Cullen's reaction. "I need a room key."

"Course you do." Brendon winked, then leaned in, his breath reeking of cigarettes. "You know, I wouldn't mind a round or two, cupcake. Who knows, maybe I'll give you what you've been needing, huh? What you can't seem to find."

Her stomach rolled. Not because of how disgusting it was, but because she knew damned well that if she ever got really desperate, she might just take him up on it.

Broken.

Anger sat with her better than pity or sadness, though, so Kara flashed her teeth. "I'm looking for a room a girl would have rented here a week or two ago. She would have paid in all cash and wanted to be on the street side."

Brendon tapped his finger on the counter. "Rings a bell, I think. Awfully hard to remember with so many comings and goings."

Kara reached into her bag and pulled out a folded fifty. She slid it across the counter.

Brendon took the money and tucked it into his pocket. "Third floor, room 312. She paid for a month up front. Hasn't returned the key yet, but I doubt that's a problem for you."

Kara nodded, then moved away from the counter.

As they hit the stairs—the elevator never worked and even if it did, she wouldn't trust it in a place like this—Reese questioned her. "Why would you pay him? I bet he'd have told us what we wanted to know." Jealousy seethed in his tone.

"This is how it works in this world. Could I have threatened him into helping? Sure, but then the next time I need a favor, he won't be eager to help me out."

"And you often need help from *him*?" Ah, it seemed Cullen had that same jealousy.

Kara might have enjoyed it if it didn't rankle her so much, if she didn't hate the idea of being the sort of woman who needed to use a place like this. She took the steps with quick hops, enjoying the way it worked her thighs, and stayed on topic. "This place is a common stop for the sort of people I deal with. Besides, I gave him a fake fifty."

"You what?" Damon sounded absolutely scandalized.

"What? He will probably be able to pass it off without a problem, but it'll be hilarious if he can't." She grinned at the way he'd glare at her later if he were caught with the fake money. The way their lives went, he wouldn't do anything directly to her, because if he was stupid enough to be taken in by a scam like that, he deserved whatever happened.

"Why do you even have counterfeit bills?" Cullen lowered his voice as if someone else in the completely vacant stairwell might hear.

"I have a buddy who pays me double by paying me with fake bills. They're easy to pass off in small denominations. With the way you guys act, you'd think I was screwing in public or something."

Which she'd done in the past, to be fair, though she wouldn't be mentioning that.

When they reached the landing for the third floor, Cullen pushed past her, going through the door first as if checking for danger.

Right, because I need a big strong alpha to watch out for me.

After a quick look down the empty, stained hallway, Cullen nodded, some tension easing from him. Hell, even though it annoyed her, he almost looked cute like that, chest puffed out like a proud puppy.

Which was the last thing Kara needed to think of him as. Instead, she patted his chest and walked toward the door at the end of the hallway, the one marked 312. "You worry too much. If anyone else had come looking for this place, the information would have cost way more than fifty bucks." She slid her picks from her bag and popped the cheap lock open without a hitch.

Then again, that was why she never trusted these locks. A strong push could open most of them. When she stayed, she used the metal latch at the top, bolted into the door frame. The cheap, hollow door would crack with a few good kicks, but that wouldn't happened without her noticing, and she never let her guard down when there.

The inside of the room looked like they all did — brown. Dingy carpet covered the floor, a dark beige with hints of orange and enough stains that it almost looked like the mix of colors was intended. An unmade bed sat with the covers twisted over it, and a bag lay open, clothing half hanging out, near the wall.

The room was messy, but not in a rifled-through sort of way.

Which was good. It meant they were probably the first to get there.

"So, you come here a lot?" Reese asked.

"That sounds like a cheesy pick-up line."

"You just pick up random men and take them to motels?" The censure in his tone was meant to wound.

She wouldn't let it, or at least she wouldn't let it show. "Sometimes. Are you telling me you're a virgin, now? Because I'm pretty damned sure you aren't, seeing as I've played in that particular playground with you." She crouched beside the bag, pulling the clothing out and setting it on the bed, looking for anything useful.

"No, but the local motels don't know me on sight."

"Oh, my," she whined theatrically, setting a hand against her chest. "You've put me in my place. I feel so terrible for doing exactly what men have been doing forever. My vagina and I have been properly shamed."

Reese rolled his eyes—an honest-to-god roll that made him look like a pre-teen girl—before going into the bathroom to search.

Cullen remained near the door, like some guard watching over them. Then again, the more time she spent with them, the more she understood their individual roles. Cullen was the military man, something that showed in the way he moved, the way he surveyed a room. Reese was the detective, the one who put all the pieces together. Damon was their tech guy, and also the one who kept them organized and on a schedule.

Still, Cullen's hard gaze didn't move from her, and she could *hear* his disapproval.

"Okay, out with it."

He lifted an eyebrow.

"You're over there pouting, so just say whatever it is so we can get over it."

Cullen shook his head, causing his hair to shift, though the gel kept it mostly back. "If you were happy with your choices, you wouldn't be so defensive."

"I'm not defensive." She winced at the venom in her voice. *Not playing it cool, are we?*

Cullen leaned back against the wall, crossing his feet at the ankles. "Is it because of what the doctor said?"

"Don't know what you're talking about." Kara checked the zippered pouches of the bag, finding nothing useful, nothing they didn't already know. Her identification, some cash, personal items. It was definitely Grace's room, and given that everything was still there, it seemed even more likely that the lab had already gotten to her.

"You could get hurt," he pressed, "going home with males you don't know anything about."

"I'm going with them to fuck them. What are they going to do, rape me?" She spoke as she traced her fingers along the lining of the bag, searching for any clues. The conversation unnerved her, but that was why she kept her back to him, why she tried to toss out the snarky, outlandish comments, to kill the conversation by either pissing him off or making it clear they weren't going to get anything from her.

"That's one risk. They could get rough with you, abduct you, even kill you."

"Rough doesn't bother me," Kara snapped.

His sigh was long, drawn-out and less annoyed than it should have been. *Am I losing my touch?* "Just because you're —"

Kara's restraint snapped. She twisted and jammed a finger in his direction. "Don't you dare say it. Just because some idiot doctor blurted out my personal information doesn't mean you get to say a word about it. That isn't your business, and neither is who I fuck, how or where. The only reason I'm even here is because your job fucked me over and put me in someone's crosshairs, and now I'm trying to clean up your mess. What makes you think you get to tell me shit?"

Cullen's face was hard, the lines carved in as though he struggled to keep his mouth shut.

"It's not about judging you," Damon offered. He'd been so quiet she'd nearly forgotten he was there. Somehow, his voice lacked the edge of Cullen's. She didn't feel quite the same explosive anger at it. "We just don't want to see you hurt."

"I've taken care of myself for a long time, pup. Trust me when I say I don't need any of you to teach me how to do it."

The conversation might have continued, because neither Kara nor the alphas seemed particularly willing to let it go, but the door to the motel room opened and all of them turned in surprise.

In walked the pretty blonde omega they'd been chasing.

Chapter Eleven

"Easy," Damon said when Grace backed away. She had the face of a girl who planned to run, and while they *could* catch her, chasing her down and grabbing her wouldn't calm her at all.

A tremble started in Grace's bottom lip, her eyes wide and frightened.

"Bran sent us." Reese stood in the doorway of her bathroom. "He was worried something had happened to you."

Grace's backtracking halted as she drew her eyebrows toward one another. "Bran did?"

Damon pulled out his phone, found the number he needed and pressed Call. One more tap put it on speaker phone, and when a male's voice answered, relief swamped Grace's face. "We've found Grace," Damon said, his voice soft. "Would you assure her we're here on your behalf?"

"Grace?" The male's voice came out frantic. "Oh, god, Grace, are you okay? I've been so worried."

Grace opened her mouth, but the sound that came out was little more than a squeak at first. She swallowed hard then tried again. "I'm okay, Bran. You shouldn't have sent them, though."

"You ran off. I had no idea what happened to you. You took my gun, Grace—what was I supposed to think?" Even with the tone the alpha on the phone used, it seemed to Damon that he wasn't aggressive. At least, no more aggressive than their protective instincts made them.

And Grace didn't appear frightened of Bran.

"I'm sorry," she whispered, though she came no closer to Damon, didn't attempt to take the phone. She seemed too hesitant about the alphas to venture closer. "I'll explain everything when I get home."

The back and forth went on until Grace made an awkward goodbye and Damon promised Bran to call him that evening.

It left Grace, Kara, Cullen, Reese and Damon in the dim, dirty motel room with far more questions than answers.

Grace sure didn't seem the sort who would run off for no reason. In fact, she looked a lot like the kind of person who might get frightened by an especially menacing shadow. What could have sent her off on her own, breaking into labs and carrying a gun?

She wrapped her arms around her sides before meeting Cullen's gaze. "I need your help," she said.

What was it about an omega in need that never failed to land alphas in trouble?

Reese sat across from Grace in their hotel suite. They had a conversation that needed to happen, and the best place for it probably wasn't in that filthy motel room.

Her plane would leave in another four hours, giving them just enough time to get the full story before getting her back to Bran and out of danger.

She had her hands in her lap and wore a flowy skirt that reached her ankles, paired with an understated white blouse. Her blonde hair was French-braided back, then brought forward to rest over her left shoulder, making her seem perfect and demure. She looked just like she had in the photo Bran had given them, down to those eyes so amber they were almost yellow in the light. What he could see of them, at least, since she rarely met any of their gazes directly.

Kara sat in the background, on the kitchen counter with her legs folded, in perfect contrast to Grace.

"I'm looking for my friend," Grace finally said, the words reluctant, as though she didn't really want to tell the story.

"Who?"

She sighed, wringing her hands as she sat there. "Kash is Bran's brother. He went missing about two years ago."

"And you think he's here? Why?" Reese sat beside Grace, though a large swath of space remained between them.

Finally, Grace met his gaze directly. "I worked at the small lab for Hythen Pharmaceuticals as an intern. The company is on the cutting edge of most omega and alpha hormone research. I was studying research on one of their newest concepts, the pheromone that's been in the news, the one that can make omegas go into heat."

Reese nodded as he recalled the drug, the one that in small doses could help alphas recognize omegas. It also had been used in the murder of a few omegas.

While Reese understood the need for research into omega and alpha hormone regulation, he didn't see much good coming from that particular drug.

At his lifted eyebrow, Grace continued. "The drug smelled like Kash."

"How can you be sure?" Damon asked.

A flush on Grace's cheeks answered that. So, even though she moved around like an innocent little doe, she at least had some feelings for the missing alpha. She traced the seams on her skirt as she answered. "He and Bran were my best friends — *are* my best friends, I mean. I'd never forget either of their scents."

"Could it be a mistake?"

"No. As soon as I got close enough to actually smell the drug, I knew it. I got everything I could about it, well, everything an intern could access. They never talked about who their 'donor' was, but the files mentioned the drug having been created from live samples from an alpha with unique properties. It has to be Kash. Even the timelines match up. They started testing two weeks after he disappeared."

"Unique properties?"

The question pulled Grace from her nerves, as though talking about facts and science gave her confidence. "Kash is what's called a prime alpha. Alphas and omegas occur on scales, like anything else. There are always outliers. The few alphas who have higher levels of certain hormones and pheromones are called primes. They happen in about one in a million, maybe. For the drug to work, it requires a concentrated dose of a prime's pheromones. Basically? Without Kash, they can't make that drug."

"Why haven't we heard about primes before?" Damon asked.

"Because we didn't have a name for them before. They're still alphas — they'll still show as alpha on tests. It's only been in the last few years we've been able to quantify the hormones enough to identify them, to realize they *are* different on a medical level."

He supposed it made sense. There were ranges to everything, so while some alphas fell low on those traits, there had to be some who ranked exceptionally high.

"Why didn't you tell Bran? Wouldn't he want to help if he thought his brother was being held against his will?" Cullen asked.

"He would, but he'd never have let me help. He needed me, because I understand the science, understand the labs. I know what I'm looking for, but he'd have made me stay home because he thought it was too dangerous."

Which Reese understood. He didn't want Grace within a state of this mess, either. The lab already knew she was onto something or they wouldn't have removed her exam information. She must have sent up flags while at the lab, and that added some credence to her claims. She'd worried someone.

"I can pay you," she said, voice desperate. "On top of whatever Bran paid you, I'll hire you to find Kash."

"You could be wrong," Cullen warned. "What if he isn't there? Or what if he's there because he's working with them willingly?"

Grace reached for her purse, which had been thrown on the couch beside her. With shaking hands, she pulled out a small picture and gave it to Cullen.

Reese caught a glimpse as it passed between them. Grace between two alphas, all of them a few years younger, all smiling.

"He and Bran were all I had, and he wouldn't have left me without a word, not if he had a choice."

Reese went to argue, to explain that people — men especially — could be unreliable even when people didn't want to think they were. Except his gaze drifted to Kara as she sat on the counter.

He wouldn't just leave her. Already, even after such a short amount of time, he wouldn't have walked away without a goodbye, without explanation.

If that alpha felt even a fraction of what Reese already did, maybe Grace was right. Maybe something had happened to him.

Before he got the chance to answer, Kara spoke up from her spot. "We'll take the job," she said.

Cullen was glad Kara had no weapons, with the way she stared daggers at him after Reese and Damon had left to take Grace to the airport.

"What is your problem?" Cullen crossed his arms as he met the annoyed gaze of the blue-haired imp who was impossible to ignore.

"Problem? Me?" She flashed him a smile that was more teeth and snark than humor. "No idea what you mean."

"You're the one who just volunteered us for a job," he groused. "I don't think you get to complain about anything right now."

"In case it has escaped your attention, the current job isn't done yet."

"The job was to find Grace. We found her."

"*I* found her. And *I* still have a price on my head, thanks to you all."

Which was true. It wasn't as if they'd planned to run out on her after getting her into trouble. Still, it was the same as everything else with her.

She acted without thinking. She didn't discuss anything with him, didn't stop to figure out a good plan. She jumped in with both feet, having no idea how deep the waters might be.

She'd drown in those waters if she kept that up, and the idea tightened his chest.

Instead of focusing on that, Cullen stayed on topic. "None of that explains why you're pissed." Though maybe it wasn't anger? She seemed to get worked up often, and Cullen's gaze dropped to her tempting body as he considered the ways they could work off all that tension.

"Don't even think about it," she snapped. "If you're hard up, why don't you go pay Miss Perfect another visit before she takes off?" Kara waved at the connecting wall between the rooms.

Jealousy? The fact hit him so fast, he nearly lost the battle against laughing at the very idea. Kara didn't seem to like him most of the time, so her being jealous tickled him in a way he doubted she'd find as funny as he did, and Kara had a mean streak if he pissed her off.

Cullen didn't bother to fight the grin that spread across his lips. "Maybe I will."

"Good," she bit out. "I'm sure she'll find you charming, and given she's useless and so are you, you seem like a perfect match." Kara turned to storm out, though where she was going, he had no clue.

Cullen caught her arm first. "You can't be jealous."

"Of course not. Why would I be jealous of her? What, just because she's perfect and pretty and perfect and —"

"You said perfect twice."

Her cheeks flushed and it stood out against the blue of her hair. "Just pointing out facts."

"Is that all?"

She cast him a look so full of malice, he might consider locking his door when he went to sleep that night. He wouldn't be shocked to wake up and find she'd cut pieces off him to sell out of spite. "Yep. Don't flatter yourself, because it's not like alphas are all that hard to come by."

She was lying through her teeth and he damned well knew it. Even though he couldn't spot her lies, her body couldn't keep secrets.

"So why do you keep looking at us like you can't wait for another shot? Like you're *starving* for another taste?"

"Because you're convenient."

"Is that what all the other men were? Just *convenient*?"

Her gaze narrowed, as sharp as her tongue. "Yes."

Cullen inhaled slowly, drawing her deep inside him. Her scent was even stronger, as though it called out, as if her jealousy had made it grow until she could claim him with it.

And despite how he told himself not to get attached, he still wanted to roll around in it. He wanted to walk away knowing her smell coated him, that anyone would know he had a mate.

Mate. The second the word entered his head, he yanked away from it as though it were a fire and might burn him.

He wanted a mate, yes, but not *her.* She'd never fit into the life he had planned out, never willingly remain safe and out of the way. She would push him constantly, fight with him over everything. He'd never have a moment of peace in his life.

It took him back for a moment, back to the horrors he'd seen overseas. How many times had innocents paid the price for others' actions? How many bodies had he seen, where he had to face the reality of how evil people could be? If people who tried to stay out of trouble got killed, what chance did a woman like Kara have?

How could he live with himself if he couldn't keep his own mate safe?

That meant no matter the pull between them, this went no further than whatever fun they could have until they finished the case. This had a time limit, and they all knew it.

That's fine with me. The lie was ash on his tongue, but he still told it to himself. Maybe if he repeated it enough, if he remembered the corpses he'd seen in his life, he'd start to believe it.

Kara stared at him, her gaze too smart, studying him as though she could pick up each thought that passed through his head. "Let go." The words were less a request and more a threat. He'd almost think his comments might have wounded her if he thought that even possible.

Cullen did as she said, not because he was afraid of her, but because each moment he touched her, it was more difficult to let go.

And he would let her go.

I have to.

Chapter Twelve

The hospital was noisy and busy, though Cullen had never minded either. Kara had rushed out after their little argument, and while he'd normally have tried to stop her, it served them well.

He waited for the other alphas to return after taking Grace to the airport. Kara being gone meant he, Damon and Reese could meet with their friend and find a few answers without her interfering. Kara did love to interfere.

Bryce stood by the door in the office that, while spacious, was still too small for all the large alpha bodies crammed into it. Still, seeing Bryce never failed to send a pang through Cullen. A longing for family, a reminder of an old life.

They'd served together, years before, and while Cullen valued his friendships with Kaidan and Joshua, the other alphas who worked with Bryce, he and Bryce had always shared a stronger bond. Maybe it was because they were similar, because they understood what it meant to feel as though they had to keep everything afloat.

It meant that when Cullen needed advice in a town that wasn't his home, he'd known exactly who to call.

Reese shook hands with Bryce, the two friendly though not close. "Good to see you."

"Likewise." Bryce turned a look on Damon, who pushed his glasses up the bridge of his nose. "Didn't realize you two were taking in cubs."

Damon didn't even flinch at the subtle jab. He smiled, the quickest flash of teeth as if to assert that while young, he was still an alpha. "I'm Damon. I take care of all the things they're not smart enough to."

A moment of silence fell at the joke before Bryce's lips cracked into a large, rare grin. "Well, we all need one of those around. Good to meet you." He gestured at the table before taking a seat himself.

"How's Claire?" Cullen had yet to meet the omega who had stolen the heart of not just Bryce, but Joshua and Kaidan as well, months before. He wondered what sort of female could manage with those three alphas.

"She's good. Tired all the time and grumpy enough to take a finger from anyone who bothers her. Joshua finished off the ice cream last week without telling her and I swear I didn't think there'd be a body left to identify when she was done with him."

Cullen chuckled at the thought of the three tough alphas all put in their place by one little pregnant omega. He'd bet they tiptoed around the house so they didn't incur her wrath. "I remember when my mom was pregnant with my little brother. The best thing you can do is offer snacks and stay the hell out of her way."

"Wise words." Bryce laughed softly, a strange sound from the normally stern alpha. "And what about you?

I have to say, when I got your call, I was expecting some help on a job, some insight into the area or the folks around here. Didn't expect to be setting you up with a doctor who specializes in omegas." The question wasn't all that subtle, but then again, Bryce hadn't ever been subtle. He was like Cullen, direct to a fault.

"Is this doctor any good?"

Bryce lifted an eyebrow at the way Cullen dodged his question. "Marshall Brown is an expert in omega care. He's dealt with about anything you can imagine. In fact, he's handling Claire's pregnancy."

That said more than anything else. If Bryce was trusting his pregnant mate to this doctor, he had complete faith in the man.

A knock on the door was the only warning before a new man came in, one who wore a white coat and a tag with *Dr. Brown* on it. He had the no-joke gait of a man who knew what he was doing.

The man shook hands with Cullen, Reese then Damon. When he did so with Bryce, however, they pulled in for a half hug with a pat on the back as well. "How's Claire?" the doctor asked.

"Good. She's out with Tiffany right now, having their nails done or something."

The doctor let out a warm laugh as he took a seat. "Yeah, Kane took them, from what I understand. He'll be complaining all night about it, I'm sure." He turned a look directly at Cullen then. "Bryce didn't tell me much about what you wanted to discuss."

Reese spoke up, which was probably for the best, as he was better at keeping things delicate. "Thanks for seeing us, Dr. Brown—"

"Call me Marshall, please."

"Marshall. We're hoping to get some understanding about what can happen to an omega who is sterile."

Marshall sat back in his chair, which was pushed away from the table so he could cross one ankle over the other knee. "It depends on why the omega is sterile. I'm going to guess this isn't a hypothetical question?"

Reese shook his head. "Wish it were. We're dealing with an omega who likes to lie. I know she's sterile because a doctor blurted it out during an exam after looking at some of her labs. She won't say a word about it, though. Even if she did, no one should trust her."

"And you're not respecting her privacy why?" The expression on the doctor's face said that while he might have a jovial attitude, he also wasn't above digging in when he needed to, and it seemed the protection of omegas was a good reason to him.

"Because we're working closely with her, and the doctor said he was surprised she was functioning so well with her condition. If this was just a case of her not being able to have kids, I'd leave it be. Her business. But it sounds like this is something that's affecting her. The last thing I want is to have her get hurt, or have any of us get hurt because she's got a condition we don't know about."

Marshall said nothing for a long while, his brown eyes studying the alphas. Finally, he nodded. "Without examining her myself, I can only give you general ideas. You said the other doctor looked at her labs? Do you know what the labs were?"

Damon answered. "He took a blood sample and put it into a machine to analyze it. He said the machine looked at hormone levels to ensure she was actually an omega."

"That means they'd be looking at a few specific hormones. Sterility can be caused by a few things. Physical, meaning there's a specific mechanical barrier—say, damaged fallopian tubes. Hormonal, which can cause the body to not release eggs or to otherwise throw an omega's cycle out of order. Lastly, there's idiosyncratic, which is a fancy way of saying an omega doesn't conceive and we aren't sure why. Given what you've said, it has to be hormonal, though there could be a physical component. Remove the ovaries, and the hormones are damaged as well. Are you with me?"

Cullen nodded, even though he was sure a good portion of what the doctor said was still above his head. He got the main parts, though. *Maybe.*

Marshall continued. "The hormonal effects associated with sterility are usually a menopausal reaction. Lower sex drive, loss of bone and muscle mass. Those can be handled through hormonal replacement therapy."

Reese shook his head. "She doesn't have any of that."

"Mood swings?"

"Mostly anger."

Bryce snorted. "Typical omega, then?"

Reese rubbed his hand over the back of his neck, as though he didn't fancy saying the next part. "She's actually got a pretty high sex drive. And her scent? It's not like any omega I've smelled before. It's not the smell of heat, but similar."

Marshall winced, his gaze softening, which was a bad fucking sign. "Well, then what the other doctor said makes sense. It sounds like she had a hysterectomy and some damage to at least one ovary. I've seen it before, and it's not a condition I enjoy seeing in omegas."

"Just say it," Cullen snapped, frustration poking at him. He didn't like not knowing, not understanding, and it seemed as though the conversation wasn't going to be a good one.

"For a typical omega, a heat occurs about once a year. That can change based on a few things, like their exposure to alphas, their health, their stress level and certain medications. When an omega goes into heat, they experience a large hormonal shift that causes heightened libido. Basically, biology demands they mate. Exposure to semen will help, and to alpha semen specifically. A heat can last twelve to forty-eight hours, usually shorter if serviced by an alpha. However, omegas with this condition don't reach a full heat state. The hormones will rise, but they won't peak. This means they don't experience the full effects of a heat, but it also means it doesn't fully abate. Depending on the individual omega, they can experience these pseudo-heats as often as every few days, and the other things, exposure to alphas and stress, can cause them to occur more often or to be stronger."

Cullen let his gaze rest on the table, his mind working as he thought about Kara's reactions. Could this be what she'd not wanted seen? Did her shirt hide a hysterectomy scar? Was that why she refused to remove it?

The scent she gave off made more sense, like the first beckoning of a heat, and her actions fit Marshall's explanation. That she'd taken males to bed and seemed to regret it later? He'd seen omegas going through heats before, knew the pain and stress and need it caused them, and even if Kara never reached that level, the thought that she suffered through even a fraction of it so often had his hands drawing into fists.

Not that he could do a damned thing about it.

"What sort of treatment is there?"

Marshall's voice was kind. "There isn't much. A lot of omegas in this condition don't last long. They often do things that are dangerous and end up in bad places. I've had some luck in the past, but there just hasn't been much research in the area. If you wanted, she could come in and I could see what I can do. There are a few hormonal regulation medications we could try, but…" He shook his head. "I wouldn't get your hopes up. This isn't something I'd wish on anyone."

Chapter Thirteen

Having Kara gone put Damon on edge, which wasn't a feeling he enjoyed. The conversation with Marshall weighed on him as he considered the discomfort she had to be in.

So far, neither Reese nor Cullen had mentioned that they smelled Damon on Kara. There was no way they'd missed it, which meant they either didn't care or had purposely chosen to ignore it.

Which hadn't sat with him any better than Kara being missing had. It felt like a weight on his shoulders he couldn't quite ignore, like a crack in their bond he had to address.

"Are you mad?" Damon blurted out as Cullen lowered himself in a pushup, pausing at the bottom.

Cullen lifted his head to look at him before pushing up again, then moving to his knees. "What?"

Really smooth. Damon groaned, giving up on trying to make the conversation easy. He'd blown that, hadn't he? "Kara," he said.

Reese chuckled from his spot in the kitchen, seated on a bar stool, an open magazine in front of him. "I win."

Cullen tossed him a glare. "No, you don't."

"I said he'd break before the end of the day."

"You said he'd *apologize*. He hasn't actually apologized, so you haven't won."

Reese huffed and looked at Damon. "He's right. Say sorry so I win."

"Win what?" Damon frowned as he tried to keep up.

"Cullen said you wouldn't say shit today, that you'd hold out for at least a week. I said nope, you were going to crack today. If you go ahead and say sorry, I'll take my fifty from Cullen."

Damon's mouth dropped open, no matter how stupid it made him look, at the alphas' bickering.

Cullen laughed, a low, dark sound that he didn't do as freely or often as Reese.

A moment later, Damon found his voice. "You bet on me? Why didn't you just say something?"

"And not get to see the whole internal struggle you had going on?" Reese shook his head. "Nope, I wouldn't miss that for anything."

Damon narrowed his gaze, a soft growl rumbling from his chest.

Cullen got to his feet and shoved Reese. "Give the kid a break, huh? We were kidding, Damon."

"He was kidding. I want my money."

And that made it impossible to stay angry at either of the other men. It snapped the tension, made the conversation accessible. Damon let out the same small laugh the others had, and it stole away the rest of the uncertainty. "So, I guess you aren't planning on firing me?"

That did kill the laughter, though. Reese and Cullen wore nearly identical expressions — surprise.

Reese straightened on his stool. "No, kid, we aren't going to fire you."

The words took a weight off Damon. He hadn't even realized before how worried he'd been about it, how he'd dreaded the idea of losing the friends he'd found. He worked so hard to keep everyone happy, to meet expectations, yet he always felt he was failing. He was always waiting for someone to send him away.

"You really thought we'd toss you out?"

"Well, I slept with the omega you two have sort of claimed." He shrugged. "We alphas tend to be possessive."

Reese shook his head. "Doesn't matter what happens with Kara — with any female — you've got a place here."

The words took a weight from Damon, the first time he'd really felt part of the group, as if he'd made the pair into a trio.

Cullen took a seat on the chair in the living room, stretching his legs out and crossing them at the ankles. "Whatever this is with Kara, it isn't long-term."

The statement didn't sound entirely true, and Cullen didn't say it like a man sure of himself. Instead, he tripped over the declaration.

"Why can't it be long-term?"

Cullen shook his head as if Damon were naïve. "You know our work is dangerous. Do you want the sort of people we deal with going after her? It isn't like she'd ever let us keep her safe, like she'd sit back and stay out of trouble."

Reese picked up the conversation. "Besides, even if something more real was possible, Kara isn't the type."

Damon's hackles rose. "Because she can't have kids?"

Reese flinched, then frowned. "Of course not. We could work around that if we had to. She's a thief, Damon, and a liar. Could you ever really sleep well? Ever trust that she was where she said she was, doing what she said she was? Every single morning I woke up, I'd need to make sure she didn't steal anything. That isn't a recipe for happiness."

While Reese said it like a bad thing, Damon couldn't fight the smile at the truth of the statement. Maybe Kara wasn't long-term, but she'd be fun for however long she stuck around, and fun was something he hadn't had much of in his life.

Damon pushed his glasses back up his nose. "All right, so if she isn't long-term, what is this? It isn't a one-night stand, either."

"I guess it's something in the middle," Cullen said. "This job is going to take a little time, and as long as we're here, we might as well enjoy it."

"How do I fit in?"

"Neither of us tried to tear your throat out for fucking her, so I guess that means we're okay with it." Reese paired the not-so-subtle threat with a grin that stole any sting. "You're not stupid. You know how Cullen and I are."

"You share?"

Reese shook his head. "No. I fuck women and Cullen just enjoys sloppy seconds."

Something sailed past Damon. Cullen had thrown one of the décor wicker balls and nailed Reese in the shoulder with it. "You asshole," Cullen tacked on.

"Call me sloppy seconds again and you'll lose something you're fond of," came a voice that had all three of them sitting up taller, as though just a few words from Kara could call them to attention. Even with the threat, she didn't look all that upset as she passed them. In fact, she only flipped them off as she emerged from the shower, her blue hair back in place, a smirk on her lips as though the comment had amused her.

As Damon watched her go, he wished there was a way to work past the issues, because he couldn't stomach the idea of losing her.

Chapter Fourteen

Reese couldn't quite forget the conversation with Cullen and Damon. They had all made good points, himself included. There were so many reasons that Kara was a piss-poor idea as a mate, even if he thought she'd want that for a minute.

The largest?

She couldn't be trusted. No matter how many times he found himself tempted by her, he always tripped over that same point. She lied. *Constantly.* She seemed to do it half for fun, as though allergic to the very idea of telling the truth.

Reese had lived through that before, dealt with a woman who couldn't be trusted. It wasn't a life he ever wanted to return to.

The memories of trying to pick himself back up afterward, when he'd had no money, nothing, they stung. Yeah, he'd been down that road once already, knew how a deceitful female could fuck up a man's life. He should know better now.

He shook his head, trying yet again to push off the thoughts. What did any of it matter?

Kara wasn't the staying type anyway, and worse yet, she wasn't the type who could be kept. Even if she wasn't who she was, even if he and Cullen and Damon all decided they wanted her, if she didn't want to stay, there was nothing they could do to change that.

Even the way she smelled didn't make anything different. All any of them had was a bit of fun while they got the contract off her head. They'd find Kash, then go the hell home.

If that meant they got to enjoy her luscious, toned body during that time? Well, no harm, no foul, right?

Which brought him to his current issue—Kara inside Damon's room and smelling like a fucking treat.

Cullen and Damon had stepped out, probably just to give him a little privacy. Both of the other alphas had taken Kara on their own, and Reese had yet to have the pleasure. He wasn't a jealous man, but that didn't mean he didn't want his own time, his chance to have her to himself for just a little while.

Kara came out of the room like a whirlwind, moving quickly and agitatedly. Frustration and anxiety hung on her, and she paced through the suite like a caged animal.

There it was, though. Clear as day, he could see right through her snarls and her slamming of items. It was that pseudo-heat the doctor had talked about. Now that he knew what to look for, he could identify the scent. It wasn't what a heat would smell like, not so sweet and demanding, but it was close enough to get his dick to wake up and take notice. *Like it's ever not taking notice of her.*

"Something wrong?"

Kara shot him a look, those blue eyes dancing like the hottest of flames. "What are you still doing here? I figured you'd be trailing after your boyfriends."

The jab only made him smile wider. "Well, aren't you grumpy when you're horny?"

That made her stand straight, not that it changed that the girl was short. "Even if I was, don't think you had anything to do with it."

Her lie scraped his nerves, but he tried to ignore it. "Don't be like that. You're soaked, I'm hard — seems like this doesn't have to be all that complicated."

"You think that's all it takes for me? Believe it or not, your dick isn't in high demand."

A lesser alpha might have winced at her words, but Reese was drawn by her challenge. Her bite only drew him to his feet and made him want to prove he could help her. "You know how good I feel. You came hard on my cock last time."

Her gaze softened, as though he chipped away her resolve. Why she even had resolve, he didn't know. It seemed she screwed anything when she wanted to, so why resist them? Why were *they* different?

He might even have liked being different if it wasn't being a cock-block right then.

Reese came forward, caging her with his body, using his size like he did everything about him — to get what he wanted.

Kara's gaze went to his lips, locking on as though that was all she could think about, which wasn't a bad idea.

"That what you need? Because I've got no issue licking you until you come all over my tongue."

A shudder ran through her, one that spread from her center and lifted goosebumps on her arms. *Such a pretty reaction.*

Which was all he really needed to know. Of course, the aching of his cock wouldn't be denied or ignored, but he had a pretty fucking good idea how to deal with it all.

Reese caught Kara around the waist and lifted her over his shoulder. She fought a little, but even a good shot to his kidney area — one hard enough to make him wince — said it was nothing more than her being difficult. If she wanted him to put her down, he had no doubt she could manage it.

Reese took her to his bed, wanting her to roll around in his sheets until everything smelled of her — only of her — and each night he lay in it afterward until they were washed, he could enjoy it.

He dropped her onto the mattress, then stripped off his jeans. He hadn't worn underwear, often didn't, but the reason that time had been obvious. The fewer layers between him and getting inside her any way he could, the better.

Kara's gaze ate up the sight like a hungry predator. She wasn't some frightened, nervous omega who wasn't sure what she wanted. Neither was she like him, someone who owned by strength and straight-forward demand. Instead, Kara was a whole different creature, lethal in her own way, like a lithe cat who walked through the darkest alleys without fear.

She wasted no time shimmying out of her own leggings. Her pale, toned thighs came into view, along with the quickest flash of her pussy, the clothing forgotten. Who cared about clothing right then?

He'd waste away to nothing with no complaints if he got to die between her legs.

Which got him moving again, the reminder of his goal. A tug of his strong arms and he'd pulled his shirt over his head, not wanting anything between them. *Well, anything except her shirt, since she still doesn't seem like she's about to take that off.* He pushed that away, not wanting to think about it, feeling as though it were yet another lie, this one of omission.

The bed dipped beneath his weight, and Kara spread her thighs for him, the best invitation he'd ever seen, offered without hesitation.

"Not what I was thinking." He grasped her hips and flipped them both, her body heavier than he'd expected given her small frame.

Then again, the girl might be small, but she carried muscle.

He ended up on his back, her knees pressed to the mattress beside his head and her waiting cunt above him.

Her startled sound when he moved her transformed into a moan as she realized the position also placed her in reach of his already hard cock.

Before he could do anything but bask in the closeness of her warm, wet pussy, Kara leaned forward and slipped his thick length past her waiting lips. The heat of her mouth was nearly too much, especially as she tightened her lips and sucked once—hard.

He lifted his hips, an unconscious demand as he wanted her to envelop all his shaft, as he wanted to feel that warm softness up his entire length.

A shift of her hips broke the spell, and he reached around her, grasping her hips in his large hands and lifting his lips to her wet pussy.

She tasted of cinnamon and honey, like something wild and untamable. Her cunt pulsed against his exploring lips, a pathetic plea from her body for more.

I'll give her more. Fuck, I'll give her everything until she is begging me to stop.

He stroked his tongue up her slit in one hard motion, gathering her wetness and swallowing it down. He swirled his tongue around her clit, wanting to touch every inch of her, every secret place on her. He wanted to wipe away the memory of all the meaningless sex she'd had and replace it with the worship of his lips and tongue and body.

She cried out, the sound muted by his large cock, but she only spread her knees wider to offer more.

And he took more. He kept one hand steady on her hips while he slipped the other between their bodies. He wanted nothing hidden, nothing kept from him. He pulled her hood back and spread her folds, then dove in with his eager, seeking tongue.

Each drop of her essence made him need more, as though instead of sating him, it only increased his hunger. He fucked into her mouth with wild thrusts, but the grip of her hand kept her from gagging.

Not that Kara needed him to slow down. She sucked on his cock as if nothing mattered but his taste, taking as much of him as she could. Her tongue, normally good only at lying and throwing insults, worked the sensitive underside of his dick while her hands stroked the base, squeezing around his aching knot, teasing it.

She took his balls in her other hand, fondling them with the same rough reverence she gave his cock. It all hurtled him toward release, even as he tried to hold off.

Reese tilted his head and latched his lips around her greedy clit, sucking hard as he plunged two fingers from the hand that had held her open into her tight cunt.

She gasped. She moaned. She made sounds like a trapped animal as her orgasm slammed into her. Not that any of it made him have mercy. He fucked into her with those fingers, scissoring them to ensure she felt as full as possible while he drew deep sucks on her clit.

Her pussy walls tightening on his fingers, the way her moans vibrated on his cock, the way his shaft muffled the sounds pushed him past that edge too.

He released her hip to grab her head, bucking up once, deep, before he came. Kara swallowed around him, the sensation milking each drop of seed from his eager cock.

Her gasp when he pulled back was sinful, and even his spent and softening dick gave a half-hearted jerk, as though it wanted to go again just from that sound.

The tension that had swamped her had slipped free, and her body—lax and sated—was a vision of contentment. He rolled them, noticing her cheeks had a pink glow and her hair was tousled so blue strands stuck every which way.

Adorable. Mine.

The second word stilled him, but he only licked his lips, tasting another drop of her sweetness before he decided the word and declaration didn't matter. They were nothing but his idiot alpha brain wanting something that he was smart enough to know wouldn't happen. Though, more of this would be good.

She couldn't lie when he had his tongue on her.

She didn't pull her thighs together, didn't hide the way the light caught on her drenched sex.

In fact, he figured a second go sounded good. By the time he licked her to another orgasm, he'd be ready for round two. He could fuck her like he needed to, deep and without mercy, and feel her sweet cunt cranking down on him.

Except as he lifted his gaze, ready to dive back in, he caught sight of where her shirt had ridden up.

Not all the way, not enough for her to notice, but enough for him to see the crisscrossing of thick white lines over her lower stomach.

He'd thought she'd hidden a hysterectomy scar, expected one long, thin line where someone had removed a part of her body, the reminder perhaps too painful for her to share.

He hadn't expected to see the evidence of nothing short of torture, where someone had carved her up and left her broken. *Another secret. Another lie.*

Kara basked in the afterglow, in the way her body tingled and even a slight breeze across her clit made her shudder in stark pleasure.

Reese had more than proven his skill. He'd eaten her out like a man starved while he'd fed her each hot inch of his hard cock. Even if he hadn't fucked her, Kara felt the same content feeling she did after full-on sex.

No, that's not quite right. She felt *more*, like he'd managed to give her something the others hadn't, like it had quenched a thirst she hadn't realized she had.

Which was foolish.

She opened her eyes, expecting to find him leering, to enjoy the way he stared at her bared sex before she tempted him into trying to get it up a second time.

Only, she found no lust in his hazel eyes, no sexy licking of his lips or anything else. Rage sat in those normally sweet eyes, one so deep that she snapped her legs closed as though protecting herself. His gaze was locked on her lower stomach, and with horror, she realized her shirt had ridden up.

The entirety of her scars weren't on display—though what did it matter, because seeing some was the same as seeing it all—but bits of the patchwork of white, jagged scars and skin not quite the right texture or color showed.

Her stomach rolled. She yanked off the bed, grabbing for the leggings she'd discarded.

"What happened?" The words came out in an angry rumble.

"Fuck off," she said back, pulling up her leggings until the high waist of them hid the ugly reminders.

Reese caught her hand, his body still nude, though his cock hadn't perked up again. Then again, what sort of guy could stay hard after seeing what she really looked like? "Talk to me."

"I don't have shit to say."

"Yeah, you really do."

"Like what?"

His fingers were tight around her wrist, an unbreakable grip that she didn't really want to escape from. "Like who the hell carved you up. Like the fact that you suffer through pseudo-heats and never said anything to us. Like your entire goddamned past!" The final one was roared out, the voice of an alpha who was so done playing.

Kara stood against the anger in that voice without a problem, though. "So you think you know anything, now? Did an internet search until you thought you understood shit about me?"

"Well, it isn't like you've been open."

"Why should I be? We are fucking, that's it. I don't owe you shit about me, my present or my past. In fact, so far all you three have done is fuck up my life, so don't you think you're on any sort of high ground with me!"

He lifted his lip in a snarl, and Kara answered with her own. She pulled her shoulders back and met every fucking ounce of his aggression with equal measure.

Sometimes she wondered if part of the reason she didn't fit in with other omegas wasn't her sterility, her broken body. Had it turned her from a normal omega into something else? Upped her aggression, her violence, her ability to ignore alpha commands?

Did it matter?

Reese let his lip drop once he saw it wouldn't get him anywhere. "I want to help."

"I don't need your help. It's nothing."

"You sure? Because last I checked, you've been fucking whatever will take you to deal with your condition. If you weren't so stubborn, if you didn't lie so damned much, you'd see that you do need us."

The words slapped her in the face. They brought up every forgettable encounter, every time she'd felt like throwing up as she'd washed herself afterward, every tear she'd refused to shed. Kara yanked again, and when he wouldn't release her, she drove her knee up and into his side.

It caused him to loosen his grip, and she took the opportunity to pull free.

As Reese leaned forward to catch his breath, his long hair obscuring his face, Kara backed a few steps away. "Like you said, I've been fucking whatever will take me. You're just the most recent in a list. Not the first, not the last and certainly not the best."

She twisted on her heel, chin held high, and stormed from the room.

Anything to not let him see how deep his words cut, especially because of how true they were.

* * * *

Damon could have killed Reese. The temptation was there, prowling around in the parts of himself he didn't like to admit to.

It wasn't that he couldn't behave as all the other alphas did—it was more that he preferred to think things through. He liked order. He liked predictability. He didn't care for the animalistic side of himself that thrived on chaos.

However, as Reese told the story, as he explained what had happened between him and Kara, Damon found that familiar anger welling up inside him.

"So you thought insulting her was a great plan?" Cullen's words came out soft, as though he were tempering them.

"No, I didn't, but I wasn't exactly thinking. You don't get it. You didn't see her fucking stomach."

The sickness inside him when he considered what Reese had said rose up again, but damn it, he wouldn't throw up all over the floor.

He'd seen injuries, scars, the proof of pain people faced. The idea of such lines sitting on Kara had him rolling his shoulders to release the tension inside him. He wasn't sure how he'd have reacted, but he was pretty sure he wouldn't have essentially called Kara a whore.

"What happened to her?" Damon mused the question out loud.

Reese sighed, rubbing his fingers against his eyelids. "I don't know, but it was fucking ugly. Honestly, I'm amazed she's alive after whatever the hell gave her those marks." He leaned forward, his elbows falling to rest on his knees. "I remember a case a long time ago, back when I first started working in missing persons. The problem with those cases is that some of the time, all you find is a body. The woman disappeared, and everyone figured she'd run off with her boyfriend, especially because her mom wasn't a fan of the boy. Young rebellion and all. Well, they were half right — it was the boyfriend, but she didn't run off. She'd broken up with him and he took a knife to her. I don't think he even meant to kill her, but no one survives that."

The horrors that washed over Reese's face said more than his words needed to about what he remembered, about what he'd seen. The body reflected in his hazel eyes, and it was clear he'd carried that guilt with him, as though it were his fault that he hadn't found her fast enough.

"So who put them on her?"

"She wasn't all that eager to discuss it. She nailed me with a knee to the side and bolted." He huffed, shaking his head. "But it sure makes a little more sense, doesn't it? Her whole 'fuck the world' attitude? I mean, look at what the world has given her."

Cullen stared out of the window. "It doesn't matter."

"What now?" Damon asked with a steel thread through his voice. Whatever Kara had suffered certainly did matter.

Cullen turned his gaze to Damon, shaking his head. "I don't mean it like that. What I meant was that whatever shitty hand she's been dealt doesn't change anything. We're still not looking for anything and neither is she. If you find a broken car, does figuring out what accident broke it make a damn bit of difference? We're still incompatible. She still doesn't want any of us or our help. She's still not what we want. So we'll keep going, we'll figure this shit out, we'll finish our job, and we *will* go home at the end of it."

Damon opened his mouth to argue, to say they could find a way to make it work.

But all his planning failed him when no steps materialized. No magic path toward success came together. Cullen was right, and knowing how or why life had twisted Kara into who she was didn't change that it had.

She *was* broken. It wasn't her body, wasn't that she couldn't have children, but rather her soul. Whatever she'd suffered had taught her that she needed to be guarded, that she needed to keep people at a distance, and Damon wasn't sure that was the sort of thing that could be fixed.

"So what now? Where do we go from here?" Reese asked.

Cullen huffed out an unhappy breath. "Whatever this is won't be forever, but that doesn't mean it's got to end tonight, either. If I know anything about our little thief, I'd bet I can guess where exactly she plans to drown her sorrows."

Reese nodded, rising to his feet and brushing his hands off on the tops of his jeans. "Let's go ruin her pity party."

Damon followed suit, feeling like part of a group for the first time, like someone wanted and valued. "She won't be happy about it."

Cullen offered a smile that was all teeth. "Oh, I'm counting on it. She's cute when she's pissed."

Chapter Fifteen

They'd checked the bar she frequented and the lobby of the hotel, only to find no sign of Kara. It reminded Cullen of how little they actually knew about their wayward thief.

If she wanted to take off, if she wanted to disappear, they couldn't do a thing to stop her. They had no access to her life, no knowledge of her friends. Hell, they didn't even know where she *lived*.

Again, he was struck with what a terrible idea this all was. Not only was she likely to get herself in trouble, but because she was so secretive, they couldn't even do much to help her.

All the searches had brought them back to the hotel room without an idea of where else to try.

A sound from Damon's room had them all freezing when they entered.

Kara? It was impossible to tell since her scent already seemed to saturate every item in their suite.

Cullen pulled his gun from the holster at his hip, nodding back toward the room despite the other alphas being on similar alert. Damon never carried a gun and Reese usually left his safely locked at home.

Another sound—a drawer closing—came as the alphas crept toward the open door. Nothing in the main suite appeared out of place, but that didn't mean anything. A smart criminal would start in the rooms.

When the figure passed the door, Cullen nodded. It had been a smart thief.

Kara went still when she spotted the three of them, her face a mask of hiding. At least toward Cullen and Damon.

She wouldn't look at Reese.

Over her shoulder was a bag. So, she'd come back only to clear her shit out? It didn't surprise Cullen but it sure did annoy him.

They all stared back and forth without saying a word, as if waiting for someone to break.

Leave it to Damon to break first. "Where are you going?"

Kara pulled the strap of her heavy pack farther up on her shoulder. "I'm leaving."

"We haven't finished the case yet."

"Yeah, well, I can handle it on my own." Even as she spoke, she averted her gaze. "I'll have Grace send you the money for it. You won't be out anything."

That was what she thought it was about? She thought they cared about some damned money? It riled Cullen's temper to realize she *still* didn't understand a damned thing. Sure, they weren't destined for romance, but the fact she actually thought they cared more about some money for the case than about her annoyed him.

She should know better. She should know *them* better than that already.

"You think we're just going to go on home, just like that?" Cullen crossed his arms, standing between her and the door she so obviously wanted to escape through.

"Why not?" The shrug of her shoulders was all defensive. "Not like there's anything between us. You finished the original job, and technically, I accepted Grace's job. So you can go."

She stood there, back straight, but eyes down on the floor. The perfect example of someone so terrified of anyone getting close to her, of seeing anything beneath that exterior she liked to hide behind. Reese had glimpsed beneath it, seen the scars—literal in this case—that she'd worked so hard to cover with attitude and posturing. It gave Cullen an understanding he'd lacked before.

The girl was terrified of the idea of people *seeing* her. She didn't want to show her wounds, show her imperfections, show any of the things she didn't like about herself.

Cullen got it. Was he any different? Fuck knew he wasn't out there telling her how much he hated to see her in danger, was he? No, he kept those worries to himself, safely hidden.

Even understanding *why* Kara might act that way didn't excuse it, though. Cullen still didn't plan on letting her get away with it.

In fact, maybe from realizing his own shortcomings, he recognized how badly he wanted to address it in her.

"So, thanks," she muttered. "I mean, for fucking things up, I guess."

She took a step toward the door, but Cullen didn't move. He kept himself planted directly in her way. She'd have to go through him to leave.

Kara met his eyes. "I'm going."

"I don't think so."

"You really think you can keep me here if I don't want to stay?"

Oh, the temptation to do so hit him. While he wasn't a kidnapping sort of man, he wanted to pit her skill against his. Worse? He didn't know who he wanted to win. Did he want to prove he could best her or would he feel better if she won? If he *knew* that despite her stubborn, stupid streak she could handle herself?

Thankfully, Reese piped up before Cullen got them in trouble. "You're pissed. I get it. That doesn't mean you should leave."

Her gaze zeroed in on Reese and, hell, Cullen was glad he wasn't the focus of all that anger. Small miracles that for once, he hadn't pissed her off.

"Well, I've got lots of men to fuck, right? Busy schedule to keep." Hurt colored the words.

Reese let out a soft sigh. "Look, I'm sorry."

"Do you know where you can shove that sorry?"

"Up my ass?"

"That's right," Kara said.

Still, Reese pushed. "I was pissed, okay? I saw the scars and you were sitting there lying to me again. In case you haven't noticed, I'm not great with lying."

She shook her head. "I don't need you to apologize, because I don't care what you think."

"If you don't care, why are you running?"

"This isn't running. It's realizing that you all have caused me far more problems than you've solved. I'd be crazy to keep sticking around."

Cullen's temper slipped another inch at the idea of her just walking out over something so small. "So you'll run off, and for what? So you can deal with killers on your own? How the hell is that a smart idea?"

She set her hands on her hips and met his gaze head on, staring up, her blue eyes flashing. "Smarter than sticking around a couple of arrogant alphas who aren't nearly as smart as you think you are."

He leaned in, towering over her, enjoying the flush on her cheeks and the way her scent exploded. "Go put your stuff down, Kara."

Her lips pressed together in a tight line. "No."

"You're being reckless. You're acting because you're pissed. Stop and think about it for one goddamned minute and you'd see it's a stupid choice."

He could tell by the look on her face she knew it was stupid. Still, she was more interested in being stubborn than in making good choices.

"Last chance. Move." She tipped her face up, so close to his that they probably looked like they were a heartbeat away from kissing.

Which he wouldn't mind. Were there better ways to work out an argument than that?

"You'll have to go through me." He said it like a dare.

A dare Kara did not back down from. She swung her head forward, but Cullen was expecting it. A yank back kept her from slamming into his face.

She was wild against him, but he had size and strength. Her elbow struck his side, her knee rising to hit him, probably in a place he didn't want struck.

He had no doubts that if they actually fought, it wouldn't have gone that way. She pulled her hits — though he'd have bruises — and of course he didn't strike her at all. It didn't take long to quell her snarling, though. He slid his fingers into her hair and tilted her face up to meet his gaze.

She bared her teeth. "You are going to be so sorry for manhandling me."

He tightened his grip in her hair. "If you really wanted to go, you would have been gone already."

"I needed my things."

"You had a few pieces of clothing. You would have left them behind. Sorry, thief, but you *wanted* us to catch you leaving."

She didn't answer that time, but the look on her face said she wanted to.

Quiet? She probably didn't want to admit she'd come there looking for them. Sure, she wanted to run, wanted to hide those wounds of hers, but she'd *still* come here.

And Cullen was tired of her acting up. Was this what she did? Push people until they turned their backs on her?

He went still as he realized that was exactly what she did. She pushed and lashed out until people wrote her off, because that was what she expected them to do anyway.

She wanted to snap and send the alphas running so she could sit back and tell herself, *See, they didn't want me, just like I knew.*

And with that, Cullen knew *exactly* what they needed to do. He released her hair, holding her arm instead as he pulled her toward his room, Reese and Damon following.

"What exactly do you think you're doing?"

"Showing you that no matter how much you snarl, you can't scare us off."

Cullen peered over at Reese, the two having spent enough time to be on a similar page. A quick nod from Reese said he was in agreement. No need to check with Damon — he wouldn't understand the question yet.

"Oh, so you all think you're tough, now?"

Damon shut the door to Cullen's room once they all entered, just as Cullen let go of Kara's arm.

She glared at each of the alphas with not a speck of fear. No, not Kara. She wasn't fragile, wouldn't wilt at a little roughness. Instead, she stood against all of it, the color on her cheeks deepening, her breath speeding. She wasn't one to win over with sweet words and gentle touches. No, Kara's life had been hard and it seemed the only way to break through those walls of hers might be that same roughness.

Reese answered her question, showing he was so on board with the plan. "If it makes you feel better, growl. Curse. Insult us. Whatever it takes you to get through it. Unless you say 'stop', sweetheart, we're going to show you that we're more than tough enough to deal with your wild streak."

The way Kara's pupils grew and the softest, prettiest moan left her lips made Cullen sure they were doing the right thing.

And he was going to enjoy every second of it.

Reese groaned at how hard he was. His cock pressed painfully against the zipper of his jeans and he cursed himself for forgoing boxers.

That fire in Kara's eyes drew him, especially when she refused to back down.

He liked her hard edges, her challenge. It was just the damned lying he hated.

He'd given her an out. As much as he'd wanted to spank her ass since he'd met her, he'd never do it if she really didn't want it. There were lines he didn't cross.

And for her part, it let Kara rage against them while still deciding if she really wanted it or not. Her reaction screamed that she wanted it, though.

The girl didn't like to accept things, but it didn't change that she wanted them.

Reese caught her with his hand behind her neck, leading her back toward the bed. She followed as if he had her leashed, her pupils wide and obscuring the blue of her lovely eyes.

He sat on the bed, and Kara bent forward. Reese kept her moving by pulling her in for a kiss before shifting her over his lap. He did it quickly before her brain caught up.

Because the moment it did, she'd kick.

Sure enough, she let out a scandalized gasp. "What the fuck do you think you're doing?"

Reese shifted her forward so her ass was up, her weight braced on his knees, and his hand on her back held her in place. "Teaching you that you can't run us off. You think you can bare those pearly whites of yours and everyone will fall in line. Guess what? We won't."

She kicked her feet but couldn't get purchase. Not to mention, Reese *had* done this before. He knew damned well how to hold a woman still.

He waited for a moment to see if she tapped out. All she had to say was 'stop.' If she uttered that, he'd let her up, and she knew it.

Despite her struggle, she didn't say it, and that didn't shock him. Kara didn't like to give in, and whether she wanted to admit it or not, she *needed* this.

Hell, maybe they all did.

Cullen pulled the chair from the desk over so he sat beside Kara, his knees brushing Reese's. He stroked his hand over her ass like a teasing promise, hinting at the things to come.

Damon, the one who seemed to give in for her, dropped to his knees in front of her. He stroked his fingers through her hair, the touch seeming to calm her.

At least, it did until Cullen caught the waist of her leggings and pulled them down her legs. Instead of taking them off, he left them around her thighs, just above her knees.

Maybe that will keep her under control. Probably not. He was starting to think nothing could make that girl behave.

The sight of her bare ass helped keep him on track.

"I swear, when you let me up—"

"Does it make you feel better to argue?" Cullen stroked his hand against the curve of her ass one more time. "Does kicking your feet and fighting against us make you feel like you can enjoy it, then? If so, feel free to keep it up, because what you've got to learn is that you don't scare us."

She opened her mouth to say something—and he was sure it was going to be something they didn't want to hear—but Cullen landed his hand hard against the flesh of her ass. The sound ricocheted through the room, followed by…a moan?

His cock hardened more, something he'd thought impossible, at the wanton sound that left Kara's lips. *And even better?* The red mark left on her skin, the one that resembled the size and shape of Cullen's hand.

One little swat wouldn't keep her still for long, though, because as soon as she cut off that sound, as if she couldn't believe it had left her lips, she resumed her posturing. She kicked her legs, she cursed, she ignored the sweet way Damon stroked his fingers through her hair.

Reese exchanged a look with Cullen, one filled with all the thrill of discovery.

Reese could have guessed Kara might enjoy this, but who really fucking knew? Mostly, the idea had been to break past those defenses of hers, to get her to realize she didn't need to fight them, because they weren't going anywhere — at least not right then.

Cullen smirked once before he repeated the action. This time he didn't slow between each slap of his hand to her ass. No, he kept a steady rhythm as he moved from one cheek to the other, her skin turning a lovely shade of pink beneath the attention.

Kara, for her part, didn't give in. Then again, she wasn't the sort of girl to give in easily. "I swear, I'll castrate you," she growled out between the gasps and shudders and moans that escaped her.

Reese kept one hand on her back, though she didn't struggle as much as she had at the start, and reached beneath her with his other. He leaned enough to capture her nearest breast, the nipple already hard and easy to find even from beneath her shirt. "Yeah, yeah," he said, dismissing her threats. "When you're done with this little temper tantrum, you just let us know. Cullen here, he spends a lot of time at the gym. Trust me when I say if it comes down to your ass or his arm wearing out first, your ass doesn't have a chance."

The shudder that ran through her was delicious, especially because he knew she fought it. That was the thing — even if bodies didn't like to admit to what they wanted, they always made it clear. Kara needed to keep the alphas at a distance, but the sweet scent of her cunt filling the room showed that she wasn't as opposed to this as she pretend.

Reese met Damon's gaze, checking in with the younger alpha. He was sweet and *not* the type to do this normally. However, Damon's eyes were filled with predatory lust, with the sort of look that reminded Reese that the other alpha was very much an alpha. He wasn't rough, offering those same gentle affections as if soothing her through it. Still, he'd lock his gaze on the fall of Cullen's hand, on the clap of sound against Kara's ass, and a soft growl would rumble from his throat.

Not quite so sweet, is he?

A hiccupping gasp left Kara. Not tears, but closer than he thought he'd ever hear from her.

"I'm sorry," she whispered, so softly Reese doubted he'd heard it.

He had, though. So had Cullen, who stopped and rubbed his hand over her ass. "What was that?"

She sniffed once, her body lax against Reese's lap, but she didn't repeat it.

Reese pulled off her leggings then shifted her until she straddled his lap before he grasped her chin between his fingers to force those red-rimmed eyes on him.

No tears, though. Hell, he didn't think he'd *ever* see her cry, no matter what happened. "What did you say?"

Another sniffle. "I'm sorry."

"For what?"

A slight defiance in her gaze, her back going straight—it all said that even if they managed to tame her for a moment, it wouldn't ever be for good. *Why do I like that?*

She hissed, and Reese chuckled to find Cullen had leaned closer and cupped her ass in his large hands, no doubt aggravating the sore skin.

Still, it seemed to work, because she answered, "For running off."

Reese shook his head. "It's not just running. You're waiting for people to fuck you over, so you think you can get them to leave first. You thought you'd show up here and we'd toss you back because you're difficult. Guess what? We aren't that weak. You can act the shrew all you want, but you aren't going to scare us away."

The shiver that ran through her was like a dream, a tiny crack in that armor. She didn't give in, didn't submit, but it was as though something in her eyes said she wanted to.

"Tell us you get it," Cullen said from behind her.

Kara nodded, a sharp jerk of her head.

Ah, the defiance still in her made Reese want to take it further. He wanted to tie her down and enjoy every luscious inch of her body, to see how her toned muscles flexed as she pulled against her bindings.

He wanted to fuck her until she gave in, until she gave them everything and realized it wasn't so bad.

But she wasn't there. In the time they had, she'd probably never get there.

Pity.

"You liked that," Reese said.

Incredulity filled her blue eyes. "Who could possibly like *that*?"

Her lie scraped at him, as always, dissipating some of those good feelings. He could call her on this one, at least. He reached between her spread thighs and pressed two of his fingers into her cunt to prove his point. "Really? Because you're as wet as I've ever felt you, hellion."

Her head dropped back and she lifted her hips — not to escape, but as if the touch was already that overwhelming.

"Admit you liked it and we'll take care of you," Damon said from where he stood beside Cullen.

Kara twisted to glare at him. "You're supposed to be the nice one."

Damon stroked his fingers down the side of her face. "I am. All you have to do is admit to all of us you enjoy it and you'll get everything you want."

Tiny shudders coursed through her, as if each inch were overwhelmed and primed. Reese pumped his fingers slowly, not enough to get her off, or even to get close to it, but enough to keep her on that edge, to make her need more.

How long would she hold out? Normally he'd think someone would have broken well before, but they weren't as stubborn as Kara.

He planned to win, though. The prize was too important.

Finally, Kara let out a pathetic whine that made his cock twitch in response. "I enjoyed it," she whispered as her little defiance.

Good enough.

Damon leaned down to take a kiss from Kara, needing to feel her lips. He'd never done something like *that* before and it unsettled him.

More so with how much he'd enjoyed it.

He, the one who never would think about striking a female, even for fun, had hardened embarrassingly quick and been far too close to coming at the sight of Cullen spanking Kara.

The flush on her cheeks, the moans from her lips — they had been the most erotic thing he'd ever witnessed.

He pulled Kara from Reese's lap as she undid the buttons of his pants.

Cullen and Reese had both touched her and Damon *needed* to feel her pussy wrapped around him.

He moved up on the bed before stretching out, Kara all but crawling on top of him. She didn't need any help figuring out what to do, splaying her knees wide around his hips before she wrapped her small hand around his hard dick. Reese was right — she was soaked. She slid him into her waiting cunt without a problem, the tightness enough to yank a snarl from him and for him to reach up and grab her hips, pulling her down, needing to be as deep as possible inside her.

Once she'd slid down his entire length and the heat and tightness of her sex surrounded every inch of him, she set her hands on his chest and rode him, staring down into his eyes.

This was what had been missing. She'd never kept her eyes open, never looked before. Maybe it wasn't much, but Damon knew damned well it meant something. Maybe Reese and Cullen's stupid idea had worked — maybe they'd managed to take down some of her defenses, at least for a while.

Cullen shifted forward behind her, his knees framing both Kara's and Damon's.

A shuddering gasp from Kara had Damon tilting so he could see.

Cullen grasped her ass, massaging her. She *had* to be sore, but the way her cunt tensed up around him, the sounds that left her sweet lips, all said she must enjoy the touch.

To their side sat Reese. He had stripped down as well, and he wrapped his hand around his cock as he watched, lust covering his features.

It all made sense, suddenly.

Before, Damon hadn't quite understood the appeal of sharing a female. He'd known Cullen and Reese did, but he'd figured there would be jealousy. No alphas could really share an omega without them getting resentful, without them wanting to tear one another apart. He'd never been able to imagine watching another alpha touch a female he wanted and being okay with it.

However, when Cullen grasped Kara's ass, when Reese reached out with his free hand to capture one of Kara's breasts, Damon couldn't find the jealousy he'd assumed he'd be filled with.

A strange sense of contentment swamped him instead. He *liked* the way she shuddered when Reese tightened his fingers on her nipple. He groaned at how Cullen pressed a hand to her back to lean her forward. The other alphas weren't in competition. It wasn't about being better than any of them.

Instead, they worked *together* to take her apart. Cullen with brute force, Reese with his charm and skill and Damon with that soft side.

They did things together none of them could on their own.

So Damon leaned up to capture Kara's lips, to swallow down those mouth-watering sounds she made and take a kiss meant to tell her the things he knew better than to say. Kara was flighty and voicing anything might just scare her off.

She curled her hands in, pressing her nails into his chest like tiny bites of pain to mix into the pleasure. *Marks.* He loved the idea of wearing her marks, of taking his shirt off the next day and seeing little crescent-shaped nail scabs in his skin, like badges of honor.

The thought alone stole his breath, and the aching in his cock couldn't be ignored any longer.

She rolled her hips again and Damon snarled against her lips before lifting his pelvis in a hard thrust, burying himself as deep as possible. He didn't need to grab her, because Cullen used his grip on her ass to press her down as Damon's knot swelled.

Her hands clutched more, a trickle of blood saying she'd probably broken his skin, but he didn't care. He locked inside her, her cunt squeezing down on his knot as she came again, triggered by that instinctual pleasure that happened between an alpha and an omega, something she couldn't get from a beta.

As he came, filling her tight pussy, he met her gaze to find those stunning blue eyes still locked to his. He took one more kiss from her, because this was something he'd never thought he'd have.

And he knew losing it would hurt.

Kara couldn't control anything.

Her cunt pulsed around Damon's thick knot, her body shivered and moans fell from her lips.

She'd *always* been in control. No matter how many males she'd used to slake her lust, she'd always put them in their place. She followed a basic truth — don't let anyone too close. Somehow, the alphas had gotten her to break that one rule.

The sting in her ass because Cullen wouldn't leave the sore skin alone kept his lesson in the forefront of her mind. Damon's dick, locked inside her, reiterated just how deeply the alphas had managed to get beneath her skin and how little she had been able to do to stop it. Reese teased her nipples, moving from one to the other as he stroked his cock, a reminder that they weren't close to done. All of it said the same thing—resisting them was pointless and they weren't going anywhere.

Would she listen to them from now on? *Fuck that.* Yet at the same time, some strange understanding had seemed to happen.

She couldn't run them off.

It had been the first time someone had truly stood against that raging inside her, when she'd bared her teeth and done whatever it took to get them to run.

The alphas hadn't run. They hadn't even bent.

Instead, they'd shown her that no matter what she dished out, they could take it.

And that *terrified* her.

Not that they'd given her time to think about it.

She focused instead on what she wanted, on what she needed right then. Locked against Damon, his cock twitching as he filled her and his knot stretching her in that delicious way that was impossible to replicate, she only needed *more*.

More of Damon's sweet lips and more of Reese's arrogant grins and more of Cullen's rough hands.

And thankfully, the alphas seemed willing to give her that without her asking.

Cullen rubbed her sore ass once again before using his grip to spread her cheeks.

She tensed against the sensation and Damon groaned when it squeezed his cock.

Cullen didn't stop, though. In fact, he stroked a finger from where Damon filled her cunt up to her ass, where she'd never let anyone take her.

Cullen must have noticed her reaction, because he chuckled. "Do I make you nervous?"

She twisted her head to glare, ready to tell him off, but Reese took that moment to offer a pinch to her nipple. The slight sting made her inhale sharply instead of saying whatever she would have said.

Cullen went down once more, stroking along her stretched cunt. When he returned to her ass, she realized he'd collected all the slick from her drenched pussy. His now wet finger rubbed against her, coaxing but insistent.

Reese released his pinch, stroking over her nipple as if to soothe it. "I can't say I'm shocked you've never done anal, hellion. Takes trust, huh? You don't strike me as the sort to let anyone get that from you."

Cullen's grip was unshakable as he kept her spread, as he teased her and made promises with that touch that had her mind racing.

It was all *too* much.

She wanted him to fuck her like this. Some frightening part of her wanted him to stretch her ass with his thick fingers before sliding his hard cock inside her. She wanted to feel Damon beneath her, locked within her, while Cullen filled her ass. She wanted to be so overtaken by them that she couldn't even think of resisting, that her brain stopped all its gymnastics looking for a reason this was stupid, why it would never work.

Then? Then she wanted Reese to push his shaft past her lips so she didn't have a single inch of space left inside her. She wanted to just…give in.

Not forever, but just for a while, just to rest, to let someone else handle everything.

Cullen pressed harder, but she still tensed against him.

Reese switched his fingers to her other nipple and once more tightened until all her attention was on the sting of his pinch. Everything else melted away as she cried out.

When he let go, though, when she shuddered in a breath, Cullen took her relaxation for granted.

He pushed forward and his finger breached the tight muscles of her ass, slipping into her in a way she'd never experienced before.

It seemed so much more personal than just sex, and she didn't like that. Physically it teased her senses, made her even more desperate, but she already felt scraped raw by the alphas.

After they'd spanked her, they'd cracked the carefully constructed walls she'd put up to keep them — and everyone else — at a distance. Now Cullen took even more of her control away, and no matter how much her body enjoyed it, her mind rebelled.

It was *too* dangerous. They'd see too much and walk out like everyone else. They'd realize she wasn't worth the effort and she'd end up hurt. Sure, lots of people had walked away from her, but always because she'd been the one to push them.

Losing someone because they really saw her, because she'd let them close and they'd still left? That was a different matter altogether.

She couldn't say it, though. That was perhaps the largest struggle. She couldn't tell them why they needed to stop, why she needed that distance and what had always worked before didn't work with them.

They didn't scare easily.

So instead, Kara's body spoke for her. She whimpered at the new sensation of Cullen's finger, at the thoughts in her head of how much more she wanted. He shifted from one to two fingers, the new stretch causing a burning.

Too much. Not enough. She warred between the two feelings. Even when she shifted, Damon's knot kept her in place, trapped her for Cullen to play.

Reese tormented her breasts through her shirt, teasing her nipples with feather-light touches before offering a tight squeeze just to keep her guessing.

Cullen withdrew his fingers, shifting behind her.

"No," she said far too quickly. It was *almost* a plea.

Cullen stilled behind her, one hand still on her ass. "No, huh?"

She shook her head, her eyes closed, trying to hide all the nonsense running amok in her mind, wanting to keep it off her face. If he went that far, she was afraid she'd shatter.

He caressed her with that large hand before shifting away and resuming his position. She jumped when his finger touched her again, but he slid it into her easily.

"You'll give in," he promised her, no anger in his voice. "Maybe not yet, but you will."

The words sank deep into her, an absolute certainty. It wasn't *about* anal and they all fucking knew it. It was about trust, about her giving in to them fully, and she just couldn't do that.

She twisted her neck to look back, to find Cullen poised behind her, his hand wrapped around his cock, stroking his hard length as he watched himself finger-fucking her ass. He seemed enthralled by it.

Her cheeks heated at the lust on his face, at how lewd it felt, but all that only added to the electric sensations running through her body.

Reese caught her chin and stole a kiss, his lips firm and unyielding. Damon took the chance to reach between them and slid his fingers along her drenched and swollen clit.

She cried out, far past overwhelmed.

Reese stroked his cock when he broke the kiss, starting down her body at where she was locked on Damon's dick, and Reese's lips curled into a dangerous smirk. He slid his fingers into Kara's hair, a grip so tight it made her scalp sting with the most deviant pleasure, before he pushed her down.

His shaft sat there like a gift, but the tug at her hair said she ought to get going. *Gladly.*

Kara took his length past her lips, though she couldn't go far because he still had his other hand wrapped around the base. It only gave her the head to work with, but it was hard to care about that.

She lavished attention on him, using her tongue to circle the thick head, to toy with the ridge and rough skin at the bottom. Each bit of pre-cum that escaped him felt like some elixir that her body reacted to.

Everything closed in on her again, and no matter how tired she was, no matter how overworked she felt, she knew she'd come again. Between them, with little control, they'd force another mind-blowing orgasm from her body no matter what.

"Look at me," Reese demanded.

She couldn't. They'd already taken too much, put her on display too entirely. She closed her eyes harder, tightening her lips and sucking at his cock in hopes he'd let it go.

His grip on her hair loosened enough for him to offer an almost sweet stroke at the same time as he sighed. "Fine," he rumbled. Maybe he realized she'd already given all she could right then, that looking at him when she already was so lost would push her past something she was not ready to face.

He stroked himself, his fist butting against her lips, his cock twitching slightly to prove how close he was.

Meanwhile, Cullen fucked her with hard and deep pumps of his fingers, as though, since he couldn't get his dick into her, he'd claim her with whatever he could.

Reese came first, his scalding cum landing on her tongue in heavy lines. She swallowed it down as quickly as she could, her tongue seeking more from the source.

As soon as it happened, though, as soon as that heavenly taste surged through her, she lost what last little scrap of control she had. She shattered beneath the orgasm that crashed over her, beneath the unyielding hands and bodies of the alphas. Her entire body tightened, sparks of pleasure so intense she felt like she was dying coursing through her.

Cullen withdrew his fingers, and when she found the blunt head of his dick pressed against her ass, she had a moment of worry. Would he ignore her no?

Except he didn't. She should have known he wouldn't, either. He stroked his cock, his free hand tight on her ass, spreading her open still, as he found his own release against her. His cum was hot and thick as it landed on her ass, and damn her, it made her almost regret her choice.

She panted hard, her arms having given out, so she rested her forehead against Damon's chest. Reese stroked his fingers through her hair and Cullen took the chance to drag his fingers through the cum on her. He pressed slightly, drawing a whine from her as he pushed his thick seed into her ass, as though that was where it damned well belonged.

And Kara could only shiver at the way her body was lax, at the absolutely sated sensation inside her, and at realizing for the first time just how dangerous these three were to her.

* * * *

Kara lounged with her head pillowed in Damon's lap, the heat of him making her want to curl against him like a cat near a fireplace.

After they'd cleaned up, they'd put on a movie and all piled onto the large fold-out couch in the living room. It was probably best, since the bedroom smelled like sex and Kara needed time to process what had happened.

Had she really enjoyed that? Had she given in so easily to the overbearing touch of the alphas? *What was I thinking?*

Even as she chastised herself for the stupidity, she found herself more relaxed than she could recall being. Tomorrow she'd think harder about it. Tomorrow she'd remember all the reasons this was an absolutely horrible idea. For tonight, she enjoyed it.

Cullen sat to her left, Reese to her right. A bowl of popcorn had been made and mostly consumed during the superhero movie she'd insisted they watch.

Cullen had offered a rom-com, but that was the last thing any of them needed. Nope, she wanted mindless ass-kicking, not romance.

While her body still responded to the alphas, the frantic need had drifted away. It meant that when Cullen's fingers danced over her side, over her hip — with her clad only in her panties and a baggy top — she could enjoy the caress for what it was. Comforting and almost sweet.

Which unnerved her all the more, especially how much she enjoyed it.

Cullen stroked her lower stomach, and her breath froze in her lungs. He didn't venture under the shirt, but the careful motions were too deliberate for him to be unaware.

Still, Cullen didn't ask. He didn't stop, didn't question the marks that they *all* knew sat just beneath the thin fabric.

The silence was thick, the ease of the movie gone until Kara couldn't fucking *think*. She couldn't breathe, couldn't figure out a way to keep going.

Torrin, Erik and Liam had seen her scars, a result of when she'd all but collapsed in their care that first night, but after the healing? After she'd gotten on her feet enough to not need them to change bandages — and they'd claim it was far too soon, really — Kara had hidden them.

She preferred her high-waisted leggings and long tops, and even when living with Torrin and Erik, even after the times she'd slept with Liam, she hadn't showed them to anyone.

But these alphas — *my alphas* — knew.

So why didn't they ask?

Probably because they had to know if they so much as opened their stupid mouths right then, she'd bolt.

Probably.

Maybe she'd knee one in the junk for good measure.

Except the longer she waited, the more she loathed the silence and the way Cullen's fingers stroked over the shirt. No, it was her reaction she hated, the feelings those strokes drew forward.

"Stop it," she whispered, her voice lacking the strength she wished it had. That was the moment for attitude, for enough 'fuck off' in her tone to keep them from even considering trying that shit again. Instead, it sounded like a plea.

Cullen paused, then pulled his hand away, a soft sigh on his lips. "Why are you trying so hard to keep us at a distance?"

His words were easier than the touches, than the caress too gentle and soft for her, for her life, for these alphas. The gunshots from the movie helped to further unwind the discomfort.

"Because it isn't your problem. *I'm* not your problem." She closed her eyes and swallowed hard, then risked offering up the words. "These are my reminders that life sucks, okay? If I forget for a second that there's always someone waiting to screw me over, all I've got to do is look under my shirt and I damn well remember."

"Life isn't fair for anyone. We just do the best we can. You can't let..." Reese hesitated, as though not sure what to say, how to phrase the statement in a way that wouldn't piss her off or send her running. "What happened stop you from living your life. We're not whoever did that to you, and you can't walk around thinking everyone is like that."

That was what they thought it was about?

If only. A little broken trust would be easy to get over.

Kara released a soft snort at the simplicity of their wrong guess. "I don't keep people at a safe distance because I'm afraid of what they'll do to me."

"You said they were a reminder?"

"Yeah, they are. The night this happened? The fucker who did it also took a blade to my brother, and it happened because my brother came back for me. He could have gotten away if he hadn't come back for me. They got to him because of me." She gulped, then squeezed her eyes tighter closed when they burned. *Fucking tears.*

Fingers trailed along her arm, thankfully not touching where the scars sat. Another hand stroked through her hair, the touch soothing her against her better judgment.

"What happened to your brother?" Reese asked.

"He pulled through, barely, but he's got no idea I'm alive. He was worse off than I was—the asshole stabbed him in the chest—and as soon as I got out of the hospital, I went and saw him. He had so many tubes going out of him, and he was so pale." Kara sat up, unable to stay flat anymore, not when the memories flooded her. She could still *smell* the disinfectant from that hospital room, the incessant beeping the only thing that told her Kane lived. She'd just kept staring, wondering how the fuck he could be alive.

Large hands stroked over her back as she hunched forward. The touches kept the words flowing. "He was the one who took care of me when we were kids, who looked out for me. I let him because I didn't know any better, and what happened? He almost died because I was weak, and he was trying to protect me."

"Where were your parents?"

"Our mom was a junkie who couldn't care less about us. It was just him and me, even before he got us out of that house. He did everything he could to take care of me, to keep a roof over our heads and food in our mouths. I know he did things he wouldn't have for any other reason but that he had to."

"That's what family does."

"Maybe," she said, shrugging. "But what it got him was almost killed. So I took off after the attack, when he assumed I was dead. I've done what I can to watch out for him, but he's better off without me."

"And the people who hurt you?" The soft growl of Cullen vibrated even through his hands. "What happened to them?"

"Dead."

"You killed them?" Damon asked.

"Not exactly." Kara let her lip curl up at the memory. She wasn't usually a killer, but she'd enjoyed knowing the assholes who had hurt her and Kane were dead. Torrin had tried to get the information from her. He'd sat by her bed one of the nights when she'd been in pain, when she'd woken from a nightmare and would have sworn she was back there with that blade slicing her up. His bright green eyes had bored into her, her chance to see what rested beneath his calm and collected exterior. He'd demanded their names — a funny thing, because Kara had no doubt he could have found them — but she'd refused.

At first, she'd thought it was because she was a coward, but later realized it was because she'd *needed* to deal with them herself. Torrin must have realized it as well, because he'd left them for her.

"What does *not exactly* mean?" Damon asked.

"I spent a couple years learning my trade from some friends. After I'd gotten better, I tracked them down. I'm not much of a killer myself, but it wasn't that hard to set them up. I got them on the wrong side of the wrong people, and they handled it for me."

Kara would never admit it, but she'd snuck in after the hit was called, after she knew the assholes were dead. She'd needed to see the people, to see their vacant stares. Not for her, despite the way her well-healed scars had burned. No, she'd wanted to spit on the bodies for what they'd done to Kane.

Reese huffed a soft sound that screamed he knew her thoughts without her voicing them. Maybe they'd shown on her face, or maybe he just knew her that well already. "Well, I'm not sorry they ended up that way."

Kara twisted to look over her shoulder at Reese, who offered her a snarky grin totally at odds with the conversation. Then again, pity would have set her off. She'd take that snark in a heartbeat.

Damon spoke next, his voice careful. "Have you ever seen a doctor?"

"Ever? Sure." Kara twisted fully to face the three, their reaction meaning she wasn't feeling the need to gut them for the conversation.

Damon didn't look amused by her avoidance. "We met a doctor who's offered to take a look at your case. He might be able to help."

"I don't need help."

"No?" Cullen lifted an eyebrow. "Because you didn't look all that in control last night."

The words didn't sound like a jab as they had before. Instead, he delivered them in as gentle a tone as he could, as though he didn't want to hurt her but needed to say it.

And…he wasn't wrong. Maybe it was her time with them, but what had used to be a tolerable but distasteful part of life had turned sickening.

When she parted ways with the alphas, could she go back to how she'd been before?

This wasn't about them. It was about her.

Reese leaned in and pressed a kiss to Kara's bare shoulder. "The doctor's an expert, the best you'll find. I'll leave his card on the table by the door, and he already agreed to see you whenever you want."

"You think you're smooth, don't you?"

His gaze heated, moving down her front, pausing on her chest as though he could see her naked already. "Yeah, I do. Seems to work pretty well for me."

His arrogance should not have been as attractive as it was…

Still, she refused to fall for it. "I don't know about that."

He grasped the front of her shirt and pulled her into a kiss, the sort that melted her resolve and turned her into a puddle of want.

When he broke the kiss, his lips tipped up into that smirk. "Lie down again, hellion. The morning is going to come too soon."

Chapter Sixteen

Reese was going to spank Kara again just for bringing up the stupid idea. "Not a chance."

Kara stared back at him, all fire after having had the night to rebuild her defenses against them. In fact, she seemed even more surly, as if she'd realized just how much she'd given up and how little she liked it. "It's the best choice!"

Cullen huffed from his spot by the bar, his arms crossed. "That's not an idea, thief. That's what people do when they don't have any ideas. Big difference."

Damon remained silent, his gaze taking in the three others. He did that a lot, liked to figure things out instead of throwing himself into the middle of the fray like the rest.

Probably for the best. They didn't need three hotheads.

Kara threw her arms up before she began to pace. "Do you know where they're keeping the alpha? Do you know *anything*?"

Reese kept his lips sealed, hating the answer. Coming up with nothing annoyed him.

She grinned, as though she enjoyed the tiny win. "All we know for sure is that they want me. That makes me the best lead we have."

"If you think we're dangling you out there like bait, you are insane."

She cocked up an eyebrow, as if her sanity was a foregone conclusion. "I'm not doing it alone, you idiots. We put out the word of where I'll be. I know enough people who can make sure it's mentioned so anyone looking for me will find it. We'll use a safehouse I know of. You guys will be set up already and waiting. When Mr. Bad Breath shows up looking for me, we turn the tables and nab him. Easy."

Reese thought about all the many ways it could go terribly wrong, and it suddenly didn't seem so easy.

The strategist in him said it was a good idea. The look on Cullen's face said it was a good idea.

Instinct said 'fuck that, she's not going anywhere near this piss-poor plan.'

"And what if they decide they're not interested in taking you alive anymore? What if they've decided they're willing to just kill you?" Cullen asked.

Which was a good point and made Reese's stomach churn.

Kara waved off the concern as if it were stupid. "They're not going to shoot first, because they've got questions and dead people aren't good at answering questions."

Which made sense.

Reese struggled to find some reason why this was stupid, some reason why they had another plan that made more sense.

"I'm doing this whether you like it or not." Kara crossed her arms and mirrored Cullen's stance.

Cullen only snorted and shook his head.

Arguing with Kara was pointless. The more they argued, the more she dug her heels in.

That she'd even come to them with the idea was a fucking miracle. Normally she did whatever the hell she wanted behind their backs, usually while offering a pretty smile to lull them into a false sense of security.

So that was progress, right?

Reese scrubbed his hands over his face at his justification, looking to find positives in a whole bucket of negatives. She'd probably come to them because she knew the back-up would be useful, not because she cared at all about being honest.

"I don't like it," Damon admitted from his spot on the sidelines. "But it's the best plan I can see right now."

"See, he understands." Kara hiked a thumb at Damon.

"He'd agree with you if you said the sky was pink," Cullen argued. "You sway him too easily."

Damon rose from his spot on the couch. "No, she doesn't. I'm just smart enough to look at this logically. The longer we all run around looking for something without any real direction, the better chance that Kara gets found by accident. If we control the situation here, if we have time to set up, then it's the safest of plans. I hate to say it, but this is the best option."

Reese hated when the youngest alpha was right. Even worse was when Reese knew damned well Damon *was* right, like now, but he didn't care for the truth. Reese wanted to find another option, one that kept Kara out of the line of fire.

But that didn't seem likely to happen, and Damon wasn't wrong. The longer it took them to wrap this up, the more opportunities they were giving Kara's pursuers.

"Fine," Reese gritted out. "But one of us is going to be inside the room with you. No, don't bother trying to argue. It's non-negotiable."

Kara pressed her lips together so tightly that the color blanched from them. Seemed she didn't care for being backed into a wall.

Too fucking bad. None of us like this plan, either. Welcome to the club.

She nodded, though she didn't look happy about it. "Okay. It'll take a couple days, so I'll get in contact with—"

Reese caught her arm before she could walk past him and pulled her up against him. All those warm curves took him back to the other hot places on her, but he stayed focused even when her eyes went wide and her pupils dilated. "You're going to listen, hellion, and you're going to follow the plan."

Her tempting tongue wet her bottom lip. "I always follow the plan."

He narrowed his eyes. "And if I catch you lying, I swear what we did to your ass last time will seem like a vacation."

Her lips parted and a thin moan escaped.

And for a second, as much as he loathed her lying, he almost hoped she'd push him to follow through on the threat.

It might just be worth it.

* * * *

Damon was entirely out of his element.

He wasn't the type to worry about his shortcomings, to fear he didn't fit the right mold, and he had long ago accepted what his limitations were.

Or perhaps it would be more accurate to say he'd grown accustomed to that. Damon was happy to let Cullen and Reese do the heavy lifting when it came to life-or-death situations.

At least, he would have been, if Kara hadn't asked him.

"Why did you want me here?" He sat in a chair in the safehouse she'd pointed out. It rested at the end of a cul-de-sac, with Cullen and Reese sitting watch in the house next door.

"You don't bug me as much as the others."

He cast her a side-eye, knowing damn well that wasn't it. "Either of them would have been more help than I am. If you need a search run, if you need to get past a security system, those things are my realm. Not this."

She didn't respond at first, slumped down in her own seat, her feet resting on the bookshelf against the wall. Cups filled the small room with the scent of over-roasted cheap coffee, but given that they'd needed to get into place five hours before the time she'd spread around to her contacts, he understood the need.

Finally, she shifted in the seat and answered while her gaze never strayed from the window. "Cullen and Reese like to be right, and I'd rather not spend the entire time arguing. I'd rather have you along because you listen."

He winced at the reminder that he *listened*. How was it that something which brought him so much happiness in the moment could drag on him?

She'd brought him because he wasn't as strong as the others, because he wasn't like them. Would she grow bored of him? Tired of him not being what it seemed every other alpha was?

"What's with that look?"

Damon tried to wipe clear any expression from his face. "Nothing."

"Was that your first lie to me? It's sort of adorable. See, I don't know why people are bothered by my lying, unless I don't look nearly that cute when I do it."

The fact she didn't demand an answer let Damon pick up one of the coffees and take a sip, to consider her words. If she'd pushed, he'd have hardened his defenses. Instead, she just waited.

"Do you ever get tired of not being what you're supposed to be?"

She snorted. "You're talking to a picture-perfect example of everything an omega isn't supposed to be, here. I got over being annoyed by it a while ago." Even as she said it, a waver in her voice said maybe she wasn't being entirely honest. Then again, maybe she'd said what she wanted to be true. "Besides, you seem pretty alpha to me."

He slid his thumb against the cup between his hands, using the mindless motions to distract him so he could ask what he needed to. "We both know that isn't true. I'm not like Reese or Cullen."

"Thank god," she muttered.

"I don't act like an alpha should."

Kara let out the loudest of sighs, one all attitude and point, as though she wanted him to know exactly how stupid she thought he was being. She twisted to look at him, and the lights from the lamp made the blue of her eyes glow. "The fact that you're not a beating-on-your-chest arrogant asshole doesn't make you not an alpha. Believe it or not, that behavior isn't some badge of honor."

"I've been with women who expected me to be something I'm not. I've seen the disappointment on their faces when I don't live up to what they thought they were getting."

"Well, people are idiots, in case you weren't already aware."

Damon set his coffee back down and risked the real fear. "Even if someone" — they both had to know he was talking about her — "accepted that I'm not like that, how long would that last? How long before they were tired of me not being a real alpha? How long before they walked away for someone who was better?"

She blinked slowly, the blue of her eyes disappearing for a split second, and he wished he could read whatever was on her face. When she answered him, her voice was soft and quiet. "You can spend your life trying to be something you're not, but it won't ever work. Eventually, that mask falls and people see you for what you really are. It's not worth it to try and hide who and what you are. If someone can't appreciate it, if they don't think it's good enough, fuck them."

"And you?" *So much for being subtle.*

"If I had any issue with you, I wouldn't give you a second look. You think I didn't know the first time I saw you what things would be like between us?"

"And it doesn't bother you?"

"Nope. I like having you at my beck and call." The curl of her lip was obvious, and the effect it had on his cock was instantaneous. "I can find alphas who want to take and take all day long, but you? You're rare, and anyone who doesn't see how fucking awesome it is, well, they can fuck off." When she finished speaking, she stilled, her smile sliding free. "I mean, this is still temporary. I might think you look amazing on your knees, but this is it. When it's over, though, it's over because it'll never work, not because of any bullshit about you not being a real alpha. Trust me, I felt your knot—you're an alpha."

He wanted to argue more, the years of feeling like he wasn't quite enough so thick it was hard for her words to truly breach them.

Except she interrupted him once more before he could. "Stop worrying. I don't ever let a good insult go to waste, so if I thought there was a damned thing wrong with you, I'd say it."

And that brought him more comfort than it should have, because she was right. While Kara might lie about nearly everything, she didn't sugar-coat. She didn't keep things quiet for the comfort of others.

Which meant she liked him, though he couldn't figure out why, and he didn't even try to hide his smile at that.

* * * *

Cullen groused at the waiting. Five hours of Kara there, and another five he'd been in place before that. He and Reese took turns, using four-hour shifts to keep their eyes from tiring out. Before long their watch would have to turn into sleeping shifts as well.

"They're never going to show," Cullen snapped, his focus on the street.

They'd set up in an abandoned house across the street, the realtor box hanging off the handle identifying it as an easy place to use. Cullen would have preferred to be stuck to Kara's hip, but he also never used a plan that didn't make sense.

They needed enough distance to see the threat coming. If he and Reese were inside the house, they'd know too late.

Instead, Damon and Kara were inside the place and he and Reese had been banished across the street to watch.

A cul-de-sac meant one way in, one way out.

"Are you sure she's even still there?" Reese seemed in an especially bad mood, something that didn't fit on his normally cheery friend.

Cullen risked moving his gaze to take in the other alpha. Reese stretched out on a folding chair they'd brought into the empty house, his head back and his eyes closed. His long hair hung loose behind him.

"She's there. Damon would have told us if she wasn't, and this is in her best interest as well." Which was one thing Cullen had learned. Kara did whatever she felt was best for her—even though she was often wrong—which meant she wouldn't do stupid things if she thought they'd hurt her.

Reese grunted. "Oh, like we can trust Damon's word, either. She's got him so wrapped around her finger."

"She isn't Gabby," Cullen said softly when he turned his gaze back outside to avoid the glare he was *sure* Reese was shooting him.

"You're right. She lies even more than Gabby did."

Some wounds didn't heal all that easily, and Reese had always seemed unwilling to let that one go. He picked at it, peeling off the scabs until it festered.

"You can't blame every single female because of the actions of one."

"I'm not. I've just dealt with one lying woman. I don't really need to deal with another. Besides, why are *you* trying to defend Kara? Last I checked you were right on board with tossing her to the curb as soon as we're done here."

Cullen went to reject that but shut his mouth as quickly. Reese was right. Whether or not Kara was like Reese's ex didn't matter. They were still letting her go as soon as they had the case done. So instead of the argument Cullen *wanted* to give to Reese's words, he went with something safer. "It doesn't have anything to do with Kara." *Liar.* "You've been looking for a reason to reject every single female we find. You've been judging them all against Gabby and seeing similarities even if there aren't any."

Reese let out a soft growl, the sort of unhappy sound that was a signal to shut up.

Cullen never listened. "Yeah, so Kara isn't the endgame here, but it's not because she's like Gabby. You've got to stop trying to see that female in every other one you meet or you're never going to get any peace. Fucking women without attachments only gets you so far."

The growling gave way to a soft sigh. "You don't get it. You've never had your heart ripped out. Turns out that isn't the sort of thing that heals very well."

"Yeah, well, you better figure out how to let it heal or you're going to end up alone."

"What? I thought we were going to be BFFs in our retirement homes." Snark bled into Reese's words and even without turning around, Cullen could *see* the bastard's grin.

"If I had to be saddled with only you for our golden years, I'd let some crooked caregiver steal my stuff as long as she put me out of *that* misery."

A huff of laughter behind him made him grin despite his best efforts. His friend was stubborn — always had been — but he deserved a lot better in life than he'd been given.

For a moment, it made Cullen think about the omega across the street.

She was nothing any of them wanted, but sometimes what a person wanted wasn't what was best for them.

His smile melted into a frown. *And sometimes what you think you want, like that curvy disaster of an omega, is really bad for you, like you thought, but you're too stupid to realize it.*

He shook his head, trying to dislodge the train of thought that was going nowhere fast. If he hadn't figured out how to deal with her over the past few days, he wouldn't figure it out then.

A car caught his gaze — the large black SUV drove slowly, no lights.

Oh, like that isn't suspicious.

"Looks like we've got company," Cullen said.

The floorboards creaked beneath Reese a moment before he came up to the window. "Finally. I hate waiting."

The SUV pulled through the cul-de-sac so it was facing the other way. *For a quick getaway?*

The passenger door opened, followed by both back doors. Four men exited the car, with the fifth, the driver, remaining there with the engine running. At the front was Thompson.

"Fuck," Reese cursed.

Cullen already had his phone out, texting a quick warning to Kara and Damon. Given that only one had attacked her at her place, they'd all expected the same to show up again.

They had *not* planned to have to deal with four men.

Cullen and Reese were on their feet quickly, but there was no way they'd make it across the yard and into the house before the men did.

And suddenly, he remembered why he'd hated this plan to start with.

Kara stared down at the text. *Four men incoming. Get out.*

The tension in Damon said he'd received the same message.

"I guess I should be flattered," she said on a laugh. "They must think I'm either a bigger threat or more important than they did the first time."

Damon cut her a glare that said he didn't find it as funny as she did. To be fair, Kara didn't find it *funny* exactly. More that humor had always been her go-to for stressful situations.

She closed her eyes for a moment, her hand already moving to her back to take the pistol there. "You can shoot, right?"

Damon stared at her gun as if it were a snake. "I *can* but I don't like to."

"Well, I don't like being killed, so let's focus on trying not to let that happen first."

Good for him, because Damon took the gun when offered. Kara went to the large dresser in the back of the room, then reached behind it. She found the hook near the bottom and flipped the latch, releasing the dresser so it slid to the left.

Ah, she did love the sight of weaponry.

At Damon's gaping looking of surprise, Kara only shrugged. "You have a safehouse when you need somewhere safe. Do you know what makes a place safe? Guns." She nodded toward the other items. "Well, I mean, and mines and grenades and knives. Whatever."

She crouched and took the pistol from the far left. While she had larger weaponry, pistols were fast, easy to use and easier to conceal.

"Reese and Cullen —"

"Are about two minutes behind the people coming. So, unless you want to just sweet-talk these guys into waiting that long, I'm going to suggest we give them a reason to think twice about coming through that door."

Damon cut her a hard look that said he thought she was crazy — a reminder that while he might not mind her taking charge in the bedroom, he was still an alpha with all the same tendencies the rest of the time.

Sure enough, he let out an unhappy snarl and checked the clip in his gun. The click when he reseated it was far more of a turn-on than it should have been, but Kara had long known she was a bit of a freak.

A creak downstairs let her know they were trying for the quiet approach. Hoping to catch her off guard?

The door handle twisted, and Kara had her weapon up a moment later.

When the door opened, Thompson stood at the front.

"What a reunion," Kara said when she met the man's gaze.

Surprise covered his features before he wiped it away with an efficiency that said he was good at his job. "So, a set-up?"

Kara shrugged but didn't let the gun move at all, keeping it trained on him. "I figured this was the best way to see why exactly you're after me."

He laughed softly before entering the room, hands up, with three others behind him. They all wore jackets, the sort that were too large and heavy to be for anything but concealing weapons.

She had to just rely on the guess that they wanted her alive.

"We have a few questions for you, that's it."

"See, I don't really like answering questions when people break into my home, when they kill my associates, when they threaten me."

"We needed to be cautious. We just want to understand what you're looking for, and if you're working for anyone."

Which was the important question. If they thought she was on her own, they had no reason not to kill her right then. Loose ends were her best friend.

"You don't want to meet the people who hired me. They aren't friendly," she lied.

A twitch in Thompson's cheek said he didn't care for the answer, but he also didn't go for his weapon. "And what is it you're looking for? Maybe we can make a deal? Come to some sort of understanding?"

His *understanding* was no doubt a lot of dead bodies.

Which was not on the top of her list of good outcomes.

"Looking for the prime alpha you took," Kara offered. Give a bit of information and sometimes she could get some back.

His lips pressed together, his tell. He knew about the alpha, at least. "I have no idea what you're talking about. I think you've gotten some bad information."

"Did you know you're a really bad liar?"

He didn't look altogether amused with Kara, though she'd become used to that reaction. It usually worked in her favor because people underestimated her.

"Come along. I didn't hurt you last time until you struggled. I don't want to hurt you this time, either. I'll bring you to my boss, we will have a conversation and that's it. They only want to know what you're after. Once we clear this up, you're free to go back to your life." His gaze moved past her to Damon then back. "You haven't returned to your apartment. You've been remaining out of sight. You have to be tired of hiding by now."

For a split second, the idea had merit. She'd spent so long stuck to the side of the alphas that a part of her *craved* that solace again. As they'd made a mockery of the defenses around her, she'd wanted to be on her own again.

If she wasn't one hundred percent sure that the man *would* kill her the moment they'd figured out what she knew, she might have considered it.

A crash downstairs pulled her attention.

The mistake was stupid. She wasn't an amateur, yet she looked away toward the sound down the stairs. She couldn't even *see* whatever it was from where she was, despite knowing damned well it was one of the other two alphas being far less stealthy than they should.

The mistake cost her.

Thompson came forward, slamming his hand against the wrist that held her pistol. Her grip loosened, and the gun sailed from her hand.

She tried to recover, but the momentum put her off balance and he took the chance to grab her and yank her against his chest.

She met the wide eyes of Damon, who held his own weapon up.

Thompson locked his arm around Kara's throat, the muzzle of his gun pressed to her temple. "Just stay put and no one gets hurt," he promised again.

Still not convincing.

They backed out of the room, with Thompson pulling Kara along. One wrong move and he'd fire that gun, and point-blank shots weren't something she could dodge.

Thompson yanked her down the stairs, pulling Kara even when she lost her balance.

At the bottom of the stars, however, he turned, leaving the other three to keep their standoff with Damon.

Cullen stood, his own weapon drawn, looking far more capable with it than Damon. Where Damon *could* shoot, Cullen had clearly spent plenty of time with his gun, holding it with the easy familiarity of a pro.

Calculations ran in his eyes, and it didn't take much for Kara to know what he was thinking. Thompson hadn't done much hostage-taking, it seemed, because despite the gun at her temple, he'd left himself exposed. A well-placed shot could miss Kara and splatter the poor asshole's head on the wall behind him.

If Kara trusted Cullen to make the shot, because it could just as easily hit her, instead.

Everything inside her screamed *no*. Trust wasn't something she gave, and certainly not to *these* alphas.

He stared at her as though asking. She'd need to relax, to not struggle so she didn't risk moving into the bullet's path.

She shook her head, the smallest movement, to let him know there was no fucking way she was going to let him try that.

His lips pressed together. *Annoyed? Too bad.*

The man yanked again, eyes trained on Cullen as he pulled Kara out through the front door. The back door sat open, the wood around the lock splintered to tell her how Cullen had gotten in.

The chill of the night air hit her as she stumbled outside in the grasp of the man, the car far too close for comfort. If they got her in the car, she was probably dead. They would have the clear advantage, control the environment—and that made escape far more difficult.

Just as she doubted her choice not to trust Cullen, everything shifted as she was thrown to the ground.

Reese had the asshole beneath him. Fury he wasn't used to swamped him at the sight of the man with his hands on Kara and a gun to her head.

He'd moved silently, from a direction the men hadn't been expecting, and taken the man to the ground.

Thompson was larger than Reese and had more muscle. He was far more in Cullen's weight-class, and after the first strike the man made to Reese's ribs, more in Cullen's skill-class too.

They rolled twice before the man landed another hit, this time to Reese's jaw, which shook him enough for the man to pull away.

Thompson's gun sat in the grass a few feet away, and he twisted to find the SUV's driver seat empty.

The man was still alive, but a good sucker punch had put him down in the front seat.

He looked back, the odds having evened.

Kara, Cullen and Damon were all armed, with Kara having picked up his gun. Thompson still had three armed men, but they looked hesitant.

People could be easy to shake if they'd expected an easy win and things didn't go that way.

Thompson lifted his hands. "Well, I guess we call this one a draw."

"Why should I let you go? Seems like a stupid plan."

"Because we leave now, no one gets seriously hurt. We start shooting? Well, you know as well as I do how bullets start changing things."

Reese wanted to argue—probably mostly because he hated the idea of the man walking free after having laid his hands on Kara twice more—but he wasn't wrong.

No one had a clear advantage.

Besides, Reese had an ace up his sleeve. "Fine. Don't let us find you sniffing around again."

"We both know this isn't over." Thompson backed the rest of the way up to the SUV, piling in, with one of the goons taking the driver's spot after shoving the unconscious man into the passenger seat.

When the SUV pulled away, they all took a deep breath.

Well, except Kara, who walked up and shoved Reese. "Why did you let them go? We did all that for nothing!"

He winced when it jostled his sore side—the punch had not done good things for his ribs, it seemed. "Do you really think so little of me?"

The look on her face said yeah, she did.

Ouch. Instead, Reese only gave her a smirk. "After I took care of the driver, I tossed my phone into the back, under the seat. We'll be able to track where they go."

Kara paused, surprise running across her face and…was she *impressed?*

Suddenly his side didn't matter anymore. It turned out he really liked impressing that omega.

He couldn't wait to get her to give him that look again.

* * * *

"Relax," Liam whispered as Kara fidgeted in her stupid gown. It wasn't the paper ones that were often used, but rather a surprisingly soft fabric.

"This is nice," she said, pulling at the hem.

"Fancy place your new friends have gotten you into."

Kara turned her gaze up to him, finding him not smiling, which felt odd. "Is that your way of asking for information?"

"Well, you've shown up smelling of the same males. They seem to have gotten you to go to a specialist, which I've tried for years to get you to do. It makes me wonder."

"Jealous?" Kara offered a wide, mocking grin.

His lips pressed together as he gave her a look that called her an idiot.

Ouch. Then again, she knew better than to think he was jealous.

Still, it helped distract her. The last place she wanted to be was at a hospital, yet that was exactly where she was. Leave it to the alphas to continue to leave her in places she wanted nothing to do with.

The card they'd left for her, the one with Dr. Marshall Brown's name and number, had taunted her on the small table by the suite door each time she'd passed it. They hadn't mentioned going again, but still, every time she left, it would mock her.

Finally, Kara hadn't said a word to the alphas. While they'd been watching the GPS from Reese's phone, waiting for a useful location, she'd picked up the card from the table and walked out of the hotel room.

She wasn't going for *them*. The only way she'd managed the nerves to call the number and set up the appointment was by reminding herself that it was for her. She was going because she was tired of living like she was. She controlled everything else about her life, yet in this one area, she felt adrift. If the doctor could help, why not?

She refused to have much hope—in her experience hope usually ended badly—but she'd called Liam because she couldn't bring herself to go alone. *Pussy.*

Before they could continue their discussion about the jealousy comment, the doctor walked in. He was younger than Kara would have expected, but that wasn't why she disliked him.

Nope, the thing that made her instantly hate him was that he looked kind. He had the sort of 'I really care about you' eyes that made Kara want to bare her teeth.

Don't hurt the doctor. The boys will be pissed.

"Kara, I'm Dr. Brown, but you can call me Marshall. I have the history the nurse took already, and we rushed your blood tests so they were ready."

The level of competence the hospital had shown amazed Kara. Then again, she'd dealt with underground doctors the past few years, going by fake names and using the few who would treat a stab wound or bullet wound without reporting, especially because if a regular hospital realized she was an omega, even a broken one, it might complicate her life. It left her seeing either vets or doctors without licenses.

Liam reached out with a card that had Torrin's company name on it. "All charges should be billed privately through this company. Any tests or treatments you need to do have already been pre-authorized."

Marshall waved the card off without looking at it. "There won't be any charges. This is a favor of a favor of a favor, I guess." He smiled, the sort that implied there was some secret joke or friendship between them. "Cullen knows Bryce who knows me. Besides, I do some pro-bono work when I can, and this is a good case for it. And, just to make it clear, everything remains confidential. Your records will be placed under a false name with only me knowing they belong to you. I don't want any omega under my care to worry about being turned over to the authorities."

"Surprisingly concerned for an alpha," Kara muttered.

Marshall laughed softly. "I have a mate, so if you were worried about me, don't be. I have my hands quite full already."

And that…did help. Especially with the way he spoke, a sweetness in his voice, the way she could almost see him thinking about whatever female had captured his attention.

Marshall shook his head as though waking up. "Let's do the physical, then we can go over the options."

The physical was less comfortable than Kara wanted to admit. In fact, when she put her feet in the stirrups, when Marshall did a pelvic exam and Liam took her hand, she let him.

If that didn't say how unnerved she was by the hospital, by her failings being on display, nothing would. He squeezed her hand, and Kara let the strength of it wash through her.

For one stupid second, so fast before she shut it down, Kara almost wished it were her alphas there. She wished it were Damon holding her hand, that it were Cullen growling at the doctor, that it were Reese making a joke to keep her relaxed.

Liam was her friend, though, and she was damned glad she'd called him. As it turned out, she wasn't quite as brave as she'd wanted to be.

"Done," Marshall said, letting Kara shoot back fast, sitting up, dizzier than she'd expected to be.

"Breathe," Liam whispered a moment before Kara tore her hand back. *Fuck panic attacks.*

Marshall stood, tossing his gloves into the small trash can in the corner. "Why don't you dress and meet me in my office?"

Whether he did that because he needed to leave or because he knew she needed the moment, Kara didn't care.

As soon as he left, Kara dropped her head into her hands.

Liam stroked his fingers through her hair the way he'd always done when she was sick.

"What if he can't fix me?" She whispered the question she'd never dared before.

"You don't need to be fixed."

Ah, sweet Liam, but he was wrong.

Kara shook her head, then said to him what she'd never say to anyone else. "I hate this. I can't do it anymore, Liam. I can't *be* this anymore. I won't."

Liam shifted, then dropped to a crouch before her, capturing her chin to lift her gaze to his. "Don't you dare say that," he said with the sort of edge that came from believing he could do anything, fix anything. Liam had never doubted his own abilities.

"I shower with scalding-hot water after each fucking time, and I still can't scrub away the scent of men I don't fucking want." The words poured from her, aided by her mild panic attack, by the things she wanted from the alphas and her fears that she'd never get them. "I can never get that off me, not fully."

"I'm here. You don't have to do that."

"You don't want me, Liam. You never have. Do you know how much I hate myself for what you've done for me? God, do you really think I want to be that at all? That I'm okay with it? Because it disgusts me that I've used you."

He moved his hands to her cheeks and caught a tear that leaked down, one of the rare few ones that ever escaped. His gaze locked on it, probably realizing he might never have seen her cry. "Why didn't you talk to me sooner? Talk to us?"

"Because it's my problem."

His eyes hardened a fraction, the look that said he wasn't happy with her response. "We're family, kid. Doesn't matter what else happens, we are family, and if I'd realized how bad you were, how you felt, I'd have had your ass in here years ago, tossed over my shoulder if you refused."

That let Kara laugh, causing a loosening in her chest. Liam always had the best jokes.

She dragged in a rough and unsteady breath before letting it out on a sigh. Liam nodded and rose, as though he could see she'd gathered herself.

She dressed, wanting nothing more than to curl up in a bed and sleep for a few days. Emotional outbursts were new for her, and she didn't seem to have the stamina for them.

They sat in the doctor's office, a large room with a well-worn couch that smelled like him.

He probably fell asleep there from time to time.

The door opened, but it wasn't Marshall who entered. Instead, a young blonde came in, beautiful enough for Liam to lift an eyebrow and Kara to suck in a breath.

She turned her gaze to Kara and stopped. "Oh, I didn't realize Marshall had patients in here. I'm so sorry," she said quickly, a flush on her cheeks.

"It's fine," Kara assured her, the young omega looking nervous, as though she'd upset someone.

"I'm Tiffany," she said, sticking her hand out. "I didn't mean to just wander in, but Dr. Brown is my mate and I didn't realize he had anyone in here."

Kara rose and clasped hands, but the moment she did, panic struck. She inhaled, now closer, able to scent below the omega. Tiffany smelled of Marshall and two other alphas.

"I've got to go," Kara blurted, making Liam rise to his feet and survey the room for danger. Then again, little panicked Kara this way. Few things could send her into a frenzied mess. "Tell Marshall I'm feeling much better, please, that everything is fine now."

"Wait a minute," Liam said, but Kara ignored him.

She darted around Tiffany's shocked face to run straight into a large body that was coming in through the door as if drawn by Tiffany's uncertainty.

The tattoos, the face, the scent. All of it was carved into Kara's mind so deep, she'd never forget it.

Kara didn't look up as she muttered quietly, "Sorry, I was just leaving."

A loud inhalation by the alpha in front of her happened moments before a large hand grasped her arm, the other gripping her chin roughly to lift her face.

"Kasey?" For the first time in so many years, her brother Kane was staring down at her.

* * * *

Cullen knew something was wrong about half a second after entering the hotel suite.

He'd expected Kara to be in a nasty mood. Even if the doctor had found a perfect cure, the fact she'd had to spend time in a hospital and that it had been the alphas' idea would have been enough to piss her off.

However, watching her flip through the pages of the room service menu as if each one had personally insulted her mother was enough for Cullen to go still. Her face was pulled into tight lines and unhappiness hung on her.

It seemed the visit hadn't gone well.

The phone from the side table of the couch was pressed to her ear, and she hadn't seemed to take notice of them at all. "Well, I don't care what fucking time it is," she snapped, then paused. "Look, buddy, I doubt you make them fresh. They're in the freezer, so what does the time of day matter? They are fresh? Then fuck it, get me some frozen ones and throw them in a toaster! Is that really *that* hard of a thing to do in a fancy place like this?"

Reese passed Cullen, plucking the phone from her before she ended up getting them kicked out of the hotel. He offered a quick 'sorry' along with a chuckled 'women' statement that seemed to smooth things over.

Kara turned her glare from the menu to Reese when he hung up. "I was talking to them."

"You were about half a second from getting us thrown out. What was that about?"

"I'm hungry."

Reese pointed at the menu and the seemingly endless number of items. "There is a lot to choose from."

"I wanted waffles."

"At five in the evening?"

She opened her mouth then snapped it shut, twisting her face so she looked at the floor instead of any of them.

Damon came and sat beside her but didn't touch her. "I take it the visit with the doctor didn't go well?"

Kara gave him a killing glare. "Can't a girl just want some waffles?" When Damon didn't shift, didn't give her an inch of space where anger or humor could wipe away her obvious upset, she let out a sigh. "I don't know how it went because I left. Because I have the sort of luck that causes people to get struck by lightning. *Twice.*"

Cullen pulled over a chair from the table so he could sit himself right in front of her. "Less dramatics, more facts, thief."

She didn't even narrow her eyes at him, and he *almost* missed that annoyance. "Turns out good old Doc Brown has a mate. A mate he shares with other alphas." She ran her fingers through her hair in a rough push that probably took at least a few strands with it. "One of them happens to be my brother."

Oh. Suddenly her reaction made sense. He thought back to the conversation about her scars, about the brother who didn't know she lived.

Reese winced. "If he saw you, how'd you manage to get out of there?"

"I ran after I punched him."

"You *punched* him? The brother you haven't seen in all these years?" Damon's voice couldn't hold enough 'are you kidding me?' for the question.

Kara threw her hands up before dropping her head into them. "I didn't know what to do, okay? He was suddenly there, calling me by my old name, and I panicked. He had the same eyes as when we were kids, and all I could think about was standing above him in that hospital room, terrified he wasn't going to make it. I thought about how much it hurt to see that, how I almost destroyed us both, and I couldn't do it. I couldn't be whatever he wanted me to be, so I ran."

All the jokes Cullen wanted to make at the idea of Kara seeing her long-lost brother and punching him vanished at the pain in her voice. Some of the time, it was so easy to think of her as that snarky, quirky omega who grinned her way through any problem. Other times, like right now, he saw beneath that. The girl had cracks that ran through her, straight to the core, and they always took his breath away. Before he could remind himself why they were doomed, a part of him wanted to take some of that from her. He couldn't fix cracks, but he could at least shoulder some of the weight.

He reached out and set his hand on her knee, a squeeze the best thing he could think of to show her that she wasn't alone, at least not right then.

She shuddered in a deep breath, her fingers curling in toward her scalp. "He's not going to stop looking for me," she whispered. "In fact, I'd bet that however you met that doctor, they're going to come looking for you. Kane doesn't get discouraged and he is relentless, and because of bros before hos, you'll all probably roll out the red carpet for him."

Cullen frowned before capturing Kara's chin and lifting her face toward his. "If we didn't turn you over to the police, do you really think we'd do it now?"

"You needed me then."

I need you now. The unwelcome thought sprang up before Cullen could stop it and froze him in his tracks.

Damon picked up the line of thought as he set his own hand on her back. "I think you should talk to your brother. You both have been through a lot, and you'll feel better to get some of that out in the open." When she opened her mouth, Damon lifted his other hand to silence her so he could continue. "However, we won't say a word to him. Your secrets are yours to keep. Whether or not I agree, I'm going to trust you to know what you want."

She went tense at the word 'trust'.

That was the root of it all, wasn't it? She didn't trust them, they didn't trust her, yet they were constantly moving in a direction that needed trust. It was a fucked-up situation with no solution he could find.

Reese stood. "I'll be right back. I'm going to smooth things over with the concierge." He left after stroking his fingers through Kara's tresses, the action sweet enough that she seemed to cringe.

Once the door shut, Cullen pulled softly on her chin so she met his gaze. "How did the appointment go before that?"

"It was long and uncomfortably thorough."

He huffed a soft laugh, unable to even be jealous when she looked so unhappy about it. "Did he have ideas?"

"I left before we got to review the results. I was waiting in his office when his mate came in, Kane on her heels." Kara fidgeted slightly. "His mate is young. A pretty blonde girl."

Cullen wished he could read her mind, because it was so hard to judge from her face what she was thinking. Not to mention the girl was forever throwing him for a loop, her mind going to places he would have never expected.

Thankfully, Kara didn't need his prompting before she continued. "I'm glad he's settled down. He deserves that, deserves to have a family, to have stability."

While she spoke, what she didn't say came through loud and clear. *She* didn't deserve those things. It was written across her features, in the cracks of her words. She was glad her brother had found them but didn't think she ever would, didn't think she even deserved to have them. Stranger? That longing to have them. For a woman so averse to the thought of being close to anyone, for the first time, he really saw that at least somewhere inside her she still craved it.

Cullen fought the desire to offer any of it, because he couldn't. He couldn't give her forever, couldn't give her anything except right then.

He shifted his grip to the back of her neck and tugged softly until she came forward, until she crawled into his lap where he could indulge in a kiss, as though that touch could say the things he wouldn't dare. Hell, the kiss was like a lie they both believed, that there was some chance for any of them to have what her brother had found.

Kara met the kiss as she always did—fire and strength. He broke it only to enjoy the way her soft whine played across his damp lips, the tiny show of need she liked to hide. She'd never hidden that she wanted them, but need?

Need was something the girl didn't care for.

Before they had to address anything, the door opened. Kara twisted in Cullen's lap to find Reese there, and the smile that crossed her lips was worth everything.

Reese held up his gift, his own grin meeting hers. "So, hellion, your choice. Waffles or sex first?"

She laughed—a real fucking laugh that melt Cullen more than he'd ever admit to. "Sex first, waffles after."

Reese tossed the waffles into the freezer, his gaze turning predatory. "You are so my kind of girl."

And that was exactly what Cullen was afraid of.

Chapter Seventeen

Kara rubbed her eyes. While living with three alphas had its perks, two being the delicious soreness between her legs and the way her pseudo-heat hormones hadn't made a peep, she needed to get to bed earlier.

The night before, she'd taken one after the other, tasting and enjoying each alpha in their own way. She'd ridden Damon on the bed, his large hands gripping her waist, his surrender sweet. She'd sucked Reese until he'd come, his hand wrapped in her hair. Cullen had gone last, since he'd seemed to enjoy the show. He'd put her on all fours, shoving her chest to the bed and fucking her with wild and untamed thrusts.

She'd savored every touch, every caress the three offered. How could something feel so good? So right? How could she so quickly lose herself to it all?

In fact, at one point, she'd realized her eyes had opened. She'd met Reese's gaze as he'd pressed his cock deep into her mouth. The moment had terrified her, the risk of a connection there, yet she hadn't broken it. She'd stared into his hazel eyes with a dangerous openness, as though he could see deep into her.

Just sex. She'd repeated it to herself like a mantra, but when she'd curled up against the alphas, when their scents and heat had surrounded her, she'd questioned if it was true at all.

She was a good liar, after all. Was she just fooling herself?

All three slept soundly, with only Cullen rousing when she'd left the bed. She'd given him a sweet kiss and whispered that she was going for a run. A frown had said he didn't like the idea, but maybe he knew that the more he tried to push her, the more she'd push back.

That was how it worked. If he said no, she'd damn well do it.

Smart or not, it was her.

So when he'd lain back down, Kara had pulled on a workout outfit and headed downstairs.

She didn't really plan on running. Instead, the familiar sounds of the city lulled her to comfort. The whir of traffic down the street, the bustle of people as they went to their jobs, as they dropped their kids off, as they did all those normal things, helped her become just another one of them.

She wasn't broken or different or confused. Just another nobody heading out for their day.

Just what she wanted. Maybe that was part of what the alphas offered her, a feeling of being...normal. When they touched her, it wasn't as a broken thing. It wasn't as a thief who couldn't fill the roles she was born to fill. Instead, they touched her like she was a woman they desired. That alone was intoxicating in an entirely too dangerous way.

She'd lost so much before. Could she lose them? Could she walk away now that she knew how it felt to be wanted?

She mused as she walked street after street. Even when her feet ached, she pushed as though some great epiphany would come to her if only she went a little farther.

She even allowed herself, as time drifted on, to imagine where things could go in some fantasy where it could work. Not that she got a clear idea. She wouldn't stop her job, and they didn't seem likely to let her continue. *Let me? Like they could stop me.* Yet, in the space between those clear obstacles, she saw Damon chuckling at her jokes, that almost shy way he smiled as he pushed up his glasses. She saw Reese's laugh and his mischievous grin. She saw Cullen's heated gaze, the way he wanted her with a primal need.

If only the world could stop on those moments in between, when the rest of the shit didn't seem so insurmountable.

Kara fell so deep into the safety of her anonymity that she ignored everything around her. A hood pulled up over her head should hide her identity in the event people were looking for her — though she was walking random streets, not going anywhere she might be recognized.

The city was large, easy to get lost in if a person wanted to, and she really wanted to.

She crossed the street, staying in the crosswalk as the little symbol signaled her turn. The soft pockets of her sweater kept her hands warm against the early morning chill.

Her body went tense. It took a moment longer than it should have for her to identify the threat she'd seen but hadn't recognized.

At the other side of the crosswalk stood three men, and the one at the front was the one she focused on. The man from her apartment, the one who had escaped the trap at the safehouse. *Persistent, isn't he?*

He opened his coat slightly, the threat obvious with the holster there.

Would he really consider opening fire on a crowded street?

Kara doubted it, but doubt wasn't certainty.

She swallowed hard as she ran through her options. There were only three of them there, so where were the rest of their buddies? Behind her, probably, given how her days had gone lately.

Getting within grabbing distance would be a *very* bad choice. Kara had experienced once already how apt that man was at close quarters, and she doubted her luck would hold out.

Between forward or backward, backward seemed the obvious choice. Kara bolted back without looking, wanting to cross as much distance as possible and use her speed as an asset.

It proved a mistake, however, when she went back fast enough to put her in front of a car making a right who hadn't expected her to move. The bumper of the large truck hit her, and she rolled onto the hood. She'd love to say it was a graceful and purposeful move, but that would be too big a lie even for her.

Instead, pain exploded on the side the car struck and after a quick roll on the hood — where at least the driver had the decency to hit his brakes — Kara went off the truck and slammed into the ground. When her head hit, the crunch it made was sickening even to her.

Everything was blurry as she lifted her head to see the man across the street. He took a step toward her before people swamped her, hands checking her, voices telling her not to move.

The man's lips pressed together in a furious line. She saw him move away a moment before everything faded to blackness.

Chapter Eighteen

The incessant noise woke Kara, and for one blissful moment, she had no idea where she was.

Then the beeping wouldn't stop, and the itching of tape on her hand and the dryness of her mouth all said something wasn't right.

She pried her lids open, the gunk that sealed them shut telling her she'd been out for a while.

Another hospital. Just wonderful.

Except it wasn't the hospital that hit her. It was the figure who sat in the chair by her side, his body lounging back, his feet kicked up on the foot of her bed.

Kane.

As soon as Kara shifted, Kane's eyes popped open, as familiar to her as her own reflection. Even after so many years, she'd know those eyes anywhere.

Kane dropped his feet from the bed and rose, gaze raking over the monitors as if he understood a fucking thing on them. He reached over and hit a button on the side of her bed, and not more than ten seconds later, Marshall came in.

"She's awake," Kane said, voice rough and closed off.

Marshall's lips tipped down at the tone, but he nodded and checked over the same screens Kane had. His gaze dropped to Kara. "How are you feeling?"

"Peachy."

Marshall's gaze lifted to Kane, then back to Kara. "Well, even if you two don't look much alike, your attitude is the same."

A soft growl from Kane got the doctor moving, though he didn't look all that chastised. Then again, Marshall and Kane shared an omega, which meant the two were almost brothers.

What did that make Marshall to her?

Did it matter? She wouldn't stick around long enough for it to make a difference what titles were used.

Marshall shone a light into Kara's eyes, did all those doctor things that Kara hated but sat still for. She didn't hurt as much as she should have, and she didn't panic, which said he'd pumped her full of the good drugs. During the exam, he spoke as if he were used to keeping up conversation.

"Do you remember what happened?"

She frowned as the accident came back to her. The crunch of her head against the pavement made her stomach roll, which was funny, as injuries didn't normally. Still, she didn't answer.

"You were hit by a car in the intersection. You have bruised ribs, some internal bleeding and a concussion. We wanted to do a transfusion because of your low blood pressure, but you have a very rare blood type.

Thankfully, as soon as I was called, I knew where we could get some." Marshall glanced over at Kane, who had a bandage over the crook of his arm.

"You're welcome, little sis," he said dryly.

Guess that says this isn't going to be a reunion to write home about. Well, I mean, if I had a home to write to.

"Where are—" Kara snapped her mouth shut before she could mutter the name of any of the alphas. Asking for them then was weak. It reeked of helplessness, of a need for connection and importance she refused to think they had.

Marshall didn't even grin. *What a professional.* "I called Cullen the moment I saw it was you. He, Reese and Damon have been sitting in the waiting room for the past few hours. You can see them when you're ready."

"How long until I'm free?" Kara went to sit up, but pain in her side told her the answer before the doctor needed to.

"You'll be weak for a while, and while none of your injuries are life-threatening, you're going to need time to heal. You'll only need to spend another day or two here if your tests look good, but don't expect to be doing anything much for a few weeks."

A few weeks? Unacceptable. Kara had shit to do, like find the missing fucking alpha, get the price off her head, ditch three asshole alphas and now slip away from a brother who was *still* just staring at her like he expected something from her.

Marshall moved his gaze from Kane to Kara a number of times before he took a step backward. "I'm going to go check on other patients and let the alphas know they can come in to visit." He hesitated by the door. "I'll have them wait about fifteen more minutes."

Once Marshall left, neither Kara nor Kane said a word.

Kane looked similar and yet different. He'd grown, and she hadn't seen him up close since the night in the hospital. He'd gotten more tattoos over the years, ones visible on his hands and even on his neck.

And yet, despite those changes, despite the truth that he was larger, more intimidating, he was still *Kane*. It showed through his eyes, the ones that would shine and crinkle at the edges when he'd try to read her a book before bed when they were still kids, despite him being shit at reading.

Kara sighed, the weight of all those years suddenly more than she could carry. "Sorry," she whispered.

He spoke fast, as though he'd been waiting for her to say something, to break the silence between them. "How could you not tell me you were alive? You knew about me, so what the fuck were you thinking, Kasey?"

Her old name hurt. Maybe Kara wasn't perfect, but she was the person she'd made, the one who had clawed her way back from almost bleeding out, the one who had refused to just lie down and die. "Kara." At Kane's look, she repeated herself. "My name is Kara now."

"Course it is," he said. "Guess you threw away everything from your old life."

Kara tried to run her fingers through her hair, but when it tugged her scalp and she winced, she recalled that crack of her skull against the pavement. "It's not like that. You were hurt because you were trying to protect me."

Oh, the spark of anger in those eyes of his took her back. "You were just a kid — *my* kid sister. It was my job to keep you safe." As quickly as the fury in him ramped up, it dissipated. There her brother was, quick to rage but just as quick to fizzle away. "Some job I did, huh?"

"I didn't want to put you in that place again," she pressed. "While you were still unconscious, I visited you in the hospital. I sat by your bed and stared down at you, and I swore I'd never make you pay that price for me again. If I'd been better, smarter, more useful, it never would have happened. If I hadn't been some naïve little thing you had to protect, you wouldn't have almost died."

"You were there?" Kane frowned, his gaze dropping as though trying to remember. "If everything I'm hearing is right about you, you've been able to take care of yourself for a while. Why not find me then?"

"I never lost you. I always knew where you were. Hell." Kara quirked her lips up. "I even helped you a time or two. Remember when you turned twenty-one, when you took a job finding that asshole pimp who was beating on the girls he managed?"

Kane nodded, his eyes narrowing. "I showed up expecting to have a bit of work on my hands. Instead, I found him hogtied in his apartment."

Kara couldn't help the soft chuckle at the memory. "Figured I owed you a gift."

Kane held her gaze for so long, she fidgeted with fear of what he saw.

She'd been so different when he'd known her before. Not perhaps naïve in the way so many other girls were, because she'd never been all that sheltered, but she'd been innocent. She'd been what omegas were *supposed* to be. She wasn't that girl anymore, and it wasn't until that second that she realized how terrified she was of how he'd react.

Would he think less of her? Would he hate what she'd become? Would he look at her like so many others had, as if she were defective?

Kane moved so fast that if she'd been armed, she'd have shot the stupid idiot. He leaned over the bed and gathered her into a hug tight enough to steal her breath. Okay, maybe part of that was the jostling of her still-healing side.

The amount of pain didn't matter a bit, though, not when his hand cupped the back of her head and he just held her. He smelled like family, like safety, like *home*.

So Kara let herself have the hug she'd avoided for so many years, no matter how much it frightened her.

Damon hated the new alpha who stood across the hallway from him. Cullen and Reese had been getting information from Marshall about how to care for Kara — though she'd adamantly refused to go home with them — when the new trio of alphas had walked in.

And they *were* alphas. It was written in their size, in the way they walked. The one in the center had worn an expensive suit, with hair so blond it was almost white and green eyes that stood out in his expressionless face. Kara had said he was Torrin when she'd offered a quick introduction before shuffling out most of them. Beside him had stood two bodyguards who looked so similar, they had to be twins.

One of them — Erik — Damon ignored, but the other? *Liam* set his teeth on edge in a way he wasn't used to and didn't much like.

Damon had been in the room with Kara when all three had walked in, and it was the absolute focus that one laid on Kara that had Damon itching to bare his teeth.

Which was not at all like him. Damon was clear-headed. Even though he was young, he'd never felt particularly jealous or possessive. Still, the way this alpha had looked at Kara had Damon refusing to take his eyes off him.

"What's your problem, cub?" The alpha lifted his gaze toward Damon, his tone saying how little he thought of Damon.

"How do you know her?"

Liam's eyebrow lifted. "Why would I tell you anything?"

Every word from Liam's lips just drove Damon's annoyance higher and he couldn't even figure out why. What was it about this guy that made him feel this way?

And worse? Liam only appeared amused by it, which pissed Damon off. He was an alpha, damn it, and he deserved a little fear when people saw his temper slipping.

Sure, maybe he wasn't the same sort of alpha as Cullen or Reese or, clearly, this guy, but that didn't change that he could be dangerous if he wanted to be.

I really want to be.

"You can growl all you want," Liam said and shrugged. "The fact is that you all are the problem."

"What problem is that?"

"Before you showed up with your little buddies, Kara wasn't getting herself put in the hospital or getting contracts on her head. Worse, because of your *interference*, she didn't come to us, who could have actually helped her."

"And what do you know about any of it?"

Liam narrowed his gaze, a hard look that had probably scared off more than a few people. "I've been keeping an eye on that girl since she was thirteen, watching her back since then. I have *never* seen her behave so foolishly before. She should have dealt with this by targeting the lab from day one to get the contract off her head. Instead, she seems to be trying to play hero with you and it has done nothing but endanger her. So why don't you just leave before you get her killed?"

That was when it hit Damon. Why had it taken him so long to figure it out? The reason for all the aggression wasn't random. While Damon couldn't have ever picked the scent out himself, not consciously, he knew right then that this alpha carried Kara's scent. They'd slept together—more than once, most likely. That, paired with Liam's possessiveness, said it was more than a quick fling.

Which was exactly what had Damon ready to tear the man's throat free with his teeth if he needed to.

"She isn't yours," Damon snapped.

"She sure as hell isn't *yours*. Despite all this territorial posturing you're doing, I can *see* how you all look at her, like she's something that needs fixing. That girl doesn't need to be changed, least of all by you lot who keep putting her in danger. The quicker she realizes that, the better."

"Are you just hoping for your own shot?"

"I don't need a shot, cub, since I've already been there more than a few times and will be long after you're gone."

Damon knew the alpha was pushing him, could spot it in the glint of the other's eyes, but knowing it didn't stop Damon from reacting. He was on Liam in a heartbeat, taking the larger alpha to the ground.

Fighting wasn't something Damon did or knew much about. Cullen and Reese had taught him a few things, mostly because they didn't want him to get himself into trouble and have no way out. Still, the way the other male moved showed Liam *did* know how to fight. As it turned out, skill against pure alpha aggression kept them fairly evenly matched. Damon landed a hard punch to Liam's face, and what surprised him was just how much that hurt him.

Not that it stopped him. If anything, the scent of blood, the red that leaked from a split on Liam's lip, made Damon want to go further. A hit from Liam knocked his glasses off, but it didn't slow him. He could only think about this alpha and Kara, about Liam's barbs and about how he had touched her. Had it been one of those times where Kara couldn't help it? Had he taken advantage of her?

Just as he was about to lose himself to the fury inside him, something hauled him off Liam. He didn't know who it was, his vision having narrowed to nothing beyond the alpha who was now standing but not being held back. Liam wiped his mouth with the back of his arm as if the fight hadn't mattered. In fact, he wasn't even breathing hard.

"Knock it off," Cullen growled, the voice waking him up, helping him to leash the rage inside him that wasn't nearly done with Liam.

Even as they stared at one another, it was Liam's words that stuck with Damon, that chipped away at him. *'So why don't you just leave before you get her killed?'*

Liam wasn't wrong, and that was the worst part about it.

Liam's scowl when he came into the room warmed Kara. While Torrin and Erik might have frowned, Liam looked downright pissed.

Which charmed her in some strange way that it probably shouldn't have.

Torrin had already checked in on her, given her the polite riot-act about being more careful and ordered her to come stay with them while she recovered. He would hire a trustworthy nurse to care for her.

Not that she'd do it.

Having the three of them bothering her might be worse than Cullen, Reese and Damon.

At least she got orgasms from *her* alphas. Torrin and the twins would mother-hen her until she wished her injuries killed her already.

When Liam neared, the red smeared across his cheek, along with the split on his lip, caught her attention. "How could you have gotten in trouble in a hospital?"

His gaze was hard, the sort of look he got when he lost prey. "Your cub outside is a bit possessive. It seems he doesn't care for our past."

"Wait. Damon punched you? The one with the glasses?"

"It turns out what he lacks in training and bulk, he makes up for in enthusiasm."

Kara chuckled at the idea of sweet and quiet Damon going up against Liam. At least the next time he got all mopey about not being a real alpha, she could point out that he also behaved like an idiot. There wasn't anything more alpha than that. Not to mention, him doing it because of jealousy, because he didn't like that someone else had been with her? Well, that sure did warm her.

"I don't know what you see in them," Liam spat toward the door.

"That's because you haven't seen them naked."

His gaze narrowed, and it only made her smile wider. While Torrin would roll his eyes and Erik would ignore her jokes, Liam rose to the occasion for her.

"I'm serious, kid." He sat on the bed beside her. "What is it about them? Because you've never attached yourself to anyone like this before. Please tell me you're not doing anything insanely stupid like bonding to them."

The idea wiped the grin from Kara's face before she blew out a breath and shook her head. "Even if I was the type to bond, I doubt I can. It's probably a package deal with the whole 'creating little spawns' thing. I need to see this through, okay? They're my best chance for getting to the bottom of whoever wants me dead."

"They aren't, and you know it. Torrin can easily pay the lab off, or I could go kill whoever made the mistake of targeting you." There were times when Kara was reminded just how scary Liam could be. Like Torrin, like Erik, he was lethal and had no issue doing whatever he had to. While Kara still retained some of those silly morals—no matter what Cullen might think—Liam had lost them long before she'd ever met him. He had a few of his own rules, but most came down to a simple fact—fuck with him or his and he'd end anyone without a second thought.

"There's more at stake than just me. There's a missing alpha."

"Since when do you care about missing people?"

Which was a fair question. "Even if we kill off whoever set the contract, don't you think they'll keep at it? This lab has too much riding on that alpha to just let it go."

"So what do you think your goody two-shoes are going to do that I can't?" Jealousy seethed in his voice. Not romantic, but something else, as though he hated the idea she might not need him, that he might be replaced.

"I don't care what they can do. I care what *I* can do. I can figure this out. When I find out where they keep the alpha, I'll have everything I need to make sure they leave me alone."

"That's really all this is about?"

Kara tried to nod, but she just couldn't. She sighed, then met his gaze. "Do you want kids?"

His eyebrows shot up, as though the question were altogether unexpected. As quickly as it happened, he tried to wipe it clean. "I don't know," he admitted. "I've thought about it, but I don't exactly live a child-friendly life, so what I want doesn't matter much. Why?"

"I never thought about kids. I don't think I'd want any no matter what, but the reality that I can't, that I had the choice stolen from me, bothers me." *Bothers is a hell of an understatement.* "They're using that alpha. They're using his nature and things he can't control and treating him like he's nothing but a science experiment. If anyone understands what that's like, it's me. Not to mention the result of all that work? A drug that doesn't have any use except to hurt omegas. If I can find the alpha, if I can stop this, maybe I can actually do something good."

"People like us don't do good," Liam said softly, setting his hand on her knee, the blanket between them. "We aren't the heroes of stories, kid."

"Why can't we be?"

"It just isn't our place. Us? We're survivors. We do what we have to, to crawl on top, and that doesn't exactly put us in a place to be heroes. And honestly? This is exactly why I don't like your new friends."

"They aren't my friends."

He grunted, a sound that didn't say he believed her, but he left what they were alone. "You didn't worry about being a hero before. Why do you care now?"

Kara leaned back against the pillow, trying to let go of the tension insider her, trying to rest her side. She didn't reply out loud, but she knew the answer.

She wanted the alphas to look at her like she was enough, and she had no other idea how to do that.

* * * *

Cullen dropped the bag of supplies to the new suite floor, having moved them all into a new hotel after the attack. They had no way of knowing exactly how much information Thompson had on Kara. *Better to play it safe and move, just in case.*

Inside the bag were the medications and bandages Kara would need. She had argued up and down about not going back with the alphas, even during the ride back.

Not that Cullen had planned to give her a say.

The injuries weren't life threatening, but she'd need help for a while. Marshall had wanted to keep her longer, but he'd agreed to let her go so long as she stayed with someone else.

Worse, that she'd been found so quickly on the street worried him. It couldn't have been a coincidence. Kara was smart enough to not do anything that would easily reveal her location, so she hadn't called anyone she shouldn't have, hadn't gone to a place anyone should know her. It meant Cullen could only assume the lab had people looking for her, contacts who kept their eyes peeled and were willing to call in when she was spotted. It meant she really needed to go nowhere.

Kara lowered herself onto the couch with Damon's help. She'd snarled at Cullen and Reese when they'd tried, as though they were far more objectionable than Damon.

Then again, she had a strange relationship with the youngest alpha, which was clear from the way she ordered him around and how he soaked up those demands. It was odd, he'd admit. Cullen much preferred to be the one giving commands than the other way around. He liked how Kara looked when he fisted her hair and forced his cock between her lips. He loved how she moaned when he fucked her hard, when he held her still beneath him. She was wild, and him holding her for even a heartbeat thrilled him.

So the way Damon melted when Kara dug her nails into him and ordered him around, the way he looked at her like a puppy — well, Cullen guessed there some things in life he'd never quite understand. It seemed good for them both, so what did it really matter? Besides, hadn't Damon served as that glue before, as the careful energy between Cullen and Reese that kept them from getting out of hand?

Funny that it seemed he served that for Kara, as well.

"This room sucks," Kara complained, the words coming out in a tight voice that said she hurt even if she'd never admit it.

Which was absurd, because the room was far better than the last. Bryce had sworn this hotel would keep their presence a secret. Without much else to trust, Cullen had accepted. No room service, no going out for her, nothing that could be used to trace back. Officially, the room was empty on all the hotel records. Cullen would still sleep lightly, however.

"This suite is larger and nicer than the last," Reese pointed out as he set the boxes of takeout Chinese food on the counter. "Plus it has four rooms, not three."

The compromise hadn't sat well with any of them. They preferred Kara moving through their space as she often did, choosing where to spend time, where to sleep.

However, with the injury, she needed rest, and she rarely did that well when beside them. Given her tendency to seduce them, and their weakness in turning her down, it was best to give her space.

"Well, I don't like it."

Cullen shook his head at her petty complaints as he dropped two of the pain pills into his palm, then poured a glass of water in the kitchen. He offered them to Kara, hoping that perhaps they might not only help with the pain, but better her mood.

Cullen took a seat beside her, twisting so he could look at her. He still couldn't spot most of her lies, but he hoped reading her might clue him in, because she was less than trustworthy with the truth, and after the hospital, he needed a few answers. "Who are those three alphas at the hospital?"

"Jealous?" Her lips tipped into the first smile she'd given since the injury.

"Yes."

At his honesty, her smile slid away, then came back full force as if it had surprised her, then pleased the hell out of her. Kara leaned back slightly, seemingly trying to get comfortable and failing miserably. "Torrin and his cousins — the two bodyguards who are always with him — are the *friends* who taught me what I know."

"So we have them to blame for how you are?"

"Oh, no, I was like this before, just not as skilled. After what happened with my brother, I broke into their place, looking for pain meds. I'd run from the hospital — slipped out when no one was looking — and I didn't have a dime to buy anything. Well, I was pretty damn terrible at the whole thief thing, and they caught me. Instead of all the things they could have done, they took care of me."

Her face had an air of contentedness he'd never seen there before. It eased some of his annoyance at her relationship with the other alphas. The idea of her being alone made his chest ache, so knowing she had someone in her life — no matter how ill-advised — was probably for the best.

She went on with her story. "I lived with them for a few years while they taught me everything, introduced me to the people I needed to know, looked out for me until I could look out for myself. I haven't had much in the way of family, not since Kane, but they filled that spot for me."

The room went quiet, but Damon posed a question that startled them all. "And what about Liam? Do you love him?"

Kara's gaze shot to Damon so fast Cullen knew the youngest had caught something the rest of them had missed. Then again, that helped explain why Damon had come to blows with Liam, didn't it?

Damon didn't lift his gaze, staring at the floor as though that made it easier to ask. "I know you've been sleeping with him. So, do you love him? I don't like the idea of being some secret, or you keeping that from us."

Kara's breath came out in a hard blow. "No, I don't love him, not like that. He doesn't love me either, never has, not as anything but family."

"But you have had sex with him."

"Yeah. More than a few times, when I needed a *fix*." She spat the word like a filthy taste from her mouth. "He did it because he was worried about me, because he wanted me safe and was afraid of what could happen to me if I kept seeking out different people. It wasn't all that good for either us."

The tension in the room from the question went down slowly, as if they could all breathe. Maybe it was the rare moment of what Cullen had to believe was truth that allowed it, the sorrow in her voice. It was hard to be jealous when she looked so damned miserable.

"I don't like being that person," she whispered quietly. "The one who has to use those I care about. That's what I've tried to avoid after Kane, and yet sometimes I think it's all I am. Liam wouldn't ever turn me down, but I know he doesn't like it any more than I do."

Cullen set a hand on her knee. "You don't have to do that anymore. You've got us."

Kara set her hand on top of his, a strangely gentle touch, sweeter than she was in general. "Thanks, but I don't really want to use anyone."

Reese chimed in, his lips having curled into a wide and mischievous grin. "Oh, hellion, you can use me any day."

The stupid remark broke what was left of the tension from the conversation, the darkness from such topics, and caused a chuckle that grew through the room. At least, it did until Kara set her hand over her side and hissed in a breath, the laughter having aggravated her wound.

The easy moment between them had him thinking that maybe there was a chance, if they could just help change her...

Chapter Nineteen

Kara groaned as she tried to stretch, her ass on the floor, her legs in front of her and bent in butterfly position. The ache in her side said it wasn't thrilled with the work, but too damn bad. She kept her back straight, her hands on her ankles, feet pressed together as she tried to inch her knees closer to the ground. The stretch in her groin both hurt and felt wonderful, the release of tension as she was able to do something, anything.

It had been a week of nothing, a week of hardly talking the alphas into letting her go to the bathroom alone. Only a threat to castrate the first one to step into that room with her had had them moving backward.

Though there had been a perverse sense of pleasure in it all that she'd never have expected or admitted to. Kara was *not* a damsel. She didn't need men falling all over her to help or care for her, and yet, whenever the alarm on Damon's watch went off, when he'd rise from whatever he was doing and retrieve her pain medication at the correct time, Kara's cheeks heated.

She felt important. Like something *worth* cherishing.

That wasn't a feeling she understood. Sure, Kane had cared for her as a child, but he'd done it by grit and determination. Softness hadn't been a part of their lives. Torrin, Liam and Erik had cared for her, but again in that big brother, tough love, 'suck it up' sort of way.

The first time Cullen had dropped to a crouch in front of her and slid a pair of soft, fuzzy socks on her feet, because Kara couldn't bend far enough to do it herself, she'd feared she was lost.

She *liked* being taken care of. Hell, maybe a few more injuries in the future were in order.

A soft growl had Kara lifting her gaze to find Cullen at the door of her room, the slash of his light brown eyebrow showing his displeasure with her exercising.

"I'm just stretching."

"You shouldn't be out of bed."

"Marshall said yesterday I could start moving."

"Marshall is an idiot." Cullen crossed his arms, his gaze hard. They both knew Marshall was an amazing doctor, but the alphas would have rather he'd told her to never move again.

"You just liked giving me sponge baths," Kara countered as she closed her eyes and slowly rolled her shoulders, twisting to ease the tightness from her back without jostling the wound in her side.

"That's true." Cullen's voice came from closer that time, as though he'd come into the room and taken a seat in front of her. "Though somewhat boring since you hadn't been cleared for sex."

Which was odd, that after a week Kara felt no strong need. Marshall hadn't started any treatments, but when she'd broached the topic, he'd mentioned that some of the bonding hormones had proven beneficial. Was that it? Was her nearness to the alphas enough to convince her body to start behaving?

"Blue balls?" Kara cocked her eyebrow despite not opening her eyes.

"You have no idea," he countered.

Kara lifted a finger to tap her nose, a sly grin across her lips. "Oh, I have some idea. However, I feel like it's only fair you all suffer. This *is* all your fault, after all."

Cullen's growl was soft and low, a sound that teased her senses. "Don't push me. In case you've forgotten, he said sex was fine now."

"I don't recall him saying that."

"I asked him in the hallway to be very clear. Not much moving on your part, but otherwise? Perfectly safe."

Kara opened her eyes to meet his green ones, his hair swept back, still damp, as though he'd just gotten out of the shower. "Not moving sounds pretty boring."

"I doubt you'd be too bored if I tied you up so you couldn't move, then licked you until you couldn't bitch anymore." He smiled at her, a rare one that made her stomach flutter. "Or I'll have Reese hold you still for me. I'd say Damon, but we both know he only listens to you, thief."

"Damon's a good boy. Maybe you ought to learn from him. Good boys get treats."

A second growl brought Kara's gaze up to find Reese there, gripping the doorframe so tight his knuckles had blanched. His long dark hair only made him look more intense, as if he were some wild animal. "You've kept us too wound up to tease, hellion."

Kara didn't break the staring, meeting Reese's hazel eyes directly, the feeling of closeness uncomfortable enough that she almost broke it. Almost.

Instead, she dragged her tongue against her bottom lip, the dampness in her panties all the evidence of her reaction. And she liked this reaction. She liked feeling the game, feeling like she wanted them because she desired *them*. Not just any knot, not just any cock, but these alphas.

"You are such a brat," Reese said, a smile across his lips. "Good thing for you I don't mind dealing with brats."

And Kara had to admit she didn't mind it either.

* * * *

Kara's wince when she went to stand was like a sky signal to Reese. Funny that despite him being involved in his own work—reviewing timelines of cases they'd been offered for after this job was done—that tiny movement of hers could break through anything. The days had moved slowly and with each one, she moved with more ease, healed more. Even better, though?

How easy things could be. Sure, they bickered, they fought over stupid things, but somehow during her healing they'd settled into a routine that he found more fulfilling than it should have been.

"Hurting?" He was already up and headed for the pill bottle on the kitchen counter before he finished the question.

Kara shook her head before she lowered herself slowly again. "Nope."

Reese gritted his teeth at the lie. Why was it that he couldn't get past that? The more time he spent with her, the more it seemed like maybe there was a future, he'd expected it to bother him less.

Instead, each time she lied — even stupid little lies that didn't matter — his chest tightened.

He still got the pills, pouring them into his palm and getting a glass of water for her. When he set them into her hand, he went to turn.

"Why do you get so mad?"

Kara's question stilled him. She rarely asked about them. To be fair, she seemed to be pretty good at figuring out things without needing to ask, but her questioning, her reaching out, felt like something he couldn't ignore no matter how annoyed he was right then.

Reese turned back to her, crossing his arms. "I don't like when you lie to me."

"But you get that pissed, you obviously can tell I'm lying, so what does it matter?"

Her logic had a point, but that didn't erase his hang ups. He huffed softly before sitting beside her. "I'm just not a fan of lying, okay? Consider it one of my sore spots."

"Why, though?"

"No reason."

She lifted her eyebrow after she swallowed the pills he'd given her. "But clearly you've got no problem with being the one who lies."

He straightened his back at the accusation — no matter how right she was. Still, he wasn't feeling all that inclined to reveal his wounds to her, not when he couldn't trust her. He tried to keep the conversation vague. "I want people around me I can trust. How can I trust someone who never tells me the truth?"

Kara crossed her legs, eyeing him with the intensity she probably used on marks. "So, I guess the question is, who fucked you over?"

"Do I need to be fucked over to know I want honesty in my life?"

"No, but to be *that* angry about it? Yep. This isn't just a random thing. It isn't a morality point you just came up with. You want to bitch at me about honesty? You've torn off more than a few of my scars. Why don't you try to do the same?"

Reese snarled softly when he couldn't find a single good reason to say no to her. He *had* insisted she let them in, that she tell them her secrets. *Guess that backfired.*

"Let's just say I've dealt with a woman who lied. I'm in no rush to repeat it."

"What, she cheated on you?" Kara asked the question without a lot of sympathy, but that almost made it easier. He didn't think he'd like pity.

"Among other things."

She didn't answer, waiting. Who the hell would have expected her to be the patient one?

The silence chipped away his resolve until he blurted out the rest in the tense silence. "I dealt with a woman who lied every other fucking word, okay? Three years with her and I lost everything. She cheated on me, nearly got me thrown in jail because she lied to me about another man stalking her and stole all my savings in the process."

Kara pulled back, the smirk sliding from her face as if she'd just realized that maybe it wasn't a joke.

Reese continued. "I was stupid, and I believed her. Even after I realized she was lying, I still thought we could figure it out. I lost everything and had to start over from scratch. So, yeah, when you lie to me? I see her. I see myself being taken in again and I wonder what exactly it's going to cost me this time."

Reese didn't know what he wanted her to say. Did he want her to swear she'd never lie to him again? *Maybe.* Not that he'd believe her. Lying was like breathing to her. He just wanted her to say something to make it okay, to make it so he didn't have to carry that fucking anger any longer.

Which was an entirely unfair weight to place on her.

"Well, I'm never going to stop lying."

Reese growled and went to stand. It was stupid to think she'd understand, to think she might actually *listen* to him.

Kara caught his wrist and tugged him back down beside her. "I'm sorry, but it's a part of me. I can't promise that I'll always be honest, because we both know that would be one hell of a lie right there. I can tell you I won't betray you, though. That's what you're really pissed about. It was never the lies – it was the betrayal."

"Aren't they the same thing?"

"Nope. I might not tell you the truth, but I'll never do it to hurt you. I'll never be dishonest to screw you over, to take shit from you, to fuck you over."

"And how am I supposed to know that's true if I can't trust anything you say?"

Kara shrugged before she slid into his lap, her weight a welcome presence, the sort that made him wonder why he ever fought against her. She brushed her lips to his. "Guess you'll just have to trust me."

He groaned at the almost kiss she teased him with, his cock hardening with more than a few ideas of how they could work out the little fight. There was always a give and take between them, with a small argument sparking make-up sex. That passion burned him and he loved it.

"Can I trust you?"

"Nope."

He heard that lie loud and clear, and when he wasn't sure what to do with it, he wrapped his fingers in her hair and pulled her tighter against him for a kiss.

He could figure it out later.

Chapter Twenty

Kara woke with a startle, a scream a breath from escaping.

Her lower stomach burned, the scars on fire as if the knife were still plunging into her.

She'd dreamed about it, about the look on the man's face as he'd carved her up.

Wetness tracked down her cheeks, and Kara brushed it away.

She thanked every fucking god there was that she'd gone to bed in her own room instead of with any of the alphas. After Kane had stayed into late into the evening, Kara and the alphas had straightened up.

It had felt domestic and sweet and altogether weird. By that time of night, Kara had been too tired for anything fun. Instead, a few toe-curling kisses had been her goodnights from the alphas, who had each taken their sweet time to offer the affection. Tearing away to crawl into a bed alone had not been high on her list of good ideas, but she had needed the sleep.

Too bad it seemed her own nightmares wouldn't let that happen, since it was only four a.m. and, with the way her heart pounded, she wasn't going to be getting back to sleep.

Kara ran her fingers through her hair, trying to erase the ghost sensations that plagued her.

Her leg bounced, the coursing energy overwhelming her moments before she rose. She pulled on workout leggings, a sport bra and a loose tank top. A bit of time on a treadmill and she could outrun those damned dreams.

She *should* wake the alphas, but then they'd ask. They'd want to know what was wrong, why she was upset, and Kara couldn't bring herself to voice that.

Every damned day with them they got *closer*. They saw more of her, they seemed more important and she already felt scraped raw.

So they could sleep while she dealt with this alone.

Kara crept through the living room space after quietly closing her door behind her.

She made it halfway through the room before a rumbled voice startled her. "Going somewhere?"

Kara pressed her hand to her chest, annoyed that she'd not noticed Cullen standing there. Then again, her heart was still pounding so loudly from her dream that she could hardly focus on anything else.

Another door opened and Reese walked out, boxers slung low on his narrow hips, followed lastly by Damon, who wore sweats and a shirt. Sleep sat in their eyes as they squinted against the brightness in the living room.

Kara looked at the floor. "Just thought I'd go to the gym."

"Without telling anywhere where you were?" Reese's words were sharp as he shook off the grogginess. "Damn it, Kara, we talked about this."

The words bubbled inside her, wanting to come out, wanting to explain. *Why the hell do I care to tell them anything?*

To cut them off, to gain control again when Kara felt like she had none, she crossed her arms. "I've gone for a run myself plenty of times. I don't need a babysitter." *Push them. Do it enough and they'll back off. People always do.*

A soft growl met her words, and she risked a glance up to find it came from Damon, which she supposed should tell her just how much trouble she was in.

Damon cut the sound off, his glasses missing from his face, making him look almost like a stranger. "How many times do we have to do this before you get it?"

"You don't have to do anything," Kara bit back. "I'm not asking you for anything."

That shut Damon up. The coldness in his eyes felt like a lash to her heart.

"It won't work." Cullen's words were soft, an odd thing in his rough voice. "You trying to push us away, it won't work."

"I don't know what you're talking about."

"Yeah, you do. It's always worked before, right? Someone gets too close, you snarl, and they run off. When are you going to figure out that doesn't work with us? What was the dream about?"

His words drove Kara a step backward. His room was beside hers. Had he heard her wake up? "I didn't have a dream."

He lifted his light eyebrow in a look that said he knew she was lying, could read it all over her face.

"Look at you, so tense you can't even pull in a full breath. Have you ever thought that maybe things would get better if you stopped trying to hide it? If you stopped trying to shoulder all this by yourself?"

Which was exactly what she'd done all her life. Even back before it all went to hell, when she'd lived with Kane, she'd never *told* him anything about her feelings.

Feelings were shit. Feelings didn't matter. *Just stupid signals in your body that get in the way of what you need to do.* So Kara had learned to bury them down where it was safest, and any time someone came close enough to get a glimpse of them, she swiped to keep them away.

"What was it about?" Reese asked this time, the frustration with her seeming to have melted away.

"It was nothing. Just a dream. Dreams happen and they don't mean shit."

"They do if they send you running," Reese said.

Kara combed her hair back with her fingers. "It was about when I was attacked, okay? Just a stupid dream about a night that's long over. See? Unimportant."

Cullen walked forward, his steps heavy on the hardwood floor of the room. He was slow enough that it heightened all of Kara's fears, her anxiety.

When he reached her, he slid a hand behind her neck and pulled her against him. His thick arms wrapped around her, and the heat of his body soothed her.

A soft rumble came from his chest, a gentle sound that seemed to steal all that fire she'd had. It was though it told her that all her snarling wouldn't do a thing to scare them off, and Kara had no idea how to react to that.

She shuddered, then spoke softly. "I remember the knife, how helpless I felt. Nothing I could do, just waiting for them to kill me, for Kane to show up."

Cullen's hand was firm against her back as he rubbed circles, and if she didn't need the touch so badly, she'd have hated it.

"Makes sense why you always want to run," Reese said from just beside her, having moved closer as well. "You're always fighting and struggling because you couldn't then. You don't want to trust anyone because of what happened then."

Kara pushed away from Cullen's chest, needing the space to say what she *needed* to say. "It wasn't just then. In my entire life, what has trusting anyone got me? I have struggled for everything I have, fought to get it and keep it. You keep talking about trust, but fuck, when exactly has trusting people ever gotten me something good? Even if I wanted to—and I sure as fuck don't think I do—I don't even know *how* to do it."

Reese caught Kara's chin, his fingers strong and sure as he brought her gaze to his. "You trust us, even if you don't want to. It's just what goes on in your head that tells you not to, that makes you fight it, that wears you out this fucking bad. You could have crawled into any of our beds after that dream, could have gotten exactly what you wanted, but instead? Instead you tried to run out of the door just to piss us off, just so you didn't have to worry about trusting us."

"How could you know what I need when I don't even know?"

"What you need is easy, hellion. You need to be taught you can trust us. You need to stop trying to hold on to everything so fucking tight that it breaks you. Let us take some of that."

The idea was so damned tempting. It seemed easy. Let them help. Could she really not feel like this anymore? Not feel crushed beneath the weight of everything she clutched? It was too good to be true, right?

Instead of saying any of that, Kara only met his gaze. "How?"

Reese ran his thumb over her bottom lip. "Let us show you. Trust us, just for tonight?"

I need to say no. One night is too dangerous. What if I can't trust them? What if I can? What if they show me something I can't live without and then it all falls apart anyway?

Kara leaped, taking the most dangerous step she'd ever taken, and nodded. "Just for tonight."

What had she gotten herself into?

Reese wished he was religious right then so he could thank whatever fucking gods he needed to.

Kara *trembled* as she stood there between the three of them, a ball of anxiety and nerves and want for things she didn't think were possible. They couldn't fix it all, especially not right then, but damn it, she needed to figure out that trusting the right person wasn't so bad, and even Reese could admit that for *him* to think that was some weird joke from fate.

With Kara, all roads led to sex. He didn't mind, and using that as the way to her figuring out she could rely on them?

Well, it seemed like a damned fun lesson.

Besides, as much as they'd enjoyed Kara, they'd never pushed her. They'd never really let themselves enjoy her as alphas, to take away all her choices, to take her to that place where she couldn't think beyond their touches.

And he'd wanted nothing more. After how she'd reacted to the spanking, he *knew* she wanted this.

He exchanged a look with Cullen, who nodded toward Reese's room. All the beds were the same size, though the more he considered a future the more he figured they'd need to put in a huge fucking bed when they got back home.

Reese nodded and moved his hand to the back of Kara's neck, his grip tight enough to set the tone as he walked her forward. Cullen went to his own room, no doubt to grab the bag of things he'd picked up days earlier. At home they had plenty of their own toys, but this wasn't home.

Nothing a stop at a good sex shop couldn't fix, though.

Damon followed Reese, and that spark in his eyes, the same one he'd had when they'd spanked Kara, said this fulfilled something for him, too.

The more time he spent around the younger alpha, the more he understood him. Damon wasn't just submissive, but rather wanted to give Kara what she *needed*. Often that was Damon's submission, but other times? Other times was this, taking care of her by taking away the control she held so dearly.

Reese released Kara in the room. "Why don't you get her stripped down."

Damon didn't hesitate before he came forward, pulling her tank top up and over her head. His hands skimmed her sides in reverence before tugging down the zipper at the front of her sports bra. He teased his thumbs over her nipples as he removed the bra, leaving her in only her leggings.

And again, Reese was struck by how stunning the girl was. Her blue hair, her striking eyes, the way the black of her leggings cut across her pale skin. Even her scars only added to how attractive he found her, as if they proved her strength, proved everything she'd survived. It made him all the more determined to take away the weight she shouldered, at least for the night.

I'd do it for far longer.

Reese stripped off his boxers as Damon crouched, pulling the fabric of her leggings down her toned legs.

The tremble continued through her, as if being naked reminded her how real this was.

Cullen entered again, bag slung over his shoulder. His lips curled up at the sight of Kara, and Reese understood that reaction.

The smile didn't seem to reassure Kara, not when her eyes landed on the bag.

Damon stole her attention and any questions he might have had when he licked up the seam of her thighs. With her legs pressed together, he couldn't get anything too focused, but it seemed enough, because she gasped.

Lovely sound.

Cullen dropped the bag on the corner of the bed, and the zipper was loud in the silent room. He removed items, digging through before setting a few out.

Anxiety seemed to tear through Kara, and if they weren't careful, she might just call it quits before they even started.

So Reese went behind her, capturing her hair in his fingers and pressing his lips to her racing pulse. "Relax," he whispered before tracing his other hand down her front. He moved to her cunt, which was still hidden by her closed thighs.

He was determined, though. He snuck two fingers into the crease there, then pulled up. She gasped, the action causing her to spread her thighs just a hair and angle her hips.

Damon dove in without needing directions. He latched his lips around her clit, the attention hard and focused. *Perfect.* Reese would love to see her worry when Damon tormented her like that.

Even as Cullen set things up on the bed, Kara only writhed against Reese's grasp. He gripped her hair tightly, baring her throat, and spread her open for Damon's eager tongue. She rolled her hips and reached back, digging her fingers into Reese's side for purchase.

When her moan stuttered, when Reese could *see* the tensing of muscles a split second before she came, Damon backed off.

The denied orgasm sizzled through her and showed in her frustrated growl.

Reese grinned. "If you can still growl, clearly we haven't gone far enough. When you're whimpering and begging, that's when we've gone far enough."

"Ready," Cullen said.

Reese turned, finding the straps hooked to the frame of the bed. *Perfect.*

Kara's gasp said she'd seen them too.

Cullen moved into Kara's space, his lips so close to hers that he must have brushed them as he spoke. He pressed something into her palm. "You can squeeze this and it means stop. That's all you get, though. You always want to fight, to keep control, and that's exactly what we plan to take away. However, if it gets to be too much, if you don't like it, squeeze that and we'll let you go. Do you understand?"

Kara nodded, squeezing the ball once so that the high-pitched noise could be heard in the room. Her shoulders dropped a bit at the sound, as if she were relieved. The fact that she didn't bitch told Reese everything about her fragile state.

Cullen wasted no time, grasping her around the waist and holding her against him before he moved her onto the bed. Reese went to one side of the bed and Damon the other. They captured her thin wrists and used the straps to bind her. Once they were fastened, she pulled at them as if testing the strength.

She wouldn't be able to break them, and the moment she became aware, her breathing sped. Not fear, and the pink on her chest was a thing of beauty.

Cullen grasped the blindfold and slid it over her eyes, stealing her sight. She twisted around as if she could see something if she tried, but the mask stayed snug.

Damon danced his fingers up and down her arm, gentle strokes as if to remind her the alphas were there even if she couldn't *see* them.

Reese reached down to cup her warm breast and tease the pointed nipple that tipped it. "We're going to enjoy this, hellion. You will too, even if you don't think so yet. Without being able to see, you're going to have to just accept whatever we do. You can't move, can't do a thing to stop us."

Her hand tightened on the ball, but she didn't squeeze it. It was if she had to remind herself she'd wanted this.

As quickly as he started to think they'd actually managed to unsettle her into silence, her wicked tongue came back to life. "First you want me to look at you, now you don't. Make up your minds."

Cullen chuckled before picking up yet another item from the bed. The red ball slid between her lips, silencing her before he reached behind her head to fasten the straps of the gag.

That got her struggling. Funny that it wasn't being bound, but stealing away her voice. Suddenly she *had* to just accept. "Don't you look good like this?" Reese smiled before closing his fingers in a pinch around her nipple until she arched up off the bed.

Cullen took one last thing, a set of headphones. "I'm going to take away all your senses but touch. You won't be able to do anything but feel, nothing but take what we give you."

A muffled sound came from her gagged mouth as Cullen put the headphones on her, taking away the last of her ability to predict anything. "You good?" Cullen turned a look on Damon, the conversation private since Kara couldn't hear it.

Damon nodded before swallowing hard. It was easy to read the kid, especially since he didn't have a deceitful bone in him. He was uneasy, probably unsure about liking it, but that didn't change that he did like it.

Cullen's lips curled into that smile of his, the one that softened his features. "Yeah, I can see you're good. I knew you'd be in for this once you saw it."

"What's the plan?"

Reese released the nipple he'd pinched, knowing damn well the most painful part of that — and the best — was when the blood rushed back into the area. "The plan? We're going to play with this little omega until she can't even think about trying to keep us at a distance."

Kara couldn't see. She couldn't hear. She couldn't *speak*.

Worse? No one did anything at first. After the pressure on her nipple was released, after one of them teased over the sore peak, nothing.

She strained to hear anything, to use all those well-honed senses of hers to figure something out.

She jumped when something stroked along her thigh, something else against her other. She tried to identify the alpha, to figure out who was touching her, but she couldn't tell *anything*.

Something closed around her thighs, pulling them wide, spreading her. Cuffs of some sort? Whatever they were, they bound her legs apart just above the knee, so her legs were bent and her cunt was on display.

She felt so vulnerable. A breeze stroked over her drenched and sensitive clit, the orgasm they'd stolen earlier still roaring through her.

The touches were light—a stroke to her right breast, a caress to her cunt that didn't touch her clit. They drove her mad with the need for more.

Insults and prodding sat on her tongue, the desire to snap, to gain back some of what they'd taken from her, but with the gag she could do *nothing*. She could only lie there and take it.

And worse? Her pussy *pulsed* with need. Each touch was a shock to her system, a surprise she couldn't predict, and yet each one felt good. Each time she tensed, ready for something bad, she was only given pleasure.

Lips latched around one nipple, soft and sweet. *Damon?* She didn't know, but the tongue lapped at the pebbled peak until she cried out through the gag. Another tongue traced her other breast, along the outside curve. A scratch of facial hair had her wondering if it was Reese, but she just couldn't tell.

Fingers danced along her spread thighs, teasing the soft skin there as her muscles jumped beneath the caress. Fingers found her cunt, pressing against the slit before filling her in a slow thrust.

It was all so much. It was too much, yet none of it hurt her. No matter how much she tried to move, no matter the sounds she made, she couldn't escape the pleasure.

Lips found her clit, which was swollen and desperate. They didn't latch on like Damon had, instead offering a reverent kiss. The tongue traced around her nub, fingers pulling the hood away, exposing her entirely. She lifted her head from the pillow, but with the blindfold, only darkness met her.

It made each touch so much deeper. She couldn't try to diminish her reaction as she normally did, couldn't focus on anything else. They'd taken everything else away.

She clutched the ball they'd given her, an out she knew she could take, so why didn't she?

As each stroke of theirs turned her defenses to dust, why didn't she tap out?

The question burned away when those lips between her legs *finally* locked onto her clit. They sucked hard, and the orgasm she'd not had earlier swallowed her whole.

She could focus on nothing else as her release surged through her, sparks of pleasure dancing in the darkness behind her eyelids. She pulled against the straps that held her, the sensations racing through her, her cunt squeezing down around nothing, the lips on her not stopping at all.

Just when she thought denying her the orgasm was the worst thing they could do, she realized *this* was torture.

That tongue that lashed her clit kept going, not giving her the slightest reprieve. At the same time, the other two focused their attention on her breasts, but there was too much to pay attention to, too many sensations to filter through her lust-filled mind.

She shook, writhing against the cuffs on her wrists and the ones on her thighs, but no matter what she did, the lips on her were relentless.

Two thick fingers filled her, fucking her hard, curling up to stroke against her G-spot. The second orgasm was harsh, scraping against her as she tensed again, already breathless.

She cried out from behind the gag, wanting to beg but unable to do so. What Reese had said made sense all of a sudden, and she was almost embarrassed by how fast they could get her to that point.

The lips pulled away from her clit, but those thick fingers still stretched her, rotating and sliding through her drenched and sensitive pussy.

The headphones were pulled free, and she expected the blindfold to be removed next.

Instead, Reese's deep voice from beside her made her jump. "You look good like this, hellion." An almost kiss pressed against her lips despite the gag. "But if you think we're done, we're not even close to it. The thing is, I want to take you entirely."

She drew her eyebrows together at the statement. *Entirely?* What did that mean?

The meaning because clear when something slid across her ass.

She responded, an immediate *no* perched on her lips, but the gag prevented her from saying anything.

Lips teased over her nipple and a stream of air blew across her clit, silencing her.

Reese kept talking. "You sure as fuck enjoyed it when we played with you. I think you know you'll like it when I'm buried deep inside your tight ass."

The lips at her breast released after one hard lick. "Are you afraid?" Damon's voice sent a shiver through her, the sound delicious after not being able to hear anything. It also gave her the first chance to pinpoint each of their positions.

Reese and Damon had been tormenting her breasts while Cullen was beneath her spread thighs.

Kara against tried to talk, the action automatic before she cursed the gag *again*.

"Squeeze the ball for yes," Damon whispered. "Are you afraid?"

Yes.

"Afraid it'll hurt?"

No answer.

He sighed softly, his fingers stroking over her still damp nipple.

Cullen pressed a kiss to her hip. "We asked you to trust us. Have we hurt you yet?"

Not physically, but damn it, she was afraid this was worse. She could handle a little pain, but what they'd done?

Cullen's tongue traced the line of her hip in a tease. "If you don't like it, you can stop it anytime. You aren't ever going to get a thing you want if you aren't willing to risk some shit, though. So, last time, squeeze that and we'll let you go."

Kara shifted on the bed, her own worries pounding against her skull, her hand gripped tight around the ball. Everything inside her screamed to squeeze it.

End this. Now.

She took a deep breath and loosened her grasp.

Reese pressed his lips to her cheek just above the strap of the gag. "Good answer, hellion."

She wished she was as sure as he was.

When Kara's body went still, Cullen groaned. This was exactly what he'd wanted, and finally, he'd have it.

He delivered one more punishing lick up her slit, enjoying that high-pitched whine that she let out.

He rose from between her thighs, no matter how much he didn't really want to move. Only the fact that he'd have more got him going.

They left the headphones off her. He had a feeling she could use a bit of connection there, with how damned nervous she seemed. She probably needed some reassurance.

Fuck, he liked the idea of that. Given her hard-ass attitude most of the time, the thought of actually *helping* her, of her using him to stay grounded and steady, sank deep into him.

Reese reached above her and undid where the cuffs connected to the straps. If she thought she was free, she was dead wrong.

He sat her up and rehooked them behind her back. She twisted, her breasts pushed forward due to the angle.

Perfect.

Cullen undid the straps at her thighs, releasing them entirely. They weren't going to need them, given she'd have three alphas more than capable of keeping her still.

He grasped her hips and tugged her closer, then rolled so she was over him. She gasped through the gag when his hard cock pressed against her cunt. The feeling of all that hot wetness against him made him growl with the need to be inside her, to fill her so deeply she'd never forget them.

He pulled her as he scooted back until he leaned against the headboard. Her breasts pressed to the flat planes of his pecs, the hard nipples yet another sign of how much she wanted it.

She had no control. She couldn't move, couldn't help as Cullen shifted her around. She had to rely on Cullen to not let her fall, since she couldn't even see.

And what he did with that was try to teach her that that she could trust them. Maybe by the end of this, when she was breathless and sated and boneless with exhaustion, she'd realize she didn't need to keep them at a distance.

He huffed as he realized even he didn't really believe that. Life with Kara would forever be tearing down the walls she put up. And when Cullen used his grasp on her waist to lift her, when he sank deep into her tight cunt, he thought it might just be worth teaching her it over and over.

She arched and inhaled as he stretched her cunt. The grip of it was the closest thing to heaven he was pretty sure he'd ever get. Reese moved in behind her, using his hands to guide her down onto Cullen's shaft.

The bed dipped beneath Damon's weight, and he caught Kara's chin and brought her face toward him. He rested his forehead on hers, the action sweet, and she responded with a slight nuzzle against him.

Reese took the lube from the bag before he pressed a hand against Kara's back, forcing her to arch. Cullen kept her still, his length buried deep inside her. It was torturous, to feel her tight around her but not be able to thrust.

Still, he pinned her against him to let Reese work.

Reese's lubed fingers pressed against her ass, and Cullen let himself peer over her shoulder to watch, enthralled by the sight. Reese was careful but sure as he slid one finger into her. The sensation teased Cullen's cock, and he groaned at the thought of how she must be feeling, caught between them and so fully taken over.

Damon reached behind her and undid the straps of the gag. Part of Cullen wanted it to stay in place. He'd sort of enjoyed the honesty she had when they took away her words, when she couldn't wield them like weapons.

Damon was still the nice one, though.

Of course, the gasping moan she released when Reese moved up to two fingers was worth giving her her voice back.

As soon as she let it out, Damon swallowed it down when he pulled her into a kiss.

Reese took the distraction as he stretched her, getting her ready to take his cock. Cullen kept her still, watching Reese, enjoying the way Kara's body writhed against him.

It didn't take long before Reese withdrew his fingers. He added more lube and stroked some over his shaft before trading a grin with Cullen.

Reese used one hand to spread her open, then pressed the head of his cock against her.

They all froze, with Damon breaking the kiss. Kara's panting breaths filled the space, and Cullen felt even more sure.

This was worth fighting for. This was worth having, worth keeping.

This was a future he wanted.

The press of Reese's cock to Kara's ass felt like an epiphany, like a moment in time. She had a choice. Would she give up that last scrap of control?

Kara relaxed against Cullen's chest, surrendering to them, to this, to the thing she'd fought so hard against.

If they broke her heart after this, she had no idea how she'd pick herself back up. Still, that fear was finally not enough to resist it. She couldn't hold it back anymore, couldn't pretend she didn't want this.

Reese pressed into her, the burn of his thick cock enough to draw whimpers from her.

Damon kissed her even though she didn't return it, the tiny acts of affection like praise that told her she could handle it.

And she let herself believe it. She let herself accept it, gave herself the chance to believe him.

Reese leaned forward and played his lips against her shoulder blade as he kept moving closer, kept sliding into her.

It took her breath away, each inch he forced her to take, especially with how full she already felt. Cullen's cock twitched inside her, his groans close to her ear as her cunt tensed around him.

"Fuck," Reese growled out. "You're so tight. I can't believe how good you look taking me."

Kara opened her mouth, wanting to snipe, but Damon chose that moment to nip her. The sting in her bottom lip only melted into yet another caress, sharp and passionate.

Finally, when Kara was sure she couldn't take any more, when she was ready to tap out, Reese's body pressed against hers. It meant she'd taken him all, and she could only whine at the way it felt.

Reese's lips danced over her shoulder, Damon still offering kisses to her that were grounding. She twisted her hands, wrists cuffed behind her, pinned between all the bulk of the alphas.

And she felt…happy.

It struck her so fast, she didn't have time to freak out, but she felt content. She didn't need to yank, to fight, to bare her teeth and struggle. Instead, she just *was*. The coaxing softness of Damon's lips soaked into her, sweet and gentle. Cullen's strong, hard body pressed to her front, flattening her breasts and offering stability she'd never had. Reese blanketed her from behind, scraping his teeth over her shoulder, his large hands on her hips.

All of it was *perfect*.

"Stop thinking," Reese whispered before he tightened his grip on her and pulled back, then thrust deep into her. It was the first *real* time he'd filled her, and the hard thrust stole her breath. The tail end of her gasp melted into a moan that surprised even her.

His chuckle said he'd caught it, and she should have known he wouldn't ever let her live it down. Instead, he repeated the movement, pressing her farther against Cullen to angle her.

The darkness of the blindfold let her focus on the feeling of Reese, especially because each of his thrusts made her move on Cullen's cock.

As Reese fucked her, hard and deep, Kara gave in. She gave in to them, to the craziness, to it all. Fuck all the nonsense in her head, fuck her fears.

She didn't feel broken for once. She was there with them, just an omega with three alphas she wanted more than anything.

The alphas' growls said they were close, and Cullen had started to lift his hips, sinking even deeper into her.

That was good, because each stroke of Cullen's pelvis against her clit drew her closer to another orgasm, despite how tired her body already was.

Reese sank deep, digging his fingers into her as he came. The stretch of her body when Cullen slammed home and his knot grew, locking into place, told her Cullen had found his end as well.

A hand slid around her neck when Reese pulled free and tugged her down. Her body bent forward, tugging against Cullen's thick knot, when she found the blunt head of a cock pressed to her lips.

Damon. He didn't wait, didn't ask, and instead slid deep into her mouth. His cock was hot and solid against her tongue, filling all her scenes. Without being able to see, with being trapped around like this, Kara lost her fight.

She came, only able to focus on not biting down on Damon's thick shaft.

A vicious snarl left Cullen when her pussy clenched down, milking his knot, making him spill more into her already full cunt.

Hot seed touched her tongue, and it set Kara's body off again, another wave of pleasure crashing over her.

Damon pulled his cock free, and Kara swallowed his cum, burning a path down her throat as she recovered, exhausted and more sated than she remembered ever being.

Reese undid her binds and Damon took off the blindfold. The darkness of the room wasn't harsh against her eyes, though she whined when—once Cullen could pull free of her—they cleaned her up.

An hour later, Kara curled against Reese's chest, Damon behind her and Cullen in the chair to the side after saying he couldn't sleep. That hadn't stopped him from dozing off, a book forgotten in his lap as if he were watching over them.

Kara stared at the alphas—*her alphas*—and the truth struck her.

Maybe it was how raw she felt after the sex, after giving in to them, after trusting them entirely and coming out the other side unscathed.

She trusted them. She might even need them.

They actually had a future, and Kara wanted it more than anything.

Chapter Twenty-One

Reese spread the map on the table, which had large Xs on each spot they'd searched. "This is pointless."

Damon shook his head and tapped the paper. "It's not."

A sound in the hotel hallway had them both pausing, listening intently. When nothing else came, they exhaled in unison.

"She won't be happy when she finds out."

"So she won't find out," Reese said, even though he knew that was a stupid plan. Kara was hard-headed and far too smart. There was no way they could keep something from her if she wanted to find out. Their best hope was to try and make it so she didn't realize she needed to find anything out.

Reese's phone had died days before and it hadn't given them anything solid. The car ran the normal errands, stayed in the same apartment building parking garage every night. They'd considered trying to tail the car, but given the people they'd already dealt with, Reese was sure they'd be spotted. They weren't amateurs, and if they were followed, it would only tip the hand they had.

The car took the same route every morning, parking in a large lot outside one of the lab's other storage buildings. From what they'd found, the building was a warehouse used to store the various medical equipment to be sent to whatever lab needed it. He'd even sat on it for a few hours at night and seen no movement, nothing to indicate anything else was done there.

Besides, it was too public for them to want to do anything illegal there. Wherever they kept the alpha, it wasn't going to be on the books. The person who drove the SUV — probably the one Reese had knocked out — had to work security there when he wasn't doing the less reputable parts of his job. *Good way to keep things looking legit.* Still, since he never showed up at wherever they kept the alpha, it left them exactly nowhere.

"She'll realize we're keeping something from her," Damon pressed, "and when she does, she isn't going to be happy."

"She's already gotten attacked, has Thompson after her and was nearly killed by that car. She's injured. Do you really think she should be doing any of this?" Reese jammed a finger down on the map. "Because she won't just help us plan. She'll want to be in the thick of it."

Damon growled softly but lowered his gaze to the map.

He was young and easily swayed by Kara. While Reese didn't love the idea of keeping the omega in the dark, it seemed the only real choice. The more time they spent with her, the more obvious it was that they wanted her.

There were issues. Cullen had been the first willing to bring them up, to mention all the reasons they weren't a great fit, but at the end?

They *could* make it work.

The alphas hadn't fully discussed the matter yet, hadn't agreed to try it, yet the more time they spent together, the more obvious it was none of them wanted to let her go. All they had to do was get her to change, just a little.

Kara could quit stealing and settle down. She'd be safe because they'd make sure she stayed safe. She wouldn't need to lie because she wouldn't have things to keep from them.

"I don't like it," Damon repeated.

"I know you don't, but you agreed just like we did. This is how it has to happen. We'll solve the case, we'll get Kara to come back home with us and we'll make it all work."

The look on Damon's face said he didn't quite believe it could all go so easily, but he said nothing. Funny that Damon had fit in so well at the end. He seemed to offer Kara something no one else did — a safe place she melted into. With the others, Kara competed. She fought. With Damon, however, she relaxed, curling around him like a body pillow. He'd admitted that his plans had never included sharing an omega, but he'd said it in the way that implied maybe his original plans weren't what he'd ever really wanted.

And Reese got that.

He'd wanted children. Or maybe he'd just expected to have them? He wasn't sure if there was a difference anymore.

Though they'd spoken to Marshall about that. Kara still had one working ovary. She couldn't carry a child, given they'd removed her uterus, but she could use a surrogate.

They could still have that life they'd wanted, with children of their own blood.

"Have you looked here?" A neon-green-painted nail tapped against a warehouse on the northern side they hadn't checked. Kara's voice was deceptively sweet, like poison covered in sugar. It screamed to tread carefully.

"Not yet," Reese said, voice slow. She reminded him of a coiled rattlesnake right then, and he sure as shit didn't want to get bitten.

"I've been thinking," she said, voice tight. "The GPS on the phone had the car stopping right here every morning and again on the way home."

"A stop light," Reese offered.

"No stop light or stop sign there. And the route is odd, not direct."

Damon frowned as he stared at the map, as though he were working out the issue in his head. "He's dropping someone off there."

"And picking them up. I'd guess he lives with a coworker, one who works at the actual lab we're looking for. Perfect out-of-the-way spot for staying off the radar there, and big enough for whatever they needed."

"For fuck's sake," Cullen muttered as he came in through the front door, telling them Kara had slipped his watch. They'd walked down to the coffee shop in the lobby for an 'outing', or so Kara had said.

It seemed she'd played them all, which shouldn't have shocked him nearly as much as it did. Why did he keep underestimating her?

Kara rose and crossed her arms, the action obscuring whatever smart-ass quip was printed across her shirt.

"Why am I actually surprised that you all would pull this?"

So, it seemed they were past her being helpful.

Cullen panted as he walked up to the dining table with the map over it, which meant he'd run all the way there. His words were broken as he answered. "It's nothing."

Kara lifted an eyebrow but remained silent, as if daring him to try that again.

Reese tried next. "You aren't even fully healed. You didn't need to be back on this case already."

"And you were just hoping, what? You'd solve it before I realized you all were plotting behind my back? Because let me tell you something, you idiots aren't nearly as sneaky as you seem to think. I knew from that first day you all were up to something. I just thought you'd come clean when Marshall cleared me. Exactly how long did you plan to keep this from me?"

No one answered.

A tic appeared in her jaw, and that mildly amused face she normally wore was nowhere to be seen. "So you weren't going to tell me at all?"

"You didn't need to know," Cullen gritted out. "We'll handle it."

"I don't need you handling my problems."

"What was the other choice? Let you get hurt again?"

Reese winced at the words, which were far too harsh even if they were accurate. "What he means —" Reese cut Cullen a hard look to get him to shut up. "Is that we wanted to deal with this so we could start over. You were hurt, and this whole mess was something we dropped on you. We thought if we could just finish the case, it all goes away."

"What do you mean 'goes away'?"

Again, no one spoke, and the answer seemed to dawn on Kara slowly.

She let out a quiet, hollow chuckle. "You think that as soon as this is finished, I'm going to, what? Sit home and behave and listen to you all the time?"

"You don't need to steal anymore," Damon said. "We make more than enough so you wouldn't have to do this anymore, wouldn't have to take jobs."

"You could have a good, safe life. You could live with us, travel with us on the safer cases, at least until we have kids—" Reese pressed.

"*Kids*?" Kara nearly choked the word out. "Have you forgotten my deficiencies in that area?"

Cullen spoke up, having regained his breath from chasing her. "We already spoke to Marshall. We can use a surrogate."

"I never even said I wanted kids."

Reese reached for her hand, but she jerked away before he could make contact. Still, he tried to explain, to make her understand. "We can talk about that later. The point is, you don't *have* to be this person anymore."

Kara went silent, her lips pressed together, her body strung so tight it might snap beneath the mounting tension. "I'm going to take a shower," she said, voice tight and carefully blank. It wasn't the easy humor in which she lied, but rather a rough and difficult cadence that said she was trying to hold it all together. Still, the emotions bled out at the seams of the words, in the glistening of her eyes.

And Reese, who hated when she lied, found none of his usual anger at the lie. She wasn't laughing, didn't have that glint she normally wore. No, it was worse. She looked *hurt*.

"Wait," Damon said, which surprised the fuck out of Reese for him to be the toughest. Reese was not anywhere near willing to tangle with Kara, not when her eyes had that steely set to them, but Damon stepped forward as though all her *keep your fucking distance* attitude meant nothing.

Kara leveled a finger at him, though she cast her gaze toward each of them when she repeated herself in a tone that left no room for arguments. "I'm taking a shower."

The click of her door was solid, just short of a slam, and it had Reese gulping.

This isn't how this is supposed to go.

Kara knew her eyes were rimmed in red, but she didn't fucking care. She was beyond caring.

Or maybe that wasn't true. She cared a hell of a lot, but not about that. It was like getting a splinter when her fucking arm had been cut off. Who cared about looking tough? Who cared about anything but the hollow space in her chest, so empty it felt as though it were imploding, as though it were dragging in everything around it?

She slung her pack over her shoulder, ignoring the subtle ache in her side that said she was likely over the ten-pound limit Marshall had given her for lifting.

Fuck it. I need to get out of here.

In the main living area of the suite, all three alphas stood uneasy and awkward, as though none of them knew what to do. The table sat clear, their little planning papers tucked away somewhere.

She wasn't stupid. They hadn't put them away because they were done with cutting her out. They'd put them away so they didn't have to argue about it.

"Look, Kara," Cullen started to say before his gaze landed on the strap over her shoulder. His eyes narrowed. "What the fuck do you think you're doing?"

"Leaving."

"Like hell," Reese said, the same absoluteness there as in Cullen's. Yeah, the two of them always thought they controlled everything.

They didn't control *her*.

"Yeah, actually, I am."

"Just stay," Damon tried, that sweet voice of his almost enough to coax her into listening. Except, if anything, he'd hurt her the worst. Reese and Cullen, they might be those sorts of alphas who beat their chests and expected an omega to obey. Damon had never been that sort, and so, for some stupid reason, Kara had really thought he respected her.

She'd thought he understood her, that he'd trusted her. Instead, he'd turned out like the rest, and that betrayal was enough to make her eyes burn again even if she cursed the foolish tears. She should have known better.

Kara shook her head, her fingers curled around the backpack strap as if it alone could keep her afloat. "This was a mistake."

Cullen leaned against the table. His green eyes, which she'd stared into so many times in the last weeks, had gone cold. Or maybe she'd gone cold and that was what reflected back out at her? "There's no reason to go running off because of one fight."

"This isn't about one fight. I just realized this was never going to work."

"Why? Because we tried to take care of you? For fuck's sake, Kara, learn to accept some help!" Cullen's voice roared through the suite, angry and frustrated. She'd bet that anger was more about his lack of control than about her.

"You aren't trying to take care of me. You're trying to change me."

"So? No one is perfect. We all could change a bit," Reese said, his tone softer, as though he were trying to talk some sense into her.

"You aren't willing to change at all, though."

"Yes, we are," Cullen said. "We're making allowances, learning to accept things about you we might not care for."

They were willing to *accept* her shortcomings? Again, the blow at how short she fell of their wants hit her. It was like always—she wasn't measuring up. Except, for once, she cared. Kara lost control of the thin grip she had on her temper, her voice coming out with the same anger as Cullen's had. "You don't want me!"

Damon took a step backward, as though her words had a physical force to them, his lips tipped down. "Of course we do. We already discussed it."

"You want some vision of a perfect omega you've concocted, and you just hope you can shove me into that box. It's not the same thing."

It took a moment for an answer to come, as if they all searched for some way to deny it. It was Cullen who took a shot, the brave, stupid asshole. "We want *you*, Kara. Just because we have certain expectations doesn't make us wrong, doesn't mean we don't want you. Are you really going to tell me that the life you've had is one worth giving us up for?"

Kara's laugh was weak and empty. "I don't know why I am so surprised. You never thought I was good enough for you—you just finally thought it was worth trying to fix me. You don't look at me and think 'that's the woman I want.' You think, 'I can turn her into what I want.' I'm no one's fix-it project. I might not be perfect, but damn it, I deserve someone who wants me."

Cullen's mouth opened, then snapped shut again. *Nothing to say? Of course not.* They thought she should just roll over, should accept that she was a shitty person with a worthless life and be happy to become their little plaything. They really thought they were doing her a favor.

Fuck that.

"You might not like my life, but guess what? It's mine. I've worked hard to get my reputation, to build my career, to learn my trade. I'm not about to walk away from it all, and for what? To fit into some picture you all made for yourselves? I'm supposed to change everything about myself so I can give you everything you want? Fuck you all! I like my life. I like what I do. I like who I am, and I'm not about to give it up for what you want."

Reese dropped his gaze for a moment, and despite all of them shuffling their feet, she knew the truth. They regretted that she was pissed, not what they'd done. They were sorry she'd found out, that she wasn't going to go along with their little plan, but not that they still looked at her like she wasn't good enough. "You're still hurt. You shouldn't be on your own."

"I'm not your problem anymore." The words were bitter on her tongue. "But I'll be staying with Torrin, so don't worry."

A knock had Kara moving past them to open the door. Torrin met her gaze, his green eyes steady. That edge to him, the almost scary side...she didn't mind it at all right then.

Torrin might frighten her, but he'd never wanted her to be anyone other than who she was.

Still, he moved his gaze past her and to the alphas, his eyes narrowed.

Kara set a hand on his chest, a clear sign of 'don't do it.' She didn't need Torrin to fight her battles, and as much as she hated the alphas in that moment, she didn't want them hurt either. Her feeling heartbroken was enough, wasn't it?

This was exactly what she'd been so afraid of. *This* had been why she'd fought against letting them close, against them seeing anything deeper than the masks she wore. If they'd walked away before, it would have been fine. It would have been like every other person who had done so, shown the door by her snark and her wild streak before they saw the real her.

But Cullen, Reese and Damon had seen the real her. They'd glimpsed beneath the layers she used to shield herself — and they'd found her lacking.

"Let's talk about this," Cullen said, his voice gentler, as if he were making a last-ditch effort to get her to stay.

"There's nothing to talk about." Kara turned back toward them once more, ignoring the way the sight of all three alphas together brought up the yearning.

"This could still work," Reese said. "Don't throw it away."

And there went her temper yet again. It seemed she'd earned her reputation as a hothead. "I'm not throwing anything away, because there isn't anything here. I'm not some piece of clay for you to turn into whatever you want, whatever will be good enough for your perfect little life."

Damon opened his mouth, but she lifted a hand to silence him.

They needed to damn well listen, and Kara was terrified that if she heard anything else from them, she might forgive them.

"Fuck you all," she muttered and turned her back to them, sliding past Torrin, moving away from the alphas, and away from the men she was pretty damn sure she loved.

Chapter Twenty-Two

Reese glowered at Cullen, as though the other alpha were to blame for the issues at hand.

He wasn't, at least no more than Reese and Damon were. They'd all managed to fuck up the situation pretty royally, but it was easier to be mad at Cullen than admit the truth.

Kara had left them.

She hadn't left in a 'I'm pissed and will come back later' sort of way. Nope, that girl had walked out of the hotel with the sure steps of a woman so over their shit.

Which didn't seem all that fair, really. People were supposed to fight for a while first. The end of things should come after a long trail of yelling and mutually hurt feelings and the sort of thing people saw weeks ahead. Instead, she'd just snapped and walked out.

They'd been happy. That was the worst part about it, that in the weeks since her injury, they'd been happy. Taking care of Kara fulfilled something inside Reese he hadn't even realized he had wanted. He liked bringing her food, and even on the rare occasions she allowed it, feeding her bites. He liked getting her the clothing she needed, reaching for things because she couldn't.

In short? He liked being useful, and he loved the way she looked at him afterward, a mixture of gratitude and annoyance, as though she was thankful but also pissed she was thankful.

Which made it all the more delicious, because it meant he was getting under her skin despite all her reluctance.

And the sex? He kept in a groan as he thought about the soft skin that covered all her toned muscles, the way her body was flexible and strong and mouthwatering. It wasn't just the physical, either. Sure, she had a killer body, but it was so much more than that.

As they'd spent time together, especially in the past weeks, even the sex had changed. She'd softened, as though she was willing to consider it as something more than just a way to work off excess energy. Her touches had turned from mindless clutching to caresses, to something so much deeper.

The best part? The way those eyes of hers had started to open, the way she'd actually *look* at them during sex. He thought back to the trust in those blue eyes as Cullen had tied her down, at the sweetest moans when he'd held her hands above her head.

The night before, when Reese had taken her while Cullen and Damon discussed plans, she'd laced her fingers behind his neck and looked up into his eyes as he'd fucked her with slow, purposeful thrusts. Her hips had rolled, a seductive lifting as though she wasn't content to only give. The light from the window had caught her, making the blue of her eyes bright and shining in the dim room. It had gone beyond need or just scratching an itch. It had meant something.

And now? Now she was gone.

"This was always how it was going to end," Cullen grated out.

Which was exactly the wrong thing to say.

Damon bit out a response first. "Only because you wouldn't back down."

"She never was going to fit into our lives, and you damned well know it. You can be angry with me all you want, but you two had issues, too. Stop thinking with your dick."

Damon flashed his teeth, the show of temper from the young alpha surprising. "If this was just about your dick, then that's *your* problem."

Despite Reese having agreed with Damon—and he really wanted to see Cullen get some sense knocked into him—Reese couldn't let them come to blows. He needed to calm them down.

As much as the end with Kara burned him, Reese and Damon were family. He couldn't lose both, especially after Kara. "It doesn't matter who caused it or why, does it?"

Damon lowered his lip, but the thin slash of his mouth said he didn't really agree.

Cullen tore his gaze from the others, choosing to stare out of the window instead. "I didn't want this," he admitted lowly, the closest to an apology they were probably ever going to get from the stubborn man. "I really thought she'd see reason. I thought she'd see we were offering her more than she had and she'd jump at it."

"Maybe she was right," Reese offered. "Maybe it was unfair to expect her to give up everything, to change."

"She never would fit with our lives unless she did." Cullen shrugged, then brushed his hands over the tops of his thighs, as though he could clear off the uncomfortable feelings so easily. "It was this or lose her anyway. This or we end up having to bury her."

"Maybe," Reese agreed. "Maybe you were right, that it was never going to work, but I can't blame her for walking out, either. Fuck, if it was reversed, if she was telling us to drop everything we'd done, everything we had, so we could fit with her, do you really think you'd have just agreed?"

Cullen didn't answer at first. Finally, a sigh that showed the stress he always tried to hide left his lips. "Does it even matter at this point? She's gone. If she hadn't been, we would either have fought with her over trying to keep her safe or she'd have kept acting as she has been and ended up dead." Cullen raked his fingers through his hair. "We are where we are, and the rest? The rest just doesn't matter."

"So what now?" Damon's question gave them all that shove, reminded them they had to think of the future instead of the past, because right about then, the past really fucking sucked.

Reese drew a breath, trying to banish the thoughts, trying not to fall into another bout of frustration at their current predicament. Getting over Kara would not be easy, and he was damned sure they'd all started to bond to the feisty, difficult little omega. Not that it mattered, since she'd left.

"We finish this case, find the alpha and get the contract off Kara's head."

Cullen and Damon nodded, especially when he said the last part.

It seemed they couldn't have her, but that didn't stop them from planning to do whatever it took to keep her safe.

Nothing else mattered.

* * * *

A folded sweater hit Kara in the face, and she flat-out refused to acknowledge it.

"Get up," Erik ordered.

"Fuck off," she countered, like some sort of negotiation.

The couch she was lounging on shifted, and everything else flipped seconds before she hit the ground. Kara twisted to glare up at Erik, who had angled the couch to dump her unceremoniously to the hardwood floor.

Not that glaring had ever worked with Erik. Liam was the softy who gave in, Torrin was the strong but silent type who would go behind her back to do what she wanted, though he'd never admit it, and Erik was the one who didn't give a fuck what someone wanted because he'd do what he damned well pleased regardless.

"You've been pouting for a week. That's more than enough."

His attempt had already worked better then Liam or Torrin, who hadn't gotten her to move from a horizontal position. The most she did was shift from one flat surface to another.

Bed sores sucked, and she planned to avoid them.

Which was why Kara flipped off Erik and lay flat again, hard ground be damned, because he would *not* win the little battle of wills.

And will was something she seemed to have in short supply at the moment. She'd used the last of hers when she'd walked out on the alphas, when she'd held it together as she'd left them behind.

Fuck, her chest hurt at the thought of it, at the way she'd forced her feet to move despite how much she wanted to just not go. Sure, she couldn't be what they wanted, but leaving had still taken more grit than she'd even known she had.

While she'd muttered *fuck them* to herself over and over, it never held weight. What should have been a rallying battle cry pushing her to move on and forget those idiots had instead been a sullen whisper.

Still, fuck them.

"You don't let anything get you like this," Erik reminded her.

But that was the point. Nothing else had ever gotten to her like that before. She'd never *let* herself feel like that, never dared to want something so much before. It was the first time she'd needed something and, in the end, she'd lost it. All because she still wasn't enough.

Kara opened one eye, the sweater having fallen somewhere in her roll off the couch. "I once again invite you to fuck right the hell off."

Erik sat on the couch, staring down at her. "You remember how I used to wake you when you refused to get up for our morning jogs?"

"You wouldn't dare."

But he did.

A minute later, dripping wet from the full pot of ice-cold water Erik had thrown on her, Kara shivered and turned her glare murderous. "This is why you were never my favorite!"

"Let me go cry about a minute about that," he deadpanned before moving on. "Stop moping around."

"Like you know anything," she snapped through chattering teeth. "You aren't exactly the person I'd go and talk to about feelings."

Erik tossed Kara a towel, the one he'd brought like some sort of apology for having been the one to drench her in the first place. "I know a lot more than you think."

A flash in his eyes had her pausing as she wrapped the towel around her shoulders. Erik had always been the one of the group who had as much depth as a cardboard cutout, and about that same range of expressions. Even worse than Torrin, which hardly seemed possible. Beneath that, something deeper showed. It took her by surprise, especially since Kara excelled at reading people and she'd never seen that before.

Even in the times when Torrin and Liam were worried about her, when they all fought, Erik never seemed to rise to the occasion. He never seemed to care about anything—not her, not the jobs, not himself.

In whatever showed in his eyes, though, Kara saw through what had to be a façade.

Erik blinked it away and shook his head. "You've gone after what you want as long as I've known you. Even when it's impossible, even when it's stupid, even when people forbid you, you've never backed down from anything. Makes me wonder why you're in here hiding and giving up."

Kara rubbed her hands over her arms, trying to use the towel to dry off the water that still dripped to the floor. *If Torrin gets mad at me about the mess, I'm blaming it all on Erik.* Even as she distracted herself with the mindless movements, she answered. "Because they don't want me. What I might want—and I'm not admitting to wanting shit—doesn't matter, because I'm not what fits into their perfect little world."

"What do they want?"

Kara dropped to the couch beside Erik, being sure she let her still wet side press against his. *Serves him right.* "A perfect omega. Someone sweet and quiet and well behaved. Someone who will sit at home safe and sound instead of being in trouble. Basically? Everything I'm not."

Erik reached into his pants pocket and held a folded piece of paper between two fingers.

"What's this?" Even as Kara asked, she took it and opened it. A time and date were written across it.

"Seems your alphas aren't calling it quits. That's when they're planning on hitting it."

"Of course not. They're the heroes, and heroes don't quit," she muttered. "How did you get this?"

"The hotel room is bugged." No shame showed in Erik's voice, as though bugging the room of strangers — the room that had been Kara's as well not long before — was the most normal thing in the world.

To him it was.

"So? What does that matter?" Kara crumpled the paper and tossed it toward the wastebasket at the corner of the room, even though she knew she'd memorized it.

"They think you're weak. They think you can't protect yourself and need them. They think you can't be trusted."

The things he said each peeled off a layer of skin with it, and that they were true — that they thought it, not the thing itself — made them all the more painful. No matter what she did, it seemed they were never going to see her as anything but a no-good, two-bit thief.

"Exactly," she said, trying to sound unaffected. "So why should I do anything when they're pretty clear about how they feel about me?"

Erik rose to his feet, a damp spot on his side a small victory to her. "Because what you do isn't about them. What they think or don't think isn't about you, and you don't need to worry about it. Do what you're going to do because it's who *you* actually are. Not who they think you are, who Liam or Torrin and I think you are, but for yourself."

"You're not making any sense."

Erik offered a rare smile to her when he reached the door. "It's simple. Are you the sort of girl who would let them have all the fun? Would you let three males you love risk themselves while you sit home alone like the good omega they want you to be? Because the girl I know? She would go raise hell, if for no other reason than to piss them off."

Kara was left sitting there, still shivering slightly, as Erik's words sank in.

It didn't take more than a minute before she grabbed the crumpled paper from the trash and rushed to get ready.

She had some alphas to piss off.

Chapter Twenty-Three

Reese remained on alert as they passed through the back door after picking the lock. The lab, from the outside, had appeared deserted. They'd watched it since the day before, seen the changes in guards, watched the scientists head home at nightfall. Cullen tended to like a lot of recon, and for once, Reese didn't mind waiting. After all, this was about taking down these bastards to keep Kara safe. What did a little bit of waiting mean?

The large building was the sort of place that had been remodeled time and time again. It seemed like an office building now. A lobby area at the front, offices and a large stockroom near the back. He'd guess the second floor was modeled the same way, with offices and conference rooms.

They searched through the darkness, listening for anything. No camera, no guards that they could see. It meant they must be hiding somewhere. *A basement?* At least it made for an easy time moving about.

As they turned another corner, they nearly ran right into a small body. Reese was already reaching for them, ready to do whatever was needed to keep their presence a secret, when the scent hit them.

Kara.

She stood in the dark, and Reese struggled to believe it had only been a week since they'd seen her, since she'd walked out on them.

Damon did what the Reese wanted but hadn't given in to. The kid was either young and foolish or maybe a lot smarter, because Damon set a hand behind her neck and pulled Kara in for a kiss without a word.

It was the sort of kiss that made even Reese want to look away, as if he were intruding, which was hilarious, since he had fucked her alongside Damon.

Kara's body softened into the kiss, but just as quickly, she pulled back. "Down, boy," she said on a breathless exhalation. "I'm not here for that."

"Why are you here?" Cullen asked, his voice careful, as though he was hiding everything he felt.

Kara took another step away from Damon, away from all three of them, as though it helped her think. "This is my job, too, and I don't quit. I'm going to help finish this, but that's it. Us? We're done."

Cullen's lips parted as though to object, but he silenced whatever he was going to say. That was probably for the best, as Cullen tended to say things that landed them all in trouble.

As much as Reese hated to hear Kara talk like that, he also knew arguing wouldn't do anything, and arguing in the middle of breaking into a secret lab was probably not the right time.

Kara nodded behind him, and while she appeared mostly unfazed, Reese caught the slight hesitation in her gaze as she looked at each alpha. "There's nothing on the upper levels. Well, there was one guard."

"Was?" Cullen's eyebrow cocked up at the past tense.

"He's still there, but he isn't guarding anything." The curl of Kara's lips showed no remorse. "He'll wake up in a couple hours with a headache. However, I got this from him." She held up a smaller keycard. "I'd guess it goes to a door on this level that's locked."

"Why is so much of this place empty?" Reese asked.

"Because they want it to look like nothing is going on. Even if someone comes in, they'll look around and see nothing noteworthy." Kara moved silently in the dark space, through the hallways and rooms, as if she'd already memorized them, the alphas following. They came to a storage room, and just inside sat the door she must have meant.

It didn't look like much, except for the keycard reader to the right of it and the camera above it that pointed down.

No way to get to the door without being seen.

"I'd guess this goes to the basement, which is where they're keeping the lab. There's no way there's enough room on this level, and being underground would hide them even better," Kara said.

"What do we do about the camera?"

Kara looked around, taking her lip between her teeth as she seemed to consider the options. Finally, she shrugged. "To get close enough to use the keycard, we'll be seen. If we manually disable the camera, they'll be alerted. They don't tend to like cameras going dead."

"So we'll be seen either way? Because I'd really prefer this not turn into a firefight," Cullen said.

"Firefights are like cardio. Good for the heart." Kara reached out and grabbed a broom from the side of the room, where actual supplies appeared to be kept. She inched to the left, to the side where the camera was, as close as she could without being seen.

Her balance was a thing of beauty. Reese couldn't help but be impressed with the way Kara leaned, one hand on a shelf behind her, the other reaching the broom out above the line of sight of the camera. Her attention was locked on the camera, on the way the broom neared it, until she was able to touch the top. She pressed, tension in her face at the effort, until the camera's hinge creaked, and it shifted down and to the side, away from the door.

She tossed the broom to the side and blew out a breath. "They'll come check it, but it'll probably take a while. A place like this doesn't see a lot of action, so guards get complacent. Even if they do come check, it'll just look like a loose hinge."

Which was smart, Reese had to admit. Disconnect the camera and they'd be found out right away. Turn the camera and it bought them a little time and could easily be chalked up to mechanical failure.

Kara moved forward first, fingers pointed to the ground where the camera's line of sight was, so the alphas could avoid it. At the door, she slid the card through the reader, and it seemed they all held their breaths as they waited.

The light flashed green and the door lock popped open.

Reese followed Kara into the darkness.

Kara had to admit, she'd missed them. As much as she chastised herself for the thought, Damon's kiss had all but curled her toes like some stupid woman in a cheesy movie.

Finish the job. Save the alpha. Get the hell out of Dodge.

All easy, doable steps that would put these three and their highly disruptive tendencies so far in her rear-view mirror she'd have to squint to see shit.

Which suited her just fine.

The stairs were steep and dark, though Kara got the sense that the place tried to stay under the radar. That meant they would be careful about the amount of power they pulled at night, during times it would be harder to explain to anyone looking too closely.

Besides, the guards probably worked twelve-hour shifts, and she doubted anyone important came by in the night. Graveyard shift guards tended toward lazy.

Not that the reasons made it any easier as her eyes struggled to adjust to the darkness. With no real source of light, the alphas' scents tantalized her even more.

When she hadn't felt the pull of the pseudo-heats, she'd called Marshall. He'd run her numbers again to tell her what she'd already feared. She'd bonded to the alphas. She'd ached from their absence, and that should have clued her in already. The only good part about bonding to males who didn't want her was that it seemed to level out her hormones, lessened the clawing need she'd felt before. *Will it last?*

She hoped so, because she couldn't imagine using strangers again like she had before. Somehow, the idea of falling into bed—or onto whatever solid surface could hold the combined weight of her and a partner that was close by—no longer seemed palatable.

Which was pretty fucking annoying. They could break her heart, but them making sex seem unappetizing pissed her off.

She missed a step, pitching forward when her distraction cost her her footing. Before she hit the floor, a strong hand grasped the back of her shirt and yanked her to a steady step.

Kara found herself pressed against a strong and familiar body that she instinctually leaned harder against.

A warm breath on her ear sent a shiver down her spine seconds before a voice accompanied it. "Careful." Cullen's voice woke her.

Pay attention, you idiot, she snapped at herself before pulling away and trailing her fingers down the wall for better balance. They made it to the bottom of the steps, where Kara peered in both directions. Dim lights cast the hallways in a subtle yellow glow, letting her see the details.

She recalled the layout of the building and where they had to be. Once she closed her eyes, she estimated how far the steps were and the direction of the walls.

To the right, unless the basement extended much farther than the building, there wasn't a lot of room. Perhaps enough for an office or two.

Kara nodded toward the left, the better chance. The alphas didn't argue, though whether that was because they trusted her or because they'd done the same calculation—or maybe they'd just figured she was picking something by dumb chance—she had no idea.

Kara stopped at the first door, pressing her ear to it. The roar of a TV came through—the news? She shook her head and kept moving. That sounded like a room with a bored guard in it, especially since no lock sat on the door.

Down the hallway, another card reader stood out on the wall.

Bingo. The door that housed the alpha would be secured. Kara slid the key through the reader, and the click of the lock said it had worked. She twisted the handle, but before she could enter, Cullen shouldered his way past.

Good. I hope he gets shot first.

Which was stupid, because she was pretty sure she didn't actually want him to be shot. At least nowhere important. Still, when she pushed her way into the room with Reese right behind her and Damon keeping an eye out on the hallway, Kara realized she hadn't needed to be worried.

The alpha in question sat on the bed, his gaze locked on the floor. The effects of the sedation on him were clear when he wavered in his spot.

"That's Kash," Reese said. "He matches the picture. Hey, we're here to help."

The alpha's eyebrows inched toward each other and he lifted his gaze, but the vacant stare made Kara doubt he saw much of anything.

"We need to move him. I doubt we have a lot of time," Cullen said, probably realizing the alpha wouldn't be moving anywhere quickly.

The growled warning was the exact wrong sound, because the alpha's tension ratcheted up, and the deep, rough sound that poured from him was quite a lot scarier than anything Kara had ever heard, and she'd once broken into a zoo and accidently ended up in a bear enclosure.

Right, alphas are territorial.

Kara ducked beneath Cullen's arm, avoiding his attempt to grab her. She crouched to meet the alpha's gaze head-on, or at least put herself right in front of him so he couldn't see anything else. "Grace is waiting for you," Kara said, trying to use the familiar bond to shake loose his thoughts.

It worked, sort of. His growling died down, though the tension didn't fully leave. His eyes cleared up a fraction, his lip dropping from the snarl. "Grace?" The name came out on a croak, as though he hadn't spoken in a long while.

Kara nodded quickly. "Yeah, Grace. She sent us to get you, but I need your help so you can see her. Can you stand?"

He frowned, and the unsteady move to his feet seemed to say he couldn't stand on his own, at least not well. He was large, taller than any alpha had a right to be, though the muscles she suspected he normally carried had atrophied due to lack of use. That was probably a part of the reason he couldn't quite keep his balance.

When it seemed like he'd topple, Kara slid to his side, wrapping an arm around his center to keep him upright.

Which none of *her* alphas seemed fond of, since all three broke into identical growls.

"Shut up," Kara snapped. "We want to get out of here alive? How about we save all snarling and growling for *enemies* instead of our own team!" When Cullen didn't back down, even as Reese and Damon did, she could feel the way the alpha at her side coiled. "He's sedated, Cullen. Most of his brain is shut off right now, which means all higher thinking is gone. Maybe don't poke the prime alpha who is literally running off instinct right now?"

"And if he decides those instincts include wanting you?" Cullen did that angry whisper thing back, which was hilarious, as it wasn't like the alpha was tracking much of anything for conversation.

Kara dug her fingers tighter into the alpha's side to keep him upright, which, given his far larger size, was not the easiest task. "He has so many drugs pumped into him, if he managed an erection, it would be a miracle. Trust me, okay? We need to get him moving and, in case you haven't noticed, he isn't doing it too well on his own. Let's argue once we are outside and safe."

Cullen's gaze narrowed but he offered a sharp nod, then backed out. None of the alphas met the prime's gaze, none of them wanting him to take it as a challenge. His feet scraped, bare and uncoordinated, against the tiled flooring. Kara wavered as she struggled with the alpha's weight hitting the wall once, when the alpha toppled toward her with no way to catch them.

The going was slow — far slower than it needed to be — but eventually they made it to the staircase. Damon had snapped pictures with his phone as they went, wanting some sort of documentation. They weren't in a place to deal with the lab as a whole just yet, but as soon as they got out, they could send someone back. Kara was sure Damon intended that to be the authorities, though Kara knew a few ball-busters who could make life hell for the lab folks. She preferred the eye-for-an-eye justice from her sort of people.

They just had to get out, first.

The trip up the stairs was long, with the alpha teetering so badly, Cullen once had to shove when he tripped backward.

The alpha showed his displeasure with another growl, this one accompanied by nearly sounded like a feral roar to go with it. Thankfully, he calmed easily enough at the mention of Grace and Kara managed him up the stairs and out of the door. They didn't bother to check the camera — what did it matter anymore? — and headed instead for the outside. They had to get the alpha into a car and the hell away as quickly as possible.

As they left the storage room, with freedom only paces away, the lights all turned on, bathing them in such brightness that Kara couldn't make anything out at first.

When her eyes did adjust, the man who had attacked her, who had dogged her every step for weeks, stood before her with more than a few armed men behind him.

Well, fuck.

Chapter Twenty-Four

Again, Cullen cursed himself. This was the exact situation he'd always been terrified of.

He had planned the job, tried to keep everyone safe, and it had turned to shit. Worse? He'd finally given in to trusting Kara, to thinking she could possibly be safe in their world, and what had it gotten them?

At gunpoint and facing off while severely outnumbered.

"Let's all just take it easy," Thompson said, his lips pulled into an arrogant grin that said he was thrilled to have won. "Hands up, please."

Cullen followed the direction, same as Reese and Damon. Kara remained against Kash's side, and the wavering of the alpha said that if she moved, he'd topple.

Two of the armed men came forward and checked the alphas for weapons. One took the pistol from Cullen, and he let it go. He had to pick his battles, and while that gun was useful, a bullet in him from fighting would end things right there.

They patted down Reese and Damon, taking their weapons as well. Reese cast a cutting look but otherwise kept his mouth shut.

The alpha let out an unhappy roar before he teetered, unsteady on his feet and suddenly upset — probably because of all the testosterone and aggression.

They went down, and the alpha's bulk took Kara, too. Cullen moved fast, trying to catch the alpha before he crushed the much smaller omega beneath him. Kara fell against him as well, and it only took a split second before one of the guards grabbed Cullen by the back of the neck and knocked him to the ground.

He stifled his need to react, to bare his teeth and snarl at the rough treatment. Instead, he only growled softly as he watched another armed guard grab Kara and shove her against the wall. He frisked her, his hands taking *far* too long on her ass.

Which did cause a snarl he couldn't hide.

"Calm down," Thompson said. "Now that we're all unarmed, let's go for a more private conversation." He looked over at one of the guards. "Take the subject back to his quarters, please."

Cullen hauled himself to his feet, ignoring the man who had thrown him down in exchange for casting a murderous glare at the one who had frisked Kara. He'd take bruises any day over someone putting their hands on her.

She was *his*.

The alpha made a few unhappy sounds as the guard escorted him back, and Cullen was reminded again how frustrating it was that Kash couldn't be more useful. Right about now, a very angry prime alpha would have been exceedingly helpful.

"Let's go," one of the guards said before smacking his hands against the back of Cullen to get him moving.

As Cullen moved forward, he noted an odd weight in the left side of his slacks. He frowned but said nothing, following the bodies as they moved through the warehouse.

As they turned the corner into one of the rooms, Cullen risked lowering his hand to his left pocket, subtly shifting the new item there. *A gun?* A small, compact pistol.

One of the guards twisted Kara hard and shoved her down into a seat. She cast a sickly-sweet look up at the man who had touched her. "Aren't you charming?" After the man huffed, she turned a side-eye glance to Cullen, and to anyone else it would look like the same smirk.

To Cullen, he *knew* it was to him. He recalled her falling against him while the alpha had toppled. She'd slid the pistol into his pocket then, since he'd already been searched.

It meant they had a chance, no matter how small.

Thompson removed his jacket and draped it over a chair. There was no table in the room, and the chairs were all folding ones. Cullen considered the fact they were all easily washable before he realized that was an unhelpful train of thought.

Thompson sat in the chair and crossed his foot over his other ankle, silent for a moment as he studied them. "I've been at this for two decades. I'm not sure anyone has given me as much trouble as you all."

"You're like forty?" Kara asked, that same mocking tone she liked to use that implied she took nothing seriously. "Your skin looks great. Not much time outside?"

The man lifted an eyebrow in her direction before dismissing her and turning his gaze back on the alphas. "While I don't care for being bested, I'll admit I hate having to destroy people who have shown such promise. If you weren't the noble type, I'd have hired you in a heartbeat."

The man's words seemed favorable, but Cullen knew better. That *if* was a sticking point. He might have the sort of personality that made him want to look into the faces of the men he was about to kill, but he'd still kill them, no doubt.

The room was less crowded than the last had been. It seemed that with them unarmed, Thompson wasn't as nervous. He'd kept only two armed guards in the room with him, and no doubt he had a weapon of his own.

One small pistol against three?

Not ideal. It meant waiting for the perfect moment when it would give them a worthwhile advantage.

"Get to the point," Reese said.

Thompson let a soft laugh escape his lips. "We all know how this is going to end. Let's not play games. You put up a good fight, got much further than I'd ever expected you to, but it's over now."

"Shooting us earlier would have been a quicker solution," Reese pointed out.

"Quicker? Yes, but not as thorough. First of all, I didn't want to risk the subject being harmed. Secondly, I need to find out exactly what you know and who else you've told. That is something for a much *longer* conversation."

Longer meaning torture, no doubt. The fact Thompson didn't look gleeful about it scored him no points, however. He said it with the same inflection as a person said they had to do laundry, as though it were an unpleasant task that nonetheless needed to be done. He rose from his seat after undoing the buttons at the cuffs of his shirt and rolling the sleeves up.

Doing that to sleeves *never* signaled anything good. He pulled a knife from its sheath at his belt, the black of the blade at least looking clean.

That Cullen was able to laugh at his predicament meant Kara had rubbed off on him far too much. The only good thing? The man seemed to have his attention locked on Cullen.

Not that getting carved up seemed like a good thing, but he'd rather take it than endure watching the other alphas or Kara suffer. Given Cullen's normal 'in-charge' attitude, he made a smart choice to start with.

Thompson stopped just in front of Cullen. "This doesn't have to happen. Tell me what I need to know, and it can be quick."

Kara's laugh broke the tension. "Do you really think it's going to be that easy?"

Thompson finally turned his gaze to her, an annoyance there like a child was interrupting his work. "Someone should have taught you to know your place. Females shouldn't get themselves into this much trouble."

Damon snorted softly at that, a reaction Cullen had to fight as well.

Still, it seemed to distract Thompson enough to put the whole knife-torture thing on hold for a moment.

"People have tried," Kara admitted. "I'm just a really slow learner, which should make it all the more embarrassing that *I've* won every time we've faced off."

Thompson pointed the tip of the knife toward Kara. "*You* didn't win. They did. You were merely lucky."

"Really? Because I recall bruising your goods the first time we tangled."

Thompson's lips pressed together, the first sign of any of this affecting him. "I had been trying to save your life. I don't care for slaughtering females when I don't have to, and I thought you were some innocent woman caught up in someone else's plan. If you'd have simply told me who hired you, I would have left you be. You escaped that only because I'd been kind."

"And round two? When I outwitted you when you tried to abduct me?"

"*They* saved you that time." He lifted the knife again when she opened her mouth for another point. "And the third time dumb luck had you hit by a car."

"Luck, skill, are they really that different? The truth is that you keep getting your ass handed to you every time you come up against me."

Thompson's knuckles whitened, signs that Kara had managed to get under his skin, which Cullen had to admit might be one of her best talents. Of course, when Thompson moved away from Cullen and toward Kara, it reminded him that it wasn't a good plan.

He went to stand but one of the guards lifted their gun in warning. It pulled a snarl from Cullen, but he sat. A hole in his chest wouldn't help the situation.

"You are a stupid girl playing in a sandbox far too big for you. No doubt you rely on those around you to do everything, surviving on their good will alone."

The statement was so preposterous that Cullen was the one to snort this time. Funny how Thompson could so wildly misunderstand Kara. The girl didn't reach out even when she really should, choosing to face things on her own instead of asking for help.

Kara's laugh mirrored Cullen's feelings. Even when Thompson stood just in front of Kara, when his knife hung in his hand by his side like a clear threat, Kara's smile wasn't wiped away.

Was she really that crazy? Did she have some plan Cullen wasn't aware of? Was he supposed to be in on something? The gun taunted him in his pocket, making him wonder when exactly he was supposed to do something.

"You just wait around for a man to ride in and save you, I bet."

Kara leaned forward, lips pulled into a grin that flashed her teeth. "Well, for once, you're right."

A sound upstairs had them all freezing. It wasn't loud, not a gunshot, but rather like something heavy dropping.

Thompson moved his gaze to Kara. "You're bluffing."

"I don't bluff," she said, which Cullen knew was a damned lie. He still couldn't read her, though, still had no idea if *this* was a bluff.

Thompson cut his gaze to one of the guards. "Go check that out."

The guard nodded and left.

Only two armed enemies now.

Thompson wrapped his fingers in the front of Kara's shirt, leaning down into her space. "This is going to end very badly for you, no matter what. We could use more omegas in our labs, and my boss would love me to put you there. The tests you had done with us show you could be very useful. Behave, and I'll kill you before you have to go through that."

"I've never been good at behaving."

312

Another crash outside, this one louder. A gunshot echoed through the walls.

Thompson turned a furious look on Kara. "What have you done?"

"What you said I'd do. Wait around until a man came to save me. Or, well, a couple of them, and trust me, they make me look like a kitten."

Thompson's face turned red, the look of someone who had just realized they held no cards. He hauled Kara up so fast it was like they were back in that safehouse again. He slid the knife into place and pulled his gun instead, pressing the weapon to her temple.

Cullen was on his feet, the pistol Kara had slipped into his pocket out and in his hand, aimed at Thompson, a heartbeat later.

They'd moved into an interior room with no windows, making the door the only exit. He had just one guard inside the room and no idea what sat outside it.

He was backed into a corner with a gun to the temple of the omega Cullen loved.

Thompson was in a very bad place.

Kara could have laughed at the repeat from before if it wasn't for the lump in her throat. She wasn't an idiot.

Last time they'd wanted her alive. This time? Thompson was done playing.

There was nothing keeping her brains nicely kept inside her skull other than him wanting her as a human shield.

Cullen had the pistol she'd planted on him out, his arm steady.

Outside the room, no doubt, there were few guards left. Erik, Liam and Kane would have done away with them quickly and quietly.

And again, it reminded her that perhaps having other people around wasn't the worst thing.

While she didn't normally call for backup, she'd never had something she was afraid of losing before, either.

Thompson and Cullen faced off, just like they had in the safehouse, when Kara had told Cullen not to take the shot.

Her fingers moved, deft and agile, as she managed to get her fingers around the knife from Thompson's sheath. Pickpocketing had its uses.

Another crash outside, closer.

She had the knife in her hand. She could act, sinking the blade into Thompson's thigh. Her angle would drive it deep. She tried to plan out how it would work, if she could twist away in time to finish him off, but she *knew* better.

He could pull the trigger well before she was able to do enough damage to put him down.

Cullen met her gaze, the question in his green eyes. Did she trust him?

Even after he'd broken her heart, after everything, did she trust him? Could she put her life in his hands, to do nothing and have faith he'd come through?

Kara took a deep breath before offering the slightest of nods, putting herself in the hands of the alphas she loved, giving in for the first time in her life.

She closed her eyes and twisted her head a hair to the side, trying to give Cullen the largest target—she really did not want to end up with a decorative hole in her face—a heartbeat before the sound of Cullen's gun shattered the room.

Chapter Twenty-Five

Everything in the room had slowed down for Damon, as if each second actually took a minute. Maybe it was the sight of a gun to Kara's head—again—or maybe it was the pounding of his heart, but the world crawled by.

Until the gunshot. Then it snapped back into motion, catapulting things so quickly he could hardly track them. A second shot echoed in his consciousness, but he tried to ignore it and focus on what he could do.

Damon threw himself into action before he could take stock. When the gun went off, Damon charged the last armed guard. Reese must have had the same idea, and two quickly advancing alphas would startle anyone.

They took the guard to the ground, and once Reese had the man's weapon, a well-placed hit from it put the guard out.

Damon twisted then, terror gripping him. What if Cullen had missed? What if he'd hit Thompson but that second shot had still taken Kara? He had no idea how to cope with what he would find, how he would react if he turned to see Kara's lifeless body on that floor.

He rose off the floor so he could see past the chairs, past Cullen.

Kara was on the floor along with Thompson, blood quickly spreading beneath them.

His breath left him and for a moment, he suspected his knees would give out.

Except, Kara moved. She pushed herself up from the ground, her face down, blood dripping, her hair obscuring her features.

She twisted, looking up toward Damon, toward Cullen and Reese, a gash across her cheek.

She didn't cry. She didn't complain about the wound dripping blood from her face. No, his wild omega wouldn't do any of that.

She stole his heart yet again when she smirked.

Fuck, I love that girl.

* * * *

Kara winced as she touched the bandage over her face. *Another scar to add to my collection, huh?*

At least she'd gotten used to Marshall. He'd poked and prodded her so many times, they were *almost* dating. She'd made the joke, but a growl from Cullen had said it wasn't appreciated.

Torrin had handled the warehouse, and when the cops arrived, they'd found lots of bodies – some alive, some not – and more than enough evidence to end the lab's work. Kash had been taken to the hospital and the alphas had remained to finish off the case. It had all been wrapped up in a neat little package.

If only her feelings were as simple to work out.

She sat on the bed in the hospital room, fully clothed but unsure what to do.

She'd thought about running. The alphas had stepped out to let her dress, and she could leave. Just walk away, never look back.

"I could buy you a few minutes," came a familiar voice that had Kara smiling even if she didn't *feel* like smiling.

"Always looking out for me, aren't you, Liam?"

He came over and sat on the bed beside her. "It's what family does, kid, and I can spot your running face from a mile away. Then again, maybe that's because it's your all-the-time face."

Kara stared out of the window, not at Liam. Conversations were easier when she didn't have to look at anyone. "How do you risk everything? How stupid is it to trust people? To give them everything knowing they can use it to destroy you?"

Liam leaned forward, mirroring her stance. "You know, you've never called for help before. You've never asked us to back you up on a job."

"I never needed it before."

His grunt called her a liar. "You've done far harder jobs, more dangerous. So, why this time?"

A lie perched on her tongue, but Kara swallowed it down. She offered the truth instead. "Because before it was just me on the line. If I failed, only I went down. This time…"

"This time you had something you cared about more than anything else? Something mattered to you enough to risk everything?"

She wanted to deny it, but that had been *exactly* the reason she'd done it, the reason she'd brought in Liam,

Erik and Kane. They'd sat in the car outside, content to wait for any sign of problems. When it had all gone to shit, Kara hadn't even hesitated to send a message from her watch.

"That doesn't mean it's worth it to keep going," she pointed out. "It's like dropping your phone. Just because I drop it doesn't mean I've got to stomp on it to. I already fucked up—they already mean way too much to me. Enough that I'll risk everything, that I'll do anything. Isn't that a good sign that I need to cut ties?"

Liam's sigh was soft. "I was bonded once."

The words shocked Kara. It wasn't that Liam was ever open with his past, with much personal stuff, yet the fact he'd had a mate and never mentioned it? Kara hadn't ever seen him bring a female home, even.

He kept speaking, staring out of the window as she had been before. It seemed they both needed privacy. "Obviously I'm not anymore, so you can draw your own conclusions from that. The thing is, the time we had? It wasn't all that much, and losing it was fucking painful, but I wouldn't trade a minute of it."

"What happened to her?"

Liam pushed himself off the bed, his features regaining that easy smile of his as if he'd managed to hide it all. "A story for another time, perhaps. So, kid, should I buy you a few minutes for you to take the fire escape, or are you going to face down your monsters?"

* * * *

How a hotel room could feel like home, Reese had no idea. It still did, though. The walls of the house where they used to live sparked nothing in Reese when he thought about them. Just rooms, walls, windows. Nothing more.

This place, though? With the scents of Kara and the alphas mingling? Well, that was where they belonged.

Or at least, that was what he'd believed.

That Kara hadn't been in the hospital room when they'd walked in, plus the open window and there being no sign of her had said she might not feel the same. Her friend Liam had distracted them, and when they'd gone in there, ready for some sort of reunion, only an empty room had met them.

He rubbed his eyes, wanting to sleep for fucking years. Would that ease the sting? Would it make him feel as if he could shake off the pain that clung to him?

Neither Damon nor Cullen had said a word about it. As many times as this had happened, as many times as they'd discussed not having her, Reese realized he'd never really thought it would happen.

Somewhere inside him, he'd always expected them to work it out, that she'd be *theirs*. Maybe it was just instinct that made him believe it, that lied to him so well.

Did it matter?

A creak caught his attention, and standing in the doorway to Kara's room was the omega herself. The bandage on her cheek remained, and she bit softly at her bottom lip.

Reese froze at the sight, like she was some ghost he wasn't sure was friendly or not.

With Kara, one could never be sure.

"You ran," Cullen grated out. "What are you even doing here?"

Kara didn't move forward, her body tense and her gaze down. "I didn't want to do this there."

"Do what?" Damon asked.

She took a deep breath, then finally met their gaze. "I love you, okay? I'm not happy about it, and I don't really know how to deal with it, but there it is."

That was the last thing Reese had ever expected her to say, and it managed to take him off balance. Sure, he'd suspected she loved them, but he hadn't figured she'd damn well say it.

Cullen recovered faster. "So why'd you run, then? Why do you always run?"

"Because I didn't want to put everything out there in the middle of another hospital. I didn't want to have this talk there, the whole stupid 'where is this going?' talk. I've never let anyone close to me, never let them matter. It's always been too dangerous."

"So why here? What are you trying to say?" Cullen's tone was careful, like he didn't dare believe her.

"I don't know how to do this. Hell, I don't know what *this* is, exactly, but I know I want you, all of you. Fuck, I think I need you, as stupid as that sounds. But I was sitting there thinking, what if I told you all that and you decided I'm too much trouble? What if I finally gave in and you realized I'm not worth it? What if after everything, you don't want me anymore?" The last words came out on a quiver.

They stole away the rest of his worries. Reese gave up on the whole distance idea—like he could ever really refuse her—and came forward to pull her into a kiss. He wrapped her thighs around his waist as he moved her backward into her room. Before he lowered onto the bed, he broke the kiss. "You're trouble, all right, but you're our kind of trouble."

She bounced slightly when he dropped her, but he was over her a moment later, sliding his hands beneath her shirt to feel all that warm, soft skin.

"I spent so long worried that you'd always lie to me, that I'd never be able to trust you."

"And now?" She gasped when he stroked his fingers over a nipple through her bra.

"Now? I've realized that your wild streak is the thing I love about you. That smirk you get when you aren't telling the truth, when you *know* that I know you're lying—fuck, I like it, because I realized that lying is like breathing for you, but at the end of the day? At the end of the day you aren't going to sell me out. You aren't going to turn on me." As he admitted it, he realized it was true.

She wasn't the omega from his past. She wasn't looking to screw him over. Her lying was like a game between them, but she had her own moral code. She'd never stab him in the back.

If she had a real problem with him, she'd damn well make sure she stabbed him in the chest where he could see it.

And that fact made him grin as he pulled off his shirt. "So yeah, I love you too, hellion."

Damon slid into the bed as Reese moved off Kara. She twisted to him so quickly it was like a rehearsed dance, like she knew exactly where to go and when. Her lips didn't find his, but rather went to his throat. She drew in deep inhalations of him, as if she needed his scent as much as his touch.

He caught the waist of her leggings in his hands and pulled, rewarded by her rising to her knees to help ease them off.

The trust she offered to them still surprised him. After everything she'd been through, all the times life had kicked her, she still could be there with them, believing it could work. If that wasn't bravery, he had no idea what was.

"I missed you," he whispered as he slid his fingers along her panties, teasing them both with the touch. "I've spent my entire life trying to get things right, trying to plan everything, thinking as long as I had a goal and steps, I could be happy. The thing is, I never was. The more I tried to be something I'm not, the more I tried to get something I didn't want, the more I realized none of that matters." Damon caught her face, careful to avoid the bandage, so she looked into his eyes. "You weren't anything I planned, but you were exactly what I needed. You accept me, flaws and differences and all."

She looked at him, her blue eyes open and honest but with a tinge of fear, as if she couldn't bring herself to really believe it.

Which was fine. They had time and he'd spend it all proving to her how much he needed her.

"I can't imagine a single plan anymore that doesn't have you in it."

Cullen's tongue felt heavy and useless. So many declarations, so many nice words.

Words hadn't ever been something Cullen was good with.

Yet after Damon, it seemed to be Cullen's turn. Kara twisted to look at him, a question in those bright blue eyes.

Did he feel the same?

She'd already risked everything, as had Reese and Damon, yet Cullen toed the edge. Could he leap?

He shifted his weight and ran his fingers through his hair, trying to figure out how to put into words something he didn't even understand himself.

They *didn't* work on paper. She was a criminal and he wasn't. She was wild and he was controlled and careful. He was forever trying to protect those he cared about and she ran toward fire like a moth.

And even as he thought about each reason it didn't work, he couldn't stop the fact that for god only knew why, it did.

"I kept thinking I'd lose you," he admitted. "I've seen a lot of death, a lot of loss. I kept thinking that I couldn't survive losing you. First, I figured I just wouldn't let myself feel anything for you. When that didn't work, I figured the best path was to try and change you. We both know how that turned out."

Kara's back went straight as she sat on the bed, clad in only the black panties and without a speck of unease about the state of her undress. She didn't seem to even mind that her scars were on display.

Cullen nodded at her bandaged cheek. "That's an example of one of a million things that could take you away. An inch to the left and you'd have been gone."

Her gaze dropped at that, her shoulders slumping.

He came forward and caught her chin, lifting her face so she looked at him. "I thought I needed someone I could control as a partner, but I was wrong. You won't stay safe, but you know what? You'll be okay because you're tough, and you're smart, and because I'll be right fucking there by your side no matter what. Whatever you want to do, I support."

"I won't ever be what you wanted," Kara said softly.

Cullen slid his hand to the back of her neck, pulling her to her knees so her front pressed against his and he could hover just above her lips. "No, you won't be, because you're a lot more than I could have ever imagined."

Kara was breathless. The words all sounded *so* good, so right. She struggled, not wanting to believe them, not wanting to let them chip away her walls.

What walls? You haven't had defenses against them from day one.

Cullen kissed her, erasing the worries, the fears.

They wouldn't have an easy life. They weren't the type to settle away and grow old in a little cottage. No, not Kara and certainly not the alphas. They'd take cases and Kara would work jobs, and sometimes they'd help each other, but it would all land them in trouble time and time again.

And yet, Kara smiled against the kiss as she considered a life where she was always in trouble with *them*.

That was a future worth having, no matter the difficulty, no matter the risk to her heart.

"What are you smiling at?" Cullen asked against her lips just as Reese pulled her back, settling her against his chest.

"That you like me."

Cullen chuckled before reaching into the nightstand and taking out a blindfold, dangling it on a finger. "What can I say? I have bad taste in women."

Damon pressed Kara's knees apart as he settled between them, stroking his fingers up and down the sensitive skin on the inside of her thighs. He pressed a kiss to her knee, sweet and yet a promise. "If you keep arguing with him, he'll just gag you again."

Reese laughed as he reached around her and cupped a breast in his large, warm hand. "Hell, I think maybe we'll do that anyway. Only way to get any peace with her around."

Kara brought her elbow back into his side even as Cullen tugged the blindfold over her eyes, as they stole her sense like they had her heart.

She relaxed against Reese's grip, against their touches. She wasn't domesticated, but she didn't mind if her alphas tamed her.

At least for a little while.

Want to see more from this author?
Here's a taster for you to enjoy!

Ready or Not: Opposites Attract
Jayce Carter

Excerpt

How is it possible for a man to be that attractive?

Tabby curled into the small chair set on her porch, a cup of tea between her palms as she watched her neighbor in front of their duplex in a way she had to convince herself was not creepy.

Gray Conners. The motorcycle-riding, tattoo-covered nuisance who had turned her life upside down since he'd moved in three weeks before.

She missed her old neighbor, the sweet elderly lady, Gayle, who never stayed up past eight and always kept the shrubs out front properly trimmed. Unfortunately, Gayle had moved in with her daughter, and the hoodlum standing in the driveway with his hair more than a little mussed and his pants undone but still somehow hiding everything important had moved in.

The tall blonde woman with a chest that seemed to defy the laws of physics set a hand on Gray's bare torso. Gayle had never done that either. She'd been past the days of early morning walks of shame, but Gray liked to parade them past Tabby's duplex every morning.

And despite knowing that—or maybe because of it—Tabby always drank her tea out front.

She justified it by reminding herself she'd used her front porch to sip her morning tea since well before he'd moved in. She liked to start her day with the quiet and peace of a rising sun. The fact that it now left her in the perfect position to see Gray's latest conquest—and usually him in some state of sinful undress—was just a lucky bonus.

The blonde—Haylee from what Tabby had overheard before—went in for a kiss. Gray didn't often have repeats, but Haylee had been there more than a few times. He must like her.

Gray gave her one, but he pulled away so fast that she tried to follow. Then again, Gray struck Tabby as the type not to care for long entanglements. In fact, the number of times she'd watched that blonde leave was surprising.

And not at all jealousy inducing. If she wants to be stupid and let a man like that ruin her life, that's her business.

Haylee turned and sauntered down the driveway—an actual, honest-to-god saunter, like she was walking a catwalk instead of a duplex driveway—with Gray staying put until she reached her car, parked on the street.

Gray had his thumbs tucked into the belt loops of his unbuttoned jeans, his chest and feet bare as though he'd pulled on the minimum amount of clothing he had to without worrying about being arrested.

And no matter how annoying the man was, how he pushed every neurotic button Tabby had, she couldn't deny he was nice to look at. He had dark brown hair, pushed back out of his face and shorter on the sides. A beard covered his jawline, dense enough to give him that wild edge but short enough to avoid the mountain-man look. His eyes were a bright icy blue that shone in the darkness no matter how far away he stood. Tattoos covered his muscular frame, all the way from neck to knuckles. They had bright pops of color mixed with deep blacks, many blending into the next. A wolf sat on his hip, its howling face over his defined abs and disappearing below the waist of his pants that sat dangerously low.

Just how far down do those tattoos go?

The thought made her take her bottom lip between her teeth, distracted by images she couldn't help of him and some faceless girl, of the things they must have gotten up to the night before. Tabby didn't have much experience, so she had no doubt that her imagination was as strait-laced as could be, but that didn't steal her desire as she considered her very vanilla fantasies.

Before she could stop it, the cup of tea slipped from her hands and crashed to the porch, shattering.

Tabby yanked her foot up to avoid the scalding liquid, cursing herself for the mistake. When she lifted her gaze, she found that her frustratingly distracting neighbor was staring right at her with a smirk that said she was in way over her head.

Gray had never found the whole nerdy thing all that sexy, so why was it that he couldn't quite stop thinking about his neighbor?

She dressed without flair, in disappointingly shapeless functional tops and leggings. Her long brown hair always hung down around her shoulders, not wavy enough to be considered curly but not straight, either. Thick black-framed glasses perched on her nose, making her look young and damned smart. She wasn't that young, not according to his aunt Cindy, the landlady. Tabby Kasey was twenty-five and had lived there for seven years. On paper, she was the perfect neighbor.

In reality, her sharp looks and never-happy glares said they didn't mesh.

Her perfectly kept porch with its fresh herbs all in matching pots without a speck of soil out of place said it, too.

Gray wasn't a perfect sort of person.

Still, each time she didn't melt for him, each time she didn't give in to his smile to win her over, Gray found himself just a bit more tempted.

His aunt, who owned both sides of their duplex, had warned him about the sweet but strung-tight girl who lived next door. He'd expected someone he hated, and despite all the reasons he should, he found her far more interesting than he had any right to.

Sure, he knew she sat outside most mornings, but ignoring her little voyeur kink was just good manners. Plus, he was perverse enough to enjoy the audience. What did that say about him, though? That he suspected he liked his neighbor's eyes on him more than he liked Haylee, the girl he'd had sex with?

Except when she went so far as to drop her cup, he couldn't keep up the entire 'I don't see you' game anymore.

And seeing the red flush up her cheeks? Worth it.

"Enjoying the show?" He leaned his shoulder against the corner of the duplex, just off her porch. Close enough to get a good look at her but not so close he crowded her. He wasn't sure if crowding would backfire or not with her.

Besides, he wasn't even trying for anything. It took one good look at her to know they didn't fit, that they'd do nothing but annoy each other.

That didn't mean he couldn't flirt, though. Flirting was like a battle, a wonderful back and forth that never failed to draw him in, and Tabby seemed like one hell of a fun opponent.

"It's not my fault. You're the one out here putting on a show." She spoke in a low voice, as if he should be embarrassed by the topic.

"You're out here every morning. You must enjoy it."

"Hardly." She rose to her feet, a large baggy sweater hanging on her thin frame with a pair of black leggings beneath that gave him no real sense of her figure. Too bad he doubted he'd get a chance for a more hands-on feel. "If you'll excuse me?"

Funny how such a polite phrase could be muttered with so much fuck you in her tone.

Suddenly, he wanted to mess up her life a bit. He wanted to put askew a few pieces of her perfectly organized world, to see her smile and laugh and come undone under his hands and his lips. A girl strung that tight would be so much fun.

"I'm having a few people over next Friday. Wouldn't be very neighborly for me not to invite you." The moment the invitation left his lips, he wondered what the hell he was doing. Sure, she could use some time around his sorts of people, but that didn't make it a good idea.

Her eyes widened in surprise before she withdrew. "No, thank you."

And there it was again, that impressive ability to make a polite statement sound like a curse. Not that her answer surprised him. She didn't strike him as the stopping-in-for-a-beer sort of girl.

She gathered up the large pieces of ceramic from her broken cup before slinking back into her house, leaving him alone in the early morning light, the scent of her chamomile tea lingering.

Her answer was for the best, but damn if he wasn't still disappointed.

Home of Erotic Romance

Sign up for our newsletter and find out about all our romance book releases, eBook sales and promotions, sneak peeks and FREE romance books!

About the Author

Jayce Carter lives in Southern California with her husband and two spawns. She originally wanted to take over the world but realized that would require wearing pants. This led her to choosing writing, a completely pants-free occupation. She has a fear of heights yet rock climbs for fun and enjoys making up excuses for not going out and socializing.

Jayce loves to hear from readers. You can find her contact information, website details and author profile page at https://www.totallybound.com